Acclaim for Sándor Márai's

Casanova in Bolzano

A *Washington Post Book World* Notable Book

"[A] novel of exquisite slowness and refreshing oddity. . . . A literary operetta." —*The New York Times*

"Márai gleefully gives life to his version of Casanova and this richly and provocatively fleshed out moment . . . that, finally, is a daring meditation in the form of disguised monologues on the meaning of love, of seduction, of the fragility of ever-threatened civilization." —*Los Angeles Times*

"[Márai] was a master. . . . Flashes of illumination, of strong perception . . . streak every page of his writing."
—*San Francisco Chronicle*

"What Márai does is create gorgeous arias of reasoned argument—sensual, psychological studies of character, which evolve into a kind of theater of the life force."
—*The Seattle Times*

SÁNDOR MÁRAI

Casanova in Bolzano

Sándor Márai was born in Kassa in the Austro-
Hungarian Empire in 1900 and died in San
Diego, California, in 1989. He rose to fame as
one of the leading literary novelists in Hungary
in the 1930s. Profoundly antifascist, he sur-
vived the war, but persecution by the Commu-
nists drove him from the country in 1948, first
to Italy, then to the United States. His novel
Embers was published for the first time in
English in 2001.

INTERNATIONAL

ALSO BY SÁNDOR MÁRAI

Embers

Casanova in Bolzano

Casanova in Bolzano

SÁNDOR MÁRAI

*Translated from the Hungarian
by George Szirtes*

VINTAGE INTERNATIONAL
Vintage Books
A Division of Random House, Inc.
New York

FIRST VINTAGE INTERNATIONAL EDITION, NOVEMBER 2005

Translation copyright © 2004 by Alfred A. Knopf, a division of Random House, Inc.

All rights reserved. Published in the United States by Vintage Books,
a division of Random House, Inc., New York, and in Canada by
Random House of Canada Limited, Toronto. Originally published in
Hungary as *Vendégjáték Bolzanóban* by Révai, Budapest, 1940.
Copyright © Heirs of Sándor Márai. Vorosvary-Weller Publishing, Toronto.
This translation originally published in hardcover in the United States by
Alfred A. Knopf, a division of Random House, Inc., New York, in 2004.

Vintage is a registered trademark and Vintage International and colophon are
trademarks of Random House, Inc.

This is a work of fiction. Names, characters, places, and incidents either are
the product of the author's imagination or are used fictitiously.

The Library of Congress has cataloged the Knopf edition as follows:
Márai, Sándor, 1900–1989.
[Vendégjáték Bolzanóban. English.]
Casanova in Bolzano / by Sándor Márai ; translated from the original
Hungarian by George Szirtes.
p. cm.
1. Casanova, Giacomo, 1725–1798—Fiction.
I. Szirtes, George, 1948– II. Title.
PH3281.M35V413 2004
894'.511334—dc22
2004044208

Vintage ISBN-10: 0-375-71296-8
Vintage ISBN-13: 978-0-375-71296-8

Book design by Virginia Tan

www.vintagebooks.com

Printed in the United States of America
10 9 8 7 6 5 4 3 2 1

AUTHOR'S NOTE

Given the appearance and behavior of my hero, the reader will no doubt identify the characteristic profile of that notorious eighteenth-century adventurer, Giacomo Casanova.

To identify, for some people, is to accuse, and it is not easy to mount a defense. My hero bears an unfortunate resemblance to that homeless, desperately roguish, and generally unhappy itinerant who, at midnight on October 31, 1756, escaped from the cells under the lead-roof ducal palace, the so-called Leads, let himself down into the lagoon by a rope ladder, and, with the help of an unfrocked friar called Balbi, fled the territory of the republic and took the road to Munich. My excuse is that it was not so much the romantic episodes in my hero's life that interested me as his romantic character.

For this reason, the only details I have taken from the infamous *Memoirs* concern the time and circumstances of his escape. Everything else the reader comes across is fable and invention.

—S.M.

Casanova in Bolzano

A Gentleman from Venice

*I*t was at Mestre he stopped thinking; the dissolute friar, Balbi, had very nearly let the police get wind of him, because he had looked for him in vain as the mail coach set off, and only found him after a diligent search, in a coffeehouse, where he was blithely sipping a cup of chocolate and flirting with the waitress. By the time they reached Treviso their money was gone; they sneaked through the gates dedicated to St. Thomas, into the fields, and, by creeping along the backs of gardens and skirting the woods, managed to reach the outskirts of Valdepiadene about dawn. Here he took out his dagger, thrust it under the nose of his disgusting companion, and told him they'd meet again in Bolzano: then they parted. Father Balbi slunk off in a bad mood through a grove of olives, brushing past their bare trunks, a shabby, slovenly figure disappearing into the distance, casting the odd sullen look behind him, like a mangy dog dismissed by his master.

Once the friar had finally gone, he made for the central part of town and with a blind, sure instinct sought accommodation at the residence of the captain of the local militia. The captain's wife, a mild-mannered woman, received him, gave him supper, had his wounds cleaned—congealed blood was sticking to his knees and ankles, from the scraping he had given them when he had leaped off the lead roof—and, before falling asleep, he learned that the captain happened to be away searching for an escaped prisoner. He stole out in the early dawn and made a few more miles. He slept over in Pergine, and, three days later, arrived—by coach this time, having extorted six gold pieces from an acquaintance—in Bolzano.

Balbi was there waiting for him. They took rooms at The Stag. He had neither baggage nor topcoat and was ragged on arrival, rags being all that remained of his fine-colored silk suit. A harsh November wind was already snapping at the narrow streets of Bolzano. The innkeeper nervously examined his tattered guests.

"The finest rooms?" he stuttered.

"The finest," came the quiet but firm answer. "And look to your kitchen staff. You tend to cook everything in rancid fat rather than in oil in these parts, and I haven't had a decent meal since leaving the republic! I want capon and chicken tonight, not one but three, with chestnuts. And get some Cyprus wine while you're at it. Are you staring at my clothes? Wondering why we have arrived without any luggage, empty handed? Don't you get news here? Don't you read the *Leyden Gazette*? Nincompoop!" he shouted in a cracked voice, having caught a chill on his journey, his windpipe seized by agonized coughing. "Have you not heard that a Venetian nobleman and his servants were robbed on the frontier? Have the police not been round yet?"

"No sir," answered the frightened innkeeper.

Balbi sniggered into his sleeve. They were eventually shown to the finest rooms: a parlor with two big casement windows giving onto the main square, furniture with gilded legs and a Venetian glass above the fireplace. There was a French four-poster in the bedchamber. Balbi's room was at the end of the corridor, at the foot of steep and narrow stairs that led to the servants' quarters. The accommodation was greatly to his satisfaction.

"My secretary," he said to the innkeeper, indicating Balbi.

"The police are very strict," apologized the innkeeper. "They'll be here any moment. They register all visitors."

"Tell them," he carelessly answered, "that you have a nobleman as guest. A gentleman . . ."

"Indeed!" enthused the innkeeper, now humble and curious, bowing deeply, his tasseled cap in his hand.

"A gentleman from Venice!" he affirmed.

He pronounced this as though it were some extraordinary title or rank. Even Balbi pricked up his ears at the tone of his voice. Then he wrote his name in a precise and expert hand in the guest book. The innkeeper was red with excitement: he wiped his temples with a fat finger and couldn't make up his mind whether to run to the police station or to go down on his knees and kiss the man's hand. Being undecided he simply stood there in silence.

Eventually he lit a lantern and escorted his guests up

the stairs. The servants were busying themselves about the apartment: they brought large gilt candlesticks, warm water in a silver jug, and canvas towels manufactured in Limburg. The visitor undressed slowly, in regal fashion, like a king at his toilette. He handed his filthy garments one by one to the innkeeper and his servants, his blood-bespotted silk pantaloons having to be cut away on both sides with scissors because they were sticking to him, and then soaked his feet in a silver bowl full of water while leaning back in an armchair, matted and solemn, almost faint with exhaustion. At certain points he dropped into sleep, mumbled, and cried out. Balbi, the innkeeper, and the servants came and went about him with open mouths, making up the bed in the chamber, drawing the curtains, and snuffing out almost all the candles. They had to knock at his door for some time when it came to supper. As soon as he had eaten he fell fast asleep, and remained sleeping till noon the next day, his face smooth and untroubled, as indifferent as a day-old corpse.

"A gentleman," said the girls, giggling, whispering, and singing as they went about their tasks in the kitchen and the cellar, washing cutlery, wiping plates, chopping up firewood, serving in the bar, now talking in low voices with fingers held to their mouths, now giggling again, eventually calming down, and passing on the news officiously then laughing: a gentleman, yes, a gentleman, from Venice. In the evening two men from the secret service appeared, drawn by his name, that name so notorious and irresistible, so dangerous and fascinating, a name redolent of adventures and flight, a name that attracted the secret service in whatever town it appeared. And they wanted to know everything about him. Is he asleep? . . . Has he no luggage?

"A dagger," replied the innkeeper. "He arrived with a dagger. That is his sole possession."

"A dagger," they repeated, nodding vigorously, bemused. "What kind of dagger?" the secret service men inquired.

"A Venetian dagger," answered the innkeeper, in awed tones.

"Nothing else?" they insisted.

"Nothing," the innkeeper said. "Nothing but a dagger. That's all he has."

The information took the secret service men by surprise. They would not have been amazed to find that he had arrived bearing loot: precious stones, spirits, necklaces, and rings that he had slipped off the fingers of innocent women as he traveled. His reputation preceded him like a herald announcing his name. The prelate had already sent word to the police chief that morning, requesting the force to send the notorious guest on his way. That same morning, and after mass in the evening, the taverns of Tyrol and Lombardy were full of tales of his escape.

"Watch him," the secret service men said. "Watch him carefully and take note of every word he says. You have to be extremely wary of him. If he receives any mail you must find out who it is from. If he sends any, you must find out where it is addressed. Observe his every movement! It seems," they whispered into the innkeeper's ear, cupping their hands, "that he has a protector. Not even his grace, the prelate, can touch him."

"Not for the time being," added the innkeeper, sagely.

"Not for the time being," echoed the secret service men, solemnly.

They departed on tiptoe, with gloomy expressions, oppressed by their cares. The innkeeper sat down in the tavern and sighed. He didn't like notorious guests who roused the prelate's or the police's suspicion. He thought of the guest himself, the dark fires and embers that flickered in his sleepy eyes, and he was afraid. He thought of the dagger, the Venetian dagger, his guest's sole possession, and was even more afraid. He thought of the news that dogged his guest's footsteps and he began, silently, to curse.

"Teresa!" he barked angrily.

A girl entered, already dressed for bed. She was sixteen and held a burning candle in one hand while clutching her nightshirt with the other.

"Listen to me," he whispered, and invited her to sit on his knee. "I can't trust anyone except you. We have dangerous guests, Teresa. That gentleman . . ."

"From Venice?" the girl asked in a singsong schoolgirl voice.

"Venice yes, Venice," he muttered nervously. "Straight from prison. Where the rats are. And the scaffold. Listen, Teresa. Mark his every word. Let your eyes and ears be ever at his keyhole. I love you like a daughter. Indeed, I have brought you up as I would my daughter, but if he calls you into the room, do not hesitate. Enter. You will take his breakfast in to him. Guard your virtue and watch him."

"I will," said the girl, then got up to return to her room, delicate as a shadow. At the door she stopped and complained in a thin, childish voice.

"I am afraid."

"Me too," said the innkeeper. "Now go to sleep. But first bring me a glass of red wine."

All the same, none of them slept well that first night.

News

They slept in flurries, snoring, panting, and puffing, and, as they slept, were aware that something was happening to them. They sensed that someone was walking through the house. They sensed someone was calling them and that they should answer in ways they had never answered before. The question posed by the stranger was insolent, saucy, aggressive, and, above all, frightening and sad. But by the time they awoke in the morning they had forgotten it.

While they were sleeping the news rapidly spread: he had arrived, had escaped the Leads, had managed to row away from his birthplace in broad daylight, had thumbed his nose at their graces the terrifying lords of the Inquisition, had run rings round Lawrence the militia chief, had sprung the unfrocked friar, had more or less strolled from the doges' citadel, had been spotted in Mestre bargaining with the driver of the mail coach, been observed sipping vermouth in a coffeehouse in Treviso, and there was one peasant who swore he had seen him at the border putting a spell on his cows. The news spread through Venetian palazzos, through suburban inns, and as it did so, cardinals, their graces the senators, hangmen, secret agents, spies, cardsharps, lovers and husbands, girls at mass and women in warm beds, laughed and exclaimed, "Hoho!" Or in full throat, with deep satisfaction, laughed out loud, "Haha!" Or giggled into their pillows or handkerchiefs, "Teehee!" Everyone was delighted he had escaped. By next evening the news had been announced to the Pope, who recalled him, remembering when he had personally presented him with some minor papal award, and he couldn't help laughing. The news spread: in Venice, gondoliers leaned on their long oars and closely analyzed all the technical details of his escape and were glad, glad because he was a Venetian, because he had outwitted the authorities, and because there was someone stronger than tyrants or stones and chains, stronger even than the Leads. They spoke quietly, spitting into the water and rubbing their palms with satisfaction. The news spread and people's hearts grew warm on hearing it. "What crime had he committed, after all?" they asked. "He gambled, and, good God, he might not have played an entirely honest hand, he certainly ran tables in low bars and wore a mask when playing with professional gamblers! But this was Venice, after all! Who didn't? . . . And yes, he roughed up a few people who betrayed him and he lured women to his rented apartment in Murano, a little way from town, but how else do you spend your youth in Venice? And of course he was impudent, had a quick tongue and talked a lot. But was anyone silent in Venice? . . ."

So they muttered and, every so often, laughed. Because there was something good about the news, something satisfying and heartwarming. Because everyone knew the Inquisition had its teeth in one or another piece of their own flesh, that one or another part of them was already living in the Leads, and now somebody had demonstrated that a man could overcome despotism, lead roofs, and the police, that he was stronger than the *messer grande,* the emissary of the hangman, and the bringer of bad news. The news spread: in police stations they were slamming files on tables, officers went round shouting, magistrates listened with reddened ears to those accused of crimes and angrily sent men to prison, into exile, to the galleys, or to the scaffold. They spoke of him in churches, preached against him after mass for having concentrated all seven deadly sins in one accursed body, which, according to the priest, would boil in its own individual cauldron, then roast in a fire especially set aside for it in hell, forever. His name was even mentioned in the confessional booth by women with heads bowed low, who beat their breasts while accepting the prescribed penance. And everyone was pleased, for something good had happened in Venice, and in every village and town of the republic he passed through.

They slept, and smiled as they dreamed. Wherever he went they took greater care than usual to close their windows and doors by night, and behind closed shutters men would spend a long time talking to their wives. It was as if every feeling that yesterday had been ashes and embers had started to smoke and spout flames. He cast no spells on cows, but cowherds swore that calves born that year were prettier and that there were more of them. Women woke, fetched water from the well in wooden buckets, kindled fires in their kitchens, warmed pans of milk, set fruit out on glazed trays, suckled their infants, fed the men, swept out the bedrooms, changed the beds, and smiled as they worked. It was a smile that took some time to disappear from Venice, Tyrol, and Lombardy. The smile spread like a highly active and harmless infection: it even spread over the borders, so that they had heard of it in Munich, and waited for it, smiling in readiness, as they did in Paris where the tale of his escape was recounted to the king while he was hunting in the deer park, and he too smiled. And it was known in Parma, and in Turin, Vienna, and Moscow. And everywhere there was smiling. And the policemen, the magistrates, the militiamen and the spies—everyone whose business it was to keep people in the grip of fear of the authorities—went about their work suspiciously and in ill temper. Because there is nothing quite as dangerous as a man who will not yield to despotism.

They knew he had nothing but a dagger to call his own, but for several weeks they doubled the guard at border posts. They knew he had no accomplices and that he did not concern himself with politics, yet the chief executive of the Inquisition drew up a complete campaign strategy to recapture him, to entice him back into the cage, dead or alive, with gold or with violence, no matter what. They explained the details of his escape to the doge, that squat figure with piercing eyes, and he beat the table with his ringed fingers and swore to send the militiamen to the galleys. Senators gripped the creases of their silk coats with delicate yellow hands and clutched them closer to their bosoms, sitting silently in their armchairs in the great hall, sniffing the air through noses yellowed with diabetes, their faces expressionless, occasionally glancing up to examine the ceiling paintings or the main joists of the council room through narrowed lids while voting for new draconian measures, shrugging their shoulders and remaining silent.

But the smile spread like influenza: the baker's wife, the goldsmith's sister, and the daughter of the doge all caught it. People in the privacy of their carefully locked rooms slapped their stomachs with delight and laughed fit to burst. There was something eerily consoling in the news that someone could spirit himself through walls a yard thick, past a set of vigilant guards wielding lances and pikes, and break the links of chains as fat as a child's arm. Then they went off to their places of work, stood in the marketplace or the bar, sipping a little Veronese wine, and the usurers among them weighed out gold dust on delicately adjusted scales, the pharmacists brewed laxatives, love potions, and deadly poisons that could be ground to a fine powder and secreted in signet rings, women with ample bellies garnished low market stalls of fish, fruit, and raw meat with scented herbs, merchants of fashion items arranged newly delivered stockings from Lyon and bodices crocheted in Bruges, displaying them in calfskin boxes perfumed with potpourri, and what with all the work, the chatter, the trade, and the administration, everyone found a moment to raise hand to mouth and have a good snigger.

The women felt that the escape and all that followed may, to some degree, have served their interests. They couldn't explain this feeling very precisely, but, being Venetian women, it was not for them to split hairs when it came to feelings, and they accepted the instinctive, half-whispered logic of heart and blood and passion. The women were glad that he had escaped. It was as if a long-shackled force contained by legends, proverbs, books, memories, dreams, and yearnings had found its way into the world at large, or as if the hidden, somewhat im-proper, yet terrifyingly true, alternative life of men and women had moved into the foreground, unmasked, with-out its powdered wig, as naked as a prisoner emerging from the solemn tête-à-tête of the torture chamber; and women glanced after him while raising hands or fans to cover mouths and eyes, their heads tipped a little to one side, without saying anything, though the veiled, misty eyes that peeked at the fugitive said, "Yes," and again, "Yes." That was why they smiled. And, for a few days, it seemed as though the world in which they lived over-flowed with tenderness. In the evening they stopped by their windows and balconies, the lagoon below them, the lyre-shaped veils of fine lace fixed to their hair by means of a comb, their silk scarves thrown across their shoulders, and gazed down into the oily, dirty, indifferent water that supported the boats, returned a glance that they would not have returned the day before, and dropped a handker-chief that was caught far below, above the reflections in the water, by a lithe brown hand: then they raised a flower to their lips, and smiled. Having done so, they closed the window and the lights went out in the room. But there was something in their hearts and their movements, in the eyes of the women and in the glances of the men, that shone. It was as if someone had sent a secret signal to tell them that life was not simply a matter of rules, prohibitions, and chains, but of passions that were less rational, less directed, and freer than they had hitherto believed. And for a moment they understood the signal and smiled at each other.

The sense of complicity did not last long: the books of the law, with all their written and unwritten rules of behavior, ensured that their hearts should forget the memory of the escaped prisoner. Within a few weeks they had forgotten it in Venice. Only Signor Bragadin, his gentle and gracious supporter, still recalled it, and a few women to whom he had promised eternal fidelity, along with the odd moneylender or gambler to whom he owed money.

"A Man"

*T*his is how he escaped, how the news preceded him, and how they remembered him, for a while at least, in Venice. But the town soon found something else to worry about and forgot its rebellious son. By the middle of the festival season everyone was talking about a certain Count B. whose body had been discovered—masked and wearing a domino cloak—hanging at dawn before the house of the French ambassador. Because, we should not forget, Venice is a cruel city.

But for now he slept, in Bolzano, in a room of The Stag Inn, behind closed shutters; and because this was the first time in sixteen months that he had slept in a properly secure, clean, and comfortable bed, he surrendered himself to the blissful underworld of dreams. He slept as if crucified, his head bathed in sweat, his legs and arms spread-eagled, lost in a passion of sleep, without a thought but with a tired and scornful smile playing on his lips, as if aware that he was being observed through the keyhole.

And indeed he was being observed, and this is how;

first by Teresa, the girl the innkeeper referred to as his own child, who played the role of servant to distant relatives in the house. The girl was well developed and, according to relatives, of an even and pleasant temper, if a little simple. They tended not to speak about this. Teresa, relative and servant, did not say very much either. She is simple, they said, and gave no reasons for their opinion, since it was not thought worthwhile, indeed not fitting, to bother about her, for the girl counted for less in The Stag than did the white mule they harnessed each morning to drive to market. Teresa, to them, was a kind of phantom relative, a figure who in some ways belonged a little to everyone and was therefore not worth bothering about or even tipping. She is simple, they said, and traveling salesmen and temporarily billeted soldiers would pinch her cheeks and arms in the dark corridors. But there was a kind of gentleness in her face and something a little severe about her mouth; her hand, too, which was always red from washing, gave off a certain nobility, and a kind of question hung about her eyes, a quiet and devout sort of question, so that one could neither address it nor forget it. Despite all that, for all her heart-shaped face and questioning eyes, she was a person of no consequence. It was a shame to waste your breath on her.

But there she was now, kneeling by the keyhole and watching the sleeping man, which might well be the reason that we ourselves are wasting breath on her. She had raised her hands to her temples so she could see better, and even her gently sloping back and strong hips were wholly given over to the task: it was as if her whole body were glued to the keyhole. What she was seeing was, in fact, of no particular interest. Teresa had observed a good many things through keyholes: she had been serving at The Stag for four years, since she was twelve years old, had kept her mouth shut, taken breakfasts into rooms, and had regularly changed the beds in which strange men and women slept, some singly, some together. She had seen much and wondered at nothing. She understood that people were as they were: that women spent a long time before the mirror, that men—even soldiers—powdered their wigs, clipped and polished their nails, then grunted or laughed or wept or beat the wall with their fists; that sometimes they would bring forth a letter or an item of clothing and soak these indifferent objects with their tears. This is what people were like when they were alone in their rooms, observed through keyholes. But this man was different. He lay sleeping, his arms extended, as though he had been murdered. His face was serious and ugly. It was a masculine face, lacking beauty and grace, the nose large and fleshy, the lips narrow and severe, the chin sharp and forceful and the whole figure small-framed and a little tubby, for in sixteen months in jail, without air or exercise, he had put on some weight. I don't understand it at all, thought Teresa. Her thoughts were slow, hesitant, and naïve. It's beyond understanding, she thought, her ears reddening with excitement: what do women see in him? For all night in the bar and all morning in the market, everywhere in town, in shops and in taprooms, he was the sole topic of conversation: the way he arrived, in rags, without money, with that other jailbird, his secretary. Best not even mention his name. But mention it they did, and most frequently, both women and men, for they wanted to know everything about him, how old he was, whether blond or dark, the sound of his voice. They talked about him as they would have some famous visiting singer or strongman, or a great castrato actor who played women's roles in the theater and sang. What is his secret? wondered the girl, and pushed her nose harder against the door and her eyes closer to the keyhole.

The man lying on the bed asleep, his arms and legs spread-eagled, was not handsome. Teresa compared him to Giuseppe the barber: now Giuseppe was clearly handsome, rosy cheeked, with soft lips and blue eyes like a girl. He often called at The Stag and always closed his eyes and blushed when Teresa addressed him. And the Viennese captain who spent the summers here: he was handsome too with his wavy, pomaded hair and the moustache he twisted into sharp points. He wore a fine satchel beside his broad sword, stomped about in boots, and spoke an unintelligible language that sounded utterly alien and savage to her ears. Later somebody told her that this savage tongue spoken by the captain was Hungarian or possibly Turkish. Teresa couldn't remember. And the prelate was a handsome man, too, with his white hair and yellow hands, with that scarlet sash around his waist and the lilac cap on his pale head. Teresa had, she thought, a working appreciation of male beauty. This man was most certainly not beautiful, no, rather ugly in fact, quite different from other men who normally appealed to ladies. The lines on the sleeping stranger's unshaved face looked hard and contemptuous, confirming an impression she had formed the previous evening. The cramps and tugs of indignation had tightened the muscles around his mouth. Suddenly he grunted in his sleep, and Teresa leaped away from the door, moved to the window, opened the shutters, and gave a signal with her mop.

It was because the women wanted to see him, those women in the fruit market, just in front of The Stag, and Teresa had promised the flower girls, Lucia and Gretel, old Helena the fruit vendor, and the melancholy widow Nanette, who sold crocheted stockings, that she would, if she could, let them into the room and allow them to look through the keyhole at him. They wanted to see him at all costs. The fruit market was particularly busy this morning and the apothecary stood in the doorway of his shop opposite The Stag holding a long conversation with Balbi the secretary, plying him with spirits flambé in the hope of discovering ever more details of the escape. The mayor, the doctor, the tax collector, and the captain of the town all dropped in at the apothecary's that morning to listen to Balbi, glancing up at the shuttered windows on the first floor of The Stag, all excited and more than a little confused in their behavior, as if unable to decide whether to celebrate the advent of the stranger with torchlight processions and night music or to send him packing, the way the dogcatcher grabs and dispatches hounds suspected of mange or rabies. They could come to no conclusion on this matter, either that morning or in the following days. And so they waited at the apothecary's, chattering and listening to Balbi, who was literally swelling with pride and passion as he gave a series of wildly different accounts of the great exploit, which hourly was being furnished with the ever-new apparatus and detail of heroic verse; and all the while they stood, their eyes darting toward The Stag with its closed shutters, or walked up and down among the fruit stalls and delicacies of the surrounding shops, acting, on the whole, in a somewhat nervous fashion, displaying as much anxiety and confusion as might be expected of respectable citizens who are responsible for the security of the town gates, for putting out fires, for the maintenance of water supplies, and for the defense of the town in case of attack by hostile forces, not knowing, all the while, whether to gag with laughter or to call the police. And so they walked and talked till noon, still lost for a plan. Then the women began to pack their stalls away and respectable citizens went off to lunch.

It was now that the stranger woke. Teresa had let the women into the darkened parlor. "Show us . . . what is he like?" the women whispered, screwing up the corners of their aprons and cramming their fists in their mouths; and so they stood in a half circle by the door that led into the bedchamber. They were pleasantly frightened, some on the point of screeching with laughter, as if someone were tickling their waists. Teresa put her finger to her lips. First she took the hand of Lucia, the hazel-eyed, plump Venus of the marketplace, and led her to the door. Lucia squatted down, her skirt billowing out like a bell on the floor, put her left eye to the keyhole, then, blushing, gave a faint scream and crossed herself. "What did you see?" they asked her, whispering, and gathered round her with a peculiar flapping like rooks settling on a branch.

The hazel-eyed beauty thought about it.

"A man," she said in a faint and nervous voice.

It was a moment before they could take this in. There was something idiotic, strange, and fearsome in the answer. "A man, dear God!" they thought and cast their eyes to the ceiling, not knowing whether to laugh or run away. "A man, well, would you believe it!" said Gretel. The ancient Helena clapped her hands together in a faintly pious gesture and mumbled meekly through her toothless gums: "A man!" And the widow Nanette stared at the floor as if recalling something, and solemnly echoed: "A man." So they mused, then started giggling, and one by one took their turn to kneel at the keyhole and take a peek into the room, and felt unaccountably good about it all. Ideally, they would have brewed up some decent coffee and sat down round the gilt-legged table with coffee mugs in their laps, waiting in a ceremonial and gently impudent manner for the foreign gentleman to walk in. Their hearts beat fast: they felt proud of having seen the stranger and of having something to talk about in town, at the market, round the well, and at home. They were proud but a touch anxious, particularly the widow Nanette and the inquisitive Lucia, and even the proud, somewhat dim Gretel felt a little nervous, as if there were something miraculous and extraordinary about the arrival in town of "a man." They knew there was something foolish and irrational about their heightened, coltish curiosity, but, at the same time, they sensed that this improper curiosity did not account for the whole feeling of excitement. It was as if finally, albeit only through the keyhole, they had actually seen a man, and that husbands, lovers, and all the strange men they had ever met, had, in that moment of glimpsing the sleeping figure, undergone a peculiar reappraisal. It was as if it were utterly unusual and somehow freakish to find a man that was ugly rather than handsome, whose features were unrefined, whose body was unheroic, about whom they knew nothing except that he was a rogue, a frequenter of inns and gambling dens, that he was without luggage and that there was something dubious even about his name, as if it were not really or entirely his own; a man about whom it was said, as of many a womanizer, that he was bold, impudent, and relaxed in the company of women: as if all this, despite all appearances, was in some way extraordinary. They were women: they felt something. Faced, as they were, with the mysterious stranger, it was as if the men they had known were coming out in their true colors. "A man," whispered Lucia, faint, anxious, and devout, and they felt the news taking wing across the market in Bolzano to the drawing rooms of Triente, through the greenrooms of theaters, through confessional booths, quickening heartbeats, telling all and sundry that he was on his way, that at this very moment a man was waking, stretching, and scratching in a room of The Stag Inn in Bolzano. "Can a man be such an extraordinary phenomenon?" asked the ladies of Bolzano in the depths of their hearts. They did not say as much, of course, but they felt it. And a single heartbeat, a heartbeat impossible to misconstrue, answered: "Yes. Most extraordinary."

For men—or so, in that moment, however mysteriously, their beating hearts told them—were fathers, husbands, and lovers who enjoyed behaving in a manly fashion: they jangled their swords like gallants and paraded their titles, rank, and wealth, chasing every skirt in sight; this was the way they were in Bolzano and elsewhere, too, if stories were to be believed. But this man's reputation was different. Men liked to act in a superior manner, bragging, sometimes almost crowing with vanity: they were as ridiculous as roosters. Under their display, though, most of them were melancholy and childish, now simple, now greedy, now dull and insensitive. What Lucia had said was true, the women felt: here was a man who was genuinely, most resolutely a man, just that and no more, the way an oak tree is just an oak tree and a rock is simply a rock. They understood this and stared at each other wide-eyed, their mouths half-open, their thoughts troubled. They understood because Lucia had said it, because they had seen it with their own eyes, and because the room, the house, and the whole town were tense with an excitement that emanated from the stranger; they understood, in short, that a genuine man was as unusual a phenomenon as a genuine woman. A man who is not trying to prove anything by raising his voice or rattling his sword, who does not crow, who asks no favors except those he himself can grant, who does not look to women for either friendship or maternal comfort, who has no wish to hide in love's embrace or behind women's skirts; a man who is only interested in buying and selling, without hustling or greed, because every atom of his being, every nerve, every spark of his spirit and every muscle of his body, is devoted to the power that is life: that kind of man is indeed the rarest of creatures. For there were mummy's boys and men with soft hands, and there were loud and boastful men whose voices had grown hoarse declaiming their feelings to women, and there were vulgar, oafish, and panting kinds of men—none of whom were as real as this. There were the handsome, who cared less for women than for their own beauty and success. And there were the merciless, who stalked women as though they were enemies, their smiles sticky as honey, who carried knives beneath cloaks wide and capacious enough to hide a pig. And then occasionally, very occasionally, there was just a man. And now they understood the reputation that preceded him and the anxiety that had spread through town: they rubbed their eyes, they sighed, their breath came in shallow gasps, and their hands flew to their breasts. Then Lucia gave a scream and they all backed away from the door. For the door had opened and behind the great white panels stood the low, tousled, unshaven, slightly stiff figure of the stranger, his eyes blinking, somewhat inflamed in the strong light, his whole body bent over as if exhausted but ready to leap.

Waking

The women backed away toward the wall and the door. The man turned his tousled head to one side, blinked—there were traces of down from the pillow in his hair, and he looked as if he had come fresh from a masked ball or some underworld carnival of dreams where he had danced like a dervish until witches had tarred and feathered him—then ran his piercing glance over the room and the furniture, turning his head this way and that at leisure as if he had all the time in the world, as if he knew that everything was of equal importance, because it is only the feelings we have about what we see that makes things seem different. At this point he noticed the women and rubbed his glazed, half-closed eyes. He stood for a moment like that, with his eyes closed. Then, his head still tilted to one side, he surveyed them in a proud, inquisitorial manner, the way a master looks at his servants, a real master, that is, who does not regard his servants as peculiarly fallible people just because he is the master and they his servants, but as people who have willingly undertaken their roles as servants. Now he raised his head and seemed to grow a little. He drew his gown over his left shoulder with a rough movement of his short arms and bony yellow hands. It was a grand, theatrical gesture. The women sensed this and it was as if they were released from the spell that had first bound them, for, with this movement, the man showed that he was not as certain of himself as he first seemed, that he was merely strutting and miming the actions of the privileged and powerful: and so they relaxed and started coughing and clearing their throats. But no one said anything. They stood like that a long time, silent, unmoving, locking eyes with him.

But now the man laughed, as easily as he might sneeze, with no intervening change of mood. He laughed silently, more with his eyes than his mouth, his eyes opening wide and filling with light: it was like a sudden opening of windows in a dark room. This light, which was good-humored, crude, blinding, and impudent, inquisitive yet confidential, touched the women. The women themselves did not laugh: they did not cry "Aha!" or exclaim "Oho!" or giggle "Tee-hee." They listened carefully and watched him. Lucia turned her eyes away a little, looked up at the ceiling as if expecting help from there, and silently, under her breath, groaned, "Mamma mia!" Nanette wrung her hands in an attitude somewhat like prayer. The man, too, kept silent and continued laughing. Now he showed his teeth, yellowing, slightly splayed, part of a large and powerful structure like an undamaged, predatory set of tusks, and his eyes, mouth, teeth, and the whole face laughed silently, with a lazy, comfortable, self-conscious good humor, as if there could be nothing finer or more amusing than this scene, here, in Bolzano, in a room of The Stag, around noon, facing a bunch of startled women who had sneaked in to watch him wake in order that they could gossip about him later in the town and around the local wells. The laughter shook his upper torso. He put his hands on his hips and leaned back gently so as to laugh better. It was as if a feeling that had long been trapped within his body had broken into pieces and was now coursing through him in hot currents, a feeling that was neither deep, nor high, nor tragic, but simply hot and pleasant, like the sense of being alive: so the laughter slowly began to bubble up his throat, found voice, cracked as it stumbled forth, then suddenly flooded out of him the way a crude, popular song might flow from the mouth of a singer. And within a few seconds, his hands still on his hips, he was bent backward and laughing out loud.

This laughter, a volley of uproarious, all-compassing, tear-wrenching, side-splitting power, filled the room and was audible down the corridor, even across the square. He was laughing as if something had just occurred to him, as if he had understood what had happened, as if the range and depth of human treachery, which was indeed infinite, had irritated him to laughter. He laughed like someone who, having woken from a nightmare, remembered where he was, saw things clearly, and would not be satisfied with mere shadows of whatever he found fearful and laughable. He laughed as though he were preparing for something, some enormous practical joke that would dazzle the world; he laughed like an adolescent, in full throat, with an oddly wolfish howl, as if he were about to sprinkle itching powder on a woman's bodice, or on the nightshirts of the great, the powerful, and the grand; he laughed as if he were set to execute a marvelous, earth-shaking caper; as if, out of sheer good humor, he were to blow earth itself to smithereens. Both hands on his hips, his belly shaking, his chest protruding, his head cocked to one side, he laughed a hoarse, long, twitching laugh. The laughter choked, then turned to coughing, for he had developed a chill during his travels, and the altitude—the air of the mountains combined with the effects of the November weather—was hard on his constitution. His face grew contorted and flushed.

When the spasm was over, his sense of humor seemed to desert him and a terrible fury took hold of him. "I see I have lady visitors," he muttered through clenched teeth, his voice cracked and sibilant. He crossed his arms across his chest. "What a privilege, dear ladies!" He bowed deeply, ornately, disposing both hands and legs in a parody of courtesy, as if he were in a corridor at Versailles, greeting ladies of the French court on a fine morning, while the king, plump-bellied and purple-faced, was still fast asleep, or as if he were idling away his time with flâneurs and toadies, practicing manners with them. "What a privilege," he repeated, "for a gentleman of the road like myself! For a fugitive who has only just escaped the hell of a damp, rat-infested prison, having seen not one friendly face nor met a single expression of tenderness in over a year and a half! What honor, and what privilege!" he mocked and minced in a somewhat threatening way.

The women felt the threat in his voice, drew closer together like hens in a storm, and slowly backed away toward the door, Lucia using the lower half of her body to feel her way along the wall. The man took slow deliberate steps toward them, pausing at every stride. "To what do I owe the good fortune," he began, then continued in a cracked but louder voice. "To what do I owe the good fortune of discovering the assembled beauties of Bolzano crowded in my room as I wake? What has prevailed upon the ladies of Bolzano to visit the fugitive, the exile, the man rejected by the rest of society, who is even now pursued by police dogs and wolf packs over borders, whose trail the mercenaries of the Holy Inquisition are trying to follow through bushes and across forest floors with pikes and lances in their hands? Are the ladies not afraid that they come upon the poor fugitive in one of his less charitable moods, at this precise time, the morning after he has spent his first night in a bed fit for human occupation, not on straw that smells of incontinent dogs? Are they not afraid of him now that he has woken and begun to remember? What do the beauties of Bolzano desire of me?" he asked, by now at full volume, his voice breaking with fury. He straightened up in a single violent movement and it was as if, for a moment, he had grown more handsome. His face was bright with anger, like a bare landscape lit by lightning. "Who, after all, am I that the ladies of Bolzano should steal into my room when I have come to claim rights of hospitality in the temporary lodging of the homeless?" It was clear to see that he was enjoying the effects of his speech, the panic it wrought in the women and the advantage it gave him in the situation. His confidence was growing: by now he was playing with them the way a swordsman plays with a lesser opponent, coming closer with every step, his every word like a swish of the blade. "Beauties of Bolzano! You, the haughty brunette, yes you! You, with your virtuous looks and the rosary beads over your cloak! You, with the ample bosom there in the corner! And you, old lady! What are you all looking at with such curiosity? A fire-eater or sword swallower might have arrived in town to demand your attention, but here you are, sneaking about, gaping at a poor feral creature like me! This is not a cage in a traveling circus, ladies. The feral creature is awake and hungry!"

He laughed again, but bitterly now and in ill humor. "Where have you come from?" he asked with quiet contempt. "From the market? From the inn? There is already talk in town that I am here: spies are sniffing round and keeping their ears open, women are gossiping in parlors and in boxes in the theater, as are you in the market, I suppose. He's here, they are saying, he's arrived, how entertaining! What honor you do me!" he repeated indifferently, with just a hint of complaint. "So, here I am. Look at me! This is what I look like! This is the way I really am, not the way I appear in the evening, wigged, lilac-coated, with a sword at my side and rings on my fingers! This is what I'm like, not a whit more handsome, not a day younger! Do you like the look of me? Do you fancy me? Do I live up to my reputation? What do you expect of me? Why don't we elope, all six of us, hop on a mailcoach and set off to see the world? Am I not Giacomo, itinerant

lover, servant to all and exploiter of all, at your ladyships'
service, whenever, wherever you desire? Go away, you
brood of hens, clear off!" he cried, his voice terrifying, his
brilliant black eyes beginning to glimmer with a faint
green light, or so Lucia said later, as she wept and trembled
in the marital bed one night, confessing all to her husband. "Imprisoned for sixteen months in the name of
virtue and morality! Have you any idea what that means?
Sixteen months, four hundred and eighty-eight days and
nights on a bed of straw with the stink of human misery in
my nostrils, prey to fleas and lice, in the company of rats;
sixteen months, four hundred and eighty-eight days in the
dark, without sunlight or even real lantern light, living
like a mole or a rat, alone with my youth, with the ambi-
tions and desires of manhood, alone with my memories,
memories of the life I lived, memories of waking to brightness and of the sweetness of retiring to bed; alone,
excluded from the world, in the name of virtue and morality, of which I am the sworn enemy—or at least that is
what the *messer grande* said when he had me arrested!
Four hundred and eighty-eight days stolen from life,
erased from it; four hundred and eighty-eight nights when
others could look upon the moon and the sea in the harbor and on people's faces illuminated by lantern light, on
women's faces at the moment the lantern goes out when
the only light remaining is that reflected in the eyes of
lovers!" His own speech had intoxicated him by now and
he was talking extremely loudly, like someone who had
been silent for a very long time. "Why are you backing
away?" he bellowed and stretched forth his arms. "Am I

not here! I have come! You, granny, why are you cowering by the door, and you, you vain silly brown-eyed creature, why don't you come closer? See, this is the arm that has squeezed many a woman's waist, these are the hands you have longed to see! Are you not frightened of them? . . . They can twirl a sword and flick through a pack of cards, but they are capable of caressing too! You, you delicate blonde powderpuff, are you acquainted with these fingers? Even in the dark they can tell clubs from spades, but they can also tickle your fancy so you scream out at their touch, and later, when you are toothless, you can lisp to your grandchildren about the time when these fingers closed about your neck! Ladies of Bolzano! Go forth into town and declare that I am here, I have arrived, the performance is about to begin! He is here, the fop, the lady's consolation, the healer of broken hearts with his arcana of remedies for heartache, the man who knows the recipe for the meal that must be fed the lackluster lover so that he may rise again, virile and amusing in bed the next night! Tell them how you managed to break in, that you have seen me with your own eyes and can certify that I am truly here and have not wasted away in prison: that you have seen this arm, this heart, these shoulders, and all the rest, all present and correct, all in working order! Spread my fame, ladies. And tell your husbands at some appropriately intimate moment, just as you undo your belts and let your skirts drop, that Giacomo, the man who was consigned to prison, darkness, and the underworld, all in the name of virtue and morality, has arrived and is now a truly virtuous and moral creature who craves their forgiveness and support. Do beg for mercy on my behalf, dear ladies, and appeal to the mighty and virtuous, those so clearly without a fault that they dare to, and are able to, pass judgment upon sinners! For a sinner is what I am; go therefore and proclaim how Giacomo repents of his sins. I am a sinner because I know all there is to know about men and women, and because my reputation says that I respect life all the more for it! Go and spread the news that I have arrived."

He went over to the window, stretched out his arms, and opened the casement wide. The cold expansive November light flooded into the room with the force of an alpine waterfall. He held the window open, his head bent back in the light, bathing his pale face in the brightness, his eyes closed to its refreshing touch, and he smiled.

"Go now!" he said without moving, with closed eyes, still smiling, to the women cowering in the corner. "Go and say that I am here. The underworld has vanished. The sun is out."

He breathed deeply. Quietly, with a touch of wonder in his voice, as if he were informing the world of a particularly rare piece of good news, he declared: "I am awake."

And so he stood with eyes closed, not bothering to turn his head toward the door over whose threshold the inquisitive women of the Bolzano market tiptoed out into the corridor. Female feet tap-tapped with sharp quick steps down the stairs. He heard their clatter, neither moving nor opening his eyes, but with half-opened mouth gulped down the cold light like someone who could see and was aware of everything that was happening in the room. Then he called out to Teresa, the young girl who had remained behind and whose red but not unshapely hands were even now on the door handle.

"You, you stay here."

He spoke casually yet commandingly, knowing that his orders were not to be countermanded. He was watching the square, scanning the clear outlines of the houses bathed in light. He gave a gentle sigh as if he were only just now waking and stirring, finally realizing that he had things to do and that the day had imposed certain obligations on him. "Come closer," he said in a distracted, friendly voice.

Five-finger Exercise

*H*e turned and moved swiftly across to the gilt-legged, floral-silk-covered armchair that stood before the fireplace and the great mirror, sat down, and crossed his right leg, which was sinewy and powerful like those of people who ride or walk a lot, over his left knee, resting his arms on the chair, keeping his eyes on the girl, solemnly inspecting her. "A little closer," he ordered her quietly. "Come right up to me." And when the girl had finally made her steady way over to him he took hold of her small red hand and lifted it lightly into the air as if he were a cavalier and she his partner at a dance, or like a tailor inspecting his latest ball gown as demonstrated by a model; he took it in an amiable, professional manner, turning the girl in a half circle with a gentle, almost incidental adjustment of his hand.

"What is your name?" he asked, and when Teresa told him, inquired further. "How old are you?"

Having heard the answer he nodded, humming and hawing as he considered it.

"Why," he eventually asked, "why did you let those women into my room?" And then, as if he were not expecting an answer, he immediately continued: "People think I am a decadent fellow, Teresa, and indeed I am just what they say. I am tired of traveling. A man gets a reputation because the world is small and because transport has very much improved these last few years, so news travels fast. Thanks to gossip in the press and in the corridors of theaters, people know everything and there are no more secrets: indeed, I do believe, there is no personal life left. It was quite different when I was young. Venice today is like a glass box with people sitting in the window, cheating, lying, stuffing their bellies, and making love in public. Have you ever been to Venice? I'll take you there sometime. From a Saturday through to a Monday," he added as an afterthought. "No, dear child, you should not believe what Venetians say. Look into my eyes. Do you see how sad they are? . . . The gossips have turned me into a figure of fun, a marketplace scandal, so that everywhere I go now, spoiled youths and spies, denizens of gambling dens, and women who prosper because there are women younger and clumsier than themselves, turn their heads to watch me; poor wallflowers and others who hang about dance halls whisper my name to each other as they promenade; from balconies and from passing coaches, with beagle eyes, they follow me; women glance at me as if shortsighted. They raise their gilded lorgnettes, turn their heads away, and lisp: 'Oh! Is that he? . . . What a disgrace! . . . Why do they tolerate such people in town?

Invite him in!' That's the way women go on. Come closer, my dear. Look into my eyes. Are you afraid of me? . . ."

"I'm not afraid," said the girl.

The stranger thought this over.

"That's not good," he responded a little anxiously.

But Teresa, who was both servant and relative at The Stag, really did not fear him. Now that she is standing there, allowing her hands to be at once caressed and grasped in this peculiar manner that seems both to give and take, perhaps it is necessary to say something about her after all. For though the girl was a person of no account, an unattached young female, there was occasionally something that played about her lips that spoke volumes to men. She was sixteen, as has already been stated, acquainted with the rank secrets of the rooms and recesses of The Stag Inn; she made and stripped beds, she emptied basins after guests had used them, she had a skirt of dark-blue cloth that was given her as a memento by a trader from Turin, she had a neatly cut pale-green bodice that was left behind at the bottom of a wardrobe by a traveling actress, she had a prayer book bound in white leather that included a portrait of the Blessed Saint of Padua, and other than that she had nothing at all to call her own. Except perhaps a Venetian comb. She slept in the attic above the guest rooms, near the space occupied by Balbi, and her home was in the southern Tyrol, in a village that practically gasped for air at the foot of a great mountain, so oppressed was it by the peak, by the condition of the land, and by poverty. Her father set off one day to become a mercenary in the service of the king of Naples and never returned. Teresa looked at the stranger and was not afraid.

The fear that had first gripped her the previous night when the innkeeper, who sometimes beat her and sometimes invited her into his widower's bed, asked her to observe the stranger; the fear that startled her when she saw the stranger half-asleep, snoring and snuffling, shortly after he had eaten his meal, had, now that the man had taken her hand, passed away. She was a little embarrassed by her hand, which was red from washing and carrying wood, and rough and scaly from the wind that eternally whistled round Bolzano, the wind she thought she would never get used to. She was therefore somewhat reluctant to yield her hand to this man whose own hand was firm yet soft, aristocratic, and smooth to the touch, like cool, finely worked leather. But touching it relaxed her. Yes, his hand, the grip of it, had about it something that would both give and take. And from his cool palm there slowly spread, across the skin and through the veins, an extraordinary warmth different from that which the stove gave out, more like when one went and sat out in the sun. This warmth radiated and extended; then, for a moment or two, it seemed to cease, as when one blows out a candle or a draft puts out a lantern—it was a sensation of approaching flames and thunder. Then it warmed again. Teresa was no longer afraid. She wasn't thinking of anything. Her favorite pastime was talking to the dog, the sharp-eared little white dog in the garden of The Stag, and to no one else; she also liked to spend an hour or two, winter or summer, in one of the chapels of the church, under the picture of the Virgin, just beneath the pulpit. At these times she closed her eyes and thought of nothing. Occasionally she did think of love but only in the way a fisherman thinks of the sea. She was acquainted with love and was not afraid of it.

Now that the man had finally touched her—the stranger was holding her hand with two fingers as if requesting the pleasure of a dance, while resting his head on his other hand—Teresa's intuition told her that she was the stronger. The feeling surprised her. The stranger, to all appearances, was powerful and elegant despite having arrived in rags; what was more, he was older, much older than Teresa, and to cap it all he was famous, and every woman desperately wanted to see him. Teresa should have had every reason to be afraid of him. He had also promised to take her to Venice, and Teresa was afraid of promises, because people who made promises were known to lie: the only people really to have given her something were those who had not said anything about it beforehand. She didn't even know what exactly the man wanted from her. For there had been those who had pinched her or patted her buttocks or wanted to kiss her or whispered lascivious words into her ear, many of which were coarse and crude, or begged her for favors or made loathsome offers, inviting her into their rooms after midnight, when everyone else had gone to bed. No, Teresa knew men, all right. But this one did not pinch her, extended no invitation, and said nothing crude. He simply gazed with an expression of close concentration on his slightly careworn face, like someone who was thinking furiously about something he had forgotten: a name, some memory, some important, life-enhancing idea.

"You're not afraid," the man muttered under his breath. With the gentlest, most courteous, almost solicitous, yet completely unambiguous gesture, he sat the girl on his knee. Teresa allowed herself to be seated. She sat in the stranger's lap quite decorously, as if visiting another person's house, prepared at any moment to run should someone ring a bell or call her. They were both solemn. They looked into each other's eyes attentively, the man slightly squinting so as to see her better, as, with two fingers, he turned Teresa's face to the light. The girl tolerated these movements exactly as if she were visiting the doctor: it was reasonable to grant reasonable requests. "It is sixteen months," said the stranger calmly, "since I looked into a woman's eyes. Yours have a nice color, Teresa, like the sky over Venice. I sometimes saw that sky from a window when they took me for exercise down the prison corridor. It was a blue sky, bluish gray to be precise, a slightly cold blue, as if somehow it were reflecting the sea. You have the color of eternity in your eyes," he told her politely. "But you don't understand this. Not that it matters whether you do or not. There is a sort of misunderstanding between us, an eternal misunderstanding as between all men and women, and I am always ashamed of myself when I am with a woman and babble on too long. Kiss me," he said in a friendly and natural fashion.

And when the girl made no move but continued staring at him with that gray-blue, glassy gaze of hers, her head held stiff and straight, he repeated, "Kiss me. Don't you understand?" in a slightly puzzled voice, but still friendly. Later Teresa recalled that it was the sort of voice in which he might have asked her for a glass of water, or told her to send in Balbi because he was bored. There was simplicity and ease in his request: "Kiss me." But Teresa had never kissed a man like this, so she continued staring, her eyes still glassy, more empty than intelligent. The man took her waist with, it seemed, half a hand, and this too he succeeded in doing in an almost incidental fashion as if reaching for a book or comb, then, amiably, in a mildly inquiring manner, asked her what she felt.

"Nothing," replied the girl.

"You don't understand," he said, a little annoyed. "You don't understand my question. I am not asking you what you feel in general about life, about men or about love. Listen here, child. What I am asking is what you feel when I touch you, when I encompass that piece of your arm above your elbow with two fingers, what you feel when I touch your heart—like this—what you are feeling now, this very moment?"

"Excuse me, sir," said the girl decorously, as she stood up, bobbed to the stranger, and with two hands, as she had sometimes seen others do in the restaurant, slightly raised the edge of her skirt. "But I feel nothing."

Now the man, too, stood up. Legs apart, arms crossed, his head bowed, his voice dark and troubled.

"That's impossible," he exclaimed, spluttering in his confusion. "It is impossible that you should feel nothing, while I . . . Wait, hang on a minute!" With a swift movement he embraced the girl, bent his head over her fresh young face, and stared deeply into the pale blue of her placid, maidenly, gently shimmering eyes.

"Not even now? Now that I have my arms around you? Can't you feel my hot breath? The pressure of my hands on your ribs? . . . Can't you feel how close I am to you? That in this mere moment we already know each other and that I am bringing you a miraculous gift, the gift of life and love? . . . You are seized by a peculiar trembling, are you not? A trembling that runs through you from your brow to the tip of your toes, a trembling you have never felt before, as if you had realized for the first time that you are alive, that this is the reason you have lived so far, the reason you came into the world?" And when he got no answer, he asked, "So what happens now?" Utterly lost, he let the girl go, allowed his hand to float to his brow, and looked about bewildered.

For the girl standing opposite him, only one step away from him, this little, slightly slatternly, raggedy, bare-footed slip of a girl, the common plaything of every innkeeper, the kind of girl he knew so well—and, if he wanted to be honest with himself, the only kind of person he ever really knew—truly did feel nothing, as he could see perfectly well. He was so confused he began groaning. The fresh young body had not shuddered pleasantly at his expert touch: not even when he had held her waist had those clear, rather glassy eyes clouded up like a mountain lake when the storm gathers above it; nor had her heart, whose pulse he had felt through her canvas blouse as he touched her warm, maidenly skin, suddenly begun to race, not even when he pressed his hot hand against her breast more firmly. The girl continued breathing evenly and stood in front of him at arm's length. He raised his arm but it stopped in midmovement, in midair. The resistance he occasionally met with in women had always encouraged him. Was there a more beautiful game, a more exciting struggle, than the duel with a woman who resisted, who slipped from his hands, who protested, and, haughtily or in panic, fended off her amorous opponent? It was at these times that he felt the full power of his humanity, when words tumbled from his mouth with the greatest ease: only at these times could he be at once bold yet submissive, demanding yet worshipping, daunted yet daring. For resistance was already a form of contact, a game half-won; resistance was a form of surrender: she who resisted knew why she resisted and already desired that from which she was escaping. . . . But this girl here, in the guest room of a hostelry in a strange town, this slim, not particularly well nourished servant girl, the first woman to whom he had opened his arms after sixteen months of prison, loneliness, misery, and obscurity—this girl wasn't even defending herself. She was not resisting. Here she stood, perfectly calmly, as if he weren't standing right opposite her, a sweet little rag doll facing a man who had not so long ago rented a palazzo in Murano for the most beautiful nun in all Venice and who, quite recently, had been taught how to pen amorous verses by a countess in Rome, at the home of a cardinal and patron. . . . Here she stood and there was nothing he could do with her because she was neither defending herself nor yielding to orders and demands; she stood like light before a shadow and no female instinct was telling her to flee. He took a deep breath and wiped his brow, covered in cold sweat.

What had happened? That which had never before happened. He looked wildly around the room as if searching for something and his eye fell on the dagger he had left on the mantelpiece the previous night. With a fluid movement he seized the dagger with both hands and began carelessly to flex the blade. He was no longer concerned with the girl but walked up and down the room with the dagger in his hand, talking quietly to himself: "Well then," he mumbled. Then: "It's impossible!" He felt truly awful. He felt like a great actor who had not appeared in public for years and who, when the time came for him to sing again, was confronted by an icy auditorium and silence in the stalls. He was not hissed off the stage, he hadn't failed, but this icy silence, this unechoing indifference was more terrifying than failure. He felt like a singer who notices with horror that something has happened to his voice, and that however much he bawls or attempts those well-practiced florid musical phrases, the warm resonance of his voice, the individual attractive timbre that once made his listeners shiver with delight so that women's eyes veiled and misted over and men stared solemnly at the ground in front of them, all paying close attention, as if the perfect moment for regret and judgment had finally arrived—was gone. . . . It was as if he had forgotten something, a voice, a pose, some secret faculty that had been his alone, which had been the secret of his success, of his very being, and he simply couldn't understand why people no longer applauded the performance when only yesterday they were cheering it to the rafters, and he knew that despite his talent, despite his practice and experience, something had gone wrong: his effect on the audience was not what it used to be! . . . What could he do? Faced as he was by the icy indifference of the auditorium, he realized that he no longer possessed his old power of attraction. He found himself groaning and raising his hands to his throat in panic, wanting to emit some sound—an aaah! or aaiigh!—but failed to make any sound whatsoever. He stood there, dagger in hand, staring at the girl.

"Impossible!" he said once more, louder this time. "You feel nothing, nothing at all? No fear? No trembling? No desire to run away? . . ." He was almost begging her to say something. He was aware what a pitiful figure he must cut, with a dagger in his hand and this imploring note in his voice. "Why don't you look me in the eye?" he asked more quietly, slightly hoarsely, the voice quite melancholy now. Noticing his tone, the girl looked up and slowly turned to face the stranger, allowing her own eyes to be explored by the solemn, piercing pair of the man before her. "Ah, you see," the man sighed with relief, shifting position as if ready to fence or to leap. "My voice has touched you," he rejoiced, the voice quieter and more tender now. "I want you to feel that I am talking to you personally. Because I know you, I would know you now among a thousand women, even at a masked ball. See, you are responding, your eyes answer mine. I knew it. How could it be otherwise?" He gave a low whistle in his joy, then resumed in the warm, deep, sad voice he seemed to deploy like a conjuror his apparatus. "For that is the only secret, my dear, that is all: there is no trick, no catch, it's always this simple. It's like touching a person. You touched me when you stepped into the room, and sometimes I think that is the most mysterious form of contact. Sometimes I think it is the cause, the very meaning, of life. Is your heart beating a little faster? . . . Are you blushing? . . . You know perfectly well that you can't go now. Come closer, return to where you were before."

And when the girl drew closer he addressed her in his calmest, most straightforward manner:

"Don't you remember? I asked you to kiss me."

Slowly, with a sure and leisurely movement, he held out his arms, gently took the girl by the shoulder, and watched tenderly as she leaned her head against his arm.

The Kiss

And now, on the third day after his escape from the notorious Leads where he had spent sixteen months, he finally kissed the maid in a room of The Stag, in Bolzano. What was it like? To begin with he simply kissed the girl's cracked lips which met the male mouth, softly, helplessly, without responding before the two mouths parted. They stayed like that a long time. He watched her eyes, catching her glance, the startled clear look of another living being, then blinked as if blinded by the strong light. Both of them shut their eyes for a moment. This was a situation both recognized, in their different ways. It was as if it were the single most natural, most sensible position in human existence, and it was impossible to understand why they had ever bothered with anything else or with any other position, having prepared themselves a long time for precisely this moment, bending every effort and every desire, awake or asleep, to this end. The girl shifted in the strange man's arms, her expression serious and relaxed. She was like someone who, after a long search and hours of puzzling, had finally sighed and declared, "Oh, I see! So this is what it was about!" Suddenly everything fell into place. She shifted her weight in the man's arms, quite carefully, with delicate, small movements, shy yet certain, feeling that every adjustment of her body had a meaning; and so the great wordless dialogue started, one established a long time ago by man and woman, the dialogue that is continued by every pair of lovers the moment one embraces the other. It was the right position she sought. To be accurate, she was not even moving but simply allowed her body to settle on his knee into the position prepared for her by the median route between resistance and attraction. She leaned her head against his arm and her youthful body readily bent back, his strong, relaxed arms supporting her without effort, taking the alien weight, almost appearing to lift it slightly as if disobeying, if only for a few moments, the force of gravity. The girl's precise position at that point might be described as collapsing in the stranger's arms, on tiptoe, head bent back, slightly off balance, keeling over to one side. Had anybody been observing them through the keyhole, he or she might have thought that the girl had fainted or had just been dragged from some invisible stream and was languishing unconscious in the arms of the person who had saved her, soon to be deposited on the bed or the floor where she would have her arms raised and her heart massaged so she might be brought back to life. Because the girl's posture suggested someone lost and unconscious yet rescued. It is, as a matter of fact, how the girl herself felt at that moment:

she felt like a would-be suicide who had plunged into the river but who had been rescued and was just now being carried to shore. Essentially, she was adjusting herself to her new situation.

Being in the arms of a strange man was both a new and yet a painfully, joyously, and frighteningly familiar situation. It is, after all, a most desirable thing for a person to be embraced by another. Teresa vaguely recalled her mother—a woman as freckled as a turkey's egg and as short and round as a Tuscany barrel—and how she once had held her in her arms like this. Yes, this new situation was familiar, as familiar as life to a newborn baby; there was nothing particularly difficult or clever to do, no need to argue: one had only to accept and to allow events to carry one along, to resign oneself, to let the two bodies discover their own equilibrium as they engaged under the pressure of his arms but according to attractions and powers beyond such pressure. And it was right, it was absolutely in order, that this man, unknown to Teresa until yesterday, who talked a great deal, waved his dagger about, and had emerged from bed that morning with down in his tousled hair, a man who slept with his legs spread and with a furious twisted expression on his face, should now have his arms locked about Teresa, and that she should only have to make a slight adjustment in the position of her head so that it rested more comfortably, to leave her mouth softly and gently open and to close her eyes, and otherwise do nothing at all, for her to feel that everything was as it should be, as was right and proper. So

much she understood. And now that she knew and understood everything she smiled, her eyes still closed, and her
breathing became lighter and faster.

They stood before the window in the fierce, cold light.
The man had his back to the window and was watching
the girl's powerfully lit face: he watched the woman in his
arms as he moved in a peculiarly encouraging and threatening manner that suggested both rescue and assault, the
movements precise and appropriate to the moment. He
too found the situation reassuringly familiar. He was no
longer afraid that lonely, empty months of damp and solitude had led him to lose his voice. He was aware that every
word, every movement of his, found favor with the audience. He looked at the girl contentedly, being in no hurry,
having plenty of time to spare. The face, that heart-shaped
face, whose every feature, every subtle shade of color, was
amplified by the strong light, was simply the face of a
woman, that was all—which did not mean that he was
lying when he said he would recognize it among a thousand women's faces, even under a mask. One woman's face
was as a hundred women's faces, faces he had bent over in
similar situations with just such tender and solemn solici-
tude, as if each were a puzzle he had to solve, an arcane
script, a word written in signs taken from the cabala or
some other realm of magic, each a word that added some
meaning to life. He watched the face patiently, solemnly.
Because these signs on a woman's face, the slightly
upturned, delicately freckled nose, the mouth which was
raw like the cut flesh of a plump fruit, the golden down

above the upper lip, and the chin, that childish little chin set among curves, the brilliant fine-drawn line of the closed eyes, the ample blonde swell of the eyelashes, and, next to the nose and the mouth, the two harsh lines that life had left as its legacy of fear and suspicion and which now, touched by light and by a strange pair of arms, seemed to soften and melt; all this was the rune, the secret script whose meaning he had to decipher. The two faces—the serious male face, gazing, and the girl's face with its closed eyes, its relaxation, its faint smile, and air of expectation—swam next to each other like two planets tied together by an unbreakable law of attraction.

"Why hurry?" thought the man. And so did she.

What was this? Was it love? . . . He was pretty sure that it was not. But now that he leaned over the girl's face and felt the warm breath of her young mouth on his skin, now that the attraction, which was gradual and irresistible, forced him to move closer to her lips, advancing very slowly, with an almost religious reverence, his whole body bending, like a fugitive dying of thirst and worshipping at the fount of water he leans over, he did consider the question. "Could this be the One? . . ." But he already knew that she wasn't, or, more precisely, that she was only one among many others who were also not the One, or, even more precisely, that she, too, was the One. He would have recognized the girl among a thousand other female faces—his powers of recollection worked with a remarkable, almost supernatural power when it came to remembering women's faces, employing precisely the same instincts as a beast of prey does when he picks up traces and scents in the jungle—but he also knew that this relationship would be as inconclusive as the rest, for no relationship was ever conclusive: whatever the power of the mysterious, dumb, yet harshly insistent voice emanating from certain women, the signal never said anything more than, "Here I am: we have something in common that we could explore, you and I." There was never any other signal but this. He always heard the voice and heeded the call, like an animal in the jungle. His ears would prick up, his eyes begin to shine and he would straighten his back. And so he would set off in the direction of the sound, following the scent, sniffing, listening, constantly on the alert, his instincts always reliable. This was the way they called to him, the young, the beautiful, the ragged, the mature, and the aging, serving maids and princesses, nuns and traveling actresses, seamstresses and serving girls, women who could be paid in gold and more discriminating women who lived in palazzos (who also, eventually, had to be paid, and more plentifully, in gold). So it had been with the baker's widow, with the canny daughter of the Jewish horse trader, with M.M. the French ambassador's favorite, with C.C. the ruined child bride in the convent, and with the dirty, lecherous creature who only recently had been swept away to be deposited in his harem at Versailles by His Most Christian Highness Louis of the Bourbons. So it had also been with the young wife of the French captain, with the lady mayoress of Cologne, and with the princess d'Urfé who was as old as the hills and so skinny that a man was likely to prick his finger on one of her bones when embracing her. . . . Each time he heard the voice and at every call he set out, never once lacking the feral excitement of sniffing the air or failing to experience the erotic trembling and the thrill of concentration when the mysterious question once again presented itself. "Could this be the One? . . ." But no sooner did he face the question than he knew that it wasn't, that not one of them was. And so he moved on.

And everywhere there were inns, and theaters with nightly performances, and every day miraculously produced someone, something, provided one wasn't afraid. No, I have never been afraid, he reflected with satisfaction, and drew the girl's unresisting body still closer to him. "But it would be good if this were finally she, the One I have been looking for," he thought. "It would be good to rest. It would be good to know that there was no more need for quick thinking and elaborate strategies, that someday the plot might be reduced to something perfectly simple, that one might live one's life with a woman who loved one back, and so desire nothing more. It would be very good," he ruefully thought. But it was as if the plot had become fatally confused at some point and had now to be straightened out, as if somewhere, at some time in the past, the fragile image of truth that he was seeking had been shattered and was lying in pieces at his feet. And now he had to bend down and recover each and every fragment of it. This girl, for example, had lovely ears, pink and childlike, a fine pair of ears with a most delicate shell-like curve, a lovely interplay between bone, cartilage, and the lobe's faintly comical, simple fleshiness: yes, her ears were a practically edible delight. What should he whisper into such ears? Should he say, "You are wonderful, unique. . . ."? He had said it so often before. But it was as if he were afraid of losing his touch, and so, more for the sake of practice, for memory's sake, he leaned toward the girl's ear and with his hot breath whispered into it: "You are wonderful, unique."

Fine and delightful as the ear was, it blushed to hear the words. Indeed, the girl blushed along her whole face. For the first time she felt embarrassed. There was something impudent, aggressive, almost improper in the words, as there is in every lie told at important moments. But there was something familiar and encouraging in them too, something reminiscent of certain patriotic songs, the kind of songs that people had been singing for centuries, in the shadow of public monuments and other sacred places. "Unique," he had said, and the girl blushed as if she had heard something deliciously risqué. She blushed because she sensed the lie, and then the man fell silent again, flushed by success and a little amazed at the inevitability of it all, knowing it could not be otherwise, that there was no greater lie to be told. And both of them felt that this lie was in some way a secret truth. So they kept silent, the pair of them, somewhat disoriented. They sensed that, in its own mysterious way, "unique" was, like all eternal verities, a truth, that is to say as much a truth as when someone pronounces the words "Motherland!" or "So it must be!" and begins dutifully to weep. And however vulgar and shameless the sentiment may be, such a person feels that the grand mendacious cliché is, in some deep way, as true as his patriotism or sense of destiny, or indeed the words "You are wonderful, unique." And so, because they could not think of anything else to say to each other, they set to kissing.

The two mouths engaged, and, almost immediately, some force started them rocking to and fro. This rocking had an incidental soothing effect, as when an adult takes a child into his arms, the evening drawing on and the child having exhausted itself and grown melancholy with running about. And the adult says something like, "That's enough play, you are tired, little one; go and rest awhile. Don't do anything, just close your eyes and rest. How hot you are! You are really flushed! And how your heart beats! . . . Once you've calmed down, a little later in the evening, I'll give you a nice piece of Neapolitan wafer." And then the girl, somewhat capriciously, even haughtily, will sometimes pull her lips away like a child protesting, "But I don't like Neapolitan wafers!" They kissed again. The rocking, that sad strange rocking, gradually drew them into the element of the kiss which was exactly like the sea, the rocking of which signifies relaxation and danger, adventure and fate. And like people who, in their dizziness, slip from the shores of reality and are amazed to observe that it is possible to survive and move in a new element, even in the alien element of fate, and that perhaps it is not really so awful to drift away from the shore with such slow rocking motions, they began to lose all contact with reality and slowly to advance, without intention, without any specific desire, toward annihilation, occasionally, between kisses, glancing dreamily round, as if raising their heads from the foam before falling back into the dangerous, joy-bringing, indifferent, rocking element, to think, "Perhaps it is not so awful being annihilated! Perhaps it is the best life can offer, this rocking and forgetting, the point at which we lose our memories and everything grows vague, familiar, and misty." The arms they had opened with such gestures of begging and inviting, gripped and held each other's heads.

And so they would have continued had not Balbi stepped in at that moment. He hesitated by the door and in a fearful voice said: "Giacomo, don't do it!"

Slowly they drew away from each other, loosened their hold, and glanced about them in confusion and curiosity. Now that he had let go of the girl, the man noticed that he was still gripping the dagger in his hand, in the left hand with which he had embraced the girl's waist.

A Writer

When the girl had left the room, her head bowed, treading as silently as only those who are used to going about barefoot can tread, Balbi spoke. "I was really frightened. You were holding that dagger in your hand as if you were about to stab her."

"I'm not a murderer," he solemnly replied, a little short of breath as he put the dagger back on the mantelpiece. "I am a writer."

"A writer?" gasped Balbi. He left his mouth open for a while. "Have you written anything?" he asked incredulously.

"Written? Of course I've written," muttered the stranger. He spoke grudgingly, as if he hardly thought it worth his while to answer a companion so far below him that he was sure he wouldn't understand. "I've written a great many things. Poems, for example," he proclaimed triumphantly, confident he had the evidence to back his claim.

"For money?" Balbi inquired.

"For money, among other things," he answered. "Real writers always write for money, you blockhead. I don't suppose you're capable of understanding writers, Balbi. It's a pity I didn't stick this knife between your ribs that time on the outskirts of Valdepiadene when we were on the run and you almost got us into trouble. Then, perhaps, I might really have been the murderer you thought I was a few moments ago. There would also have been one less idiotic rogue in the world and the world would have thanked me for it! I never cease to regret the day I rescued you from that rat-infested gutter."

"You would not have escaped without me, either," the friar answered calmly. He was not easily insulted. He sat down in the armchair, spread his legs, and crossed his hands over his full belly, blinking and twiddling his thumbs.

"True enough," came the matter-of-fact answer. "When a man is in trouble he will grasp at anything, even the hangman's rope."

They were weighing each other up. "Yes, it was a pity," he repeated, and shrugged his shoulders to demonstrate how pointless it was for a man to dwell on all the things he had failed to do in life. "And you, potbelly, you don't understand, are incapable of understanding, that I am a writer. What have you ever written in your life? Love letters, two-a-penny, to sell on the market to servants with holes in their shoes, a few fake contracts to self-employed tradesmen and petty criminals, some begging letters with which you might trouble your betters, people who were sufficiently easygoing and forgetful not to send you to the galleys."

"All the same," replied the friar in his mildest, friendliest manner, "it was writing that saved me, Giacomo. Cast your mind back. We wrote each other such letters, we might have been lovers. Long, ardent letters they were, and Lorenzo the warder, was our go-between. We made our acquaintance through those letters, told each other everything, both past and present. If I were incapable of writing I would never have started a correspondence with you, nor would I ever have escaped. You despise me and look down on me. I know you would happily kill me. You are not being fair. I know as well as you do that writing is very important, a great source of power."

"Power?" his fellow fugitive repeated, and surveyed the friar haughtily from under suspicious, half-closed eyelids, his head thrown right back. "It's far greater than that. It is not a matter of 'sources,' Balbi, but power itself. Writing is the one and only power. You are right, it is writing that freed you. I really hadn't thought of that. The scriptures, the sacred writings, are right when they tell us that even fools are not without grace. Writing is the greatest power there is: the written word is greater than king or pope, greater than the doge. We are living proofs of that. It was in writing that we plotted our escape, letters formed the teeth that cut through our chains, letters were the ladder and the rope on which we let ourselves down, it was letters that led us back from hell to earth. Some say," he continued, "that letters can lead us from earth up to heaven too. But I don't believe in their power to do that."

"What then do you believe in?" asked the friar conversationally.

"In fate," he answered without hesitation, "in the fate we create for ourselves and thenceforth accept. I believe in life, in the multifariousness of things that eventually, miraculously, chime in harmony, in the various fragments that finally combine to make one man, one life. I believe in love and in the wheel of fortune. And I believe in writing, because the power of writing is greater than that of fate or time. The things we do, the things we desire, the things we love, the things we say, all pass away. Women pass, affairs pass. Time's dust settles over all we have done, over everything that once excited us. But words remain. I tell you, I am a writer," he declared with delight and satisfaction, as if he had just discovered the fact.

He ran his fingers through his uncombed hair and threw back his head like a great musician about to raise the violin to his chin and assault the strings with his bow. It was a pose he had learned to strike in his youth when he played the instrument in a band in Venice. Agitated, he paced in a somewhat peculiar limping manner across the room, then added quietly, "Sometimes it surprises even me."

"What surprises you?" asked Balbi like a curious child.

"I am surprised to find that I am a writer," he replied without thinking. "I cannot help it, Balbi, there is nothing I can do about it, so I beg you to keep the secret to yourself since I don't like the idea of bragging and complaining in the same breath. I am telling this to you alone, because I have absolutely no respect for you. There are many ways of

62

writing. Some people sit in a room and do nothing but write. They are the happy ones. Their lives are sad because they are lonely, because they gaze at women the way dogs gaze at the moon, and they complain bitterly to the world, singing their woes, telling us how much suffering they undergo on account of the sun, the stars, autumn and death. They are the saddest of men but the happiest of writers because their lives are dedicated to words alone: they breakfast on proper nouns and go to sleep with a well-fleshed adjective in their arms. They smile in a faintly wounded manner when they dream. And when they wake in the morning they raise their eyes to heaven because they are under a permanent spell and live in some cockeyed rapture, believing that by grunting and stuttering their way through all those adjectives and proper nouns they will continue to succeed in articulating that which God himself has succeeded in articulating once and once only. Yes, the happy writers are those who walk about looking sad, and women deal gently with them, taking considerable care of them as they might of their simpleminded nearest and dearest, as if they were the writers' more fortunate, wiser sisters, obliged to comfort them and prepare them for death. I wouldn't want to be a writer who does nothing but write," he declared a little contemptuously. "Then there are writers who run you through with their pens as they would with a sword or dagger, writing in blood, spattering the page with bile, the kind of writers you find in the study with tasseled nightcaps on their heads, berating kings and parasites, traitors and usurers, writers who enter the service of ideas or of human causes as either volunteers or mercenaries. . . . I've known some of them. I once spent some time in the company of that scarecrow, Voltaire. Don't interrupt me, you've never even heard of him. He had no teeth left but that did not stop him biting: kings and queens sought to earn his approval, and this toothless wretch with a single quill between his gouty knotted fingers could hold the world to account with it. Do you understand? . . . I do. Writing, for these people, was a means of changing the world, but the writers who exercised power on the basis of their strength and intellect were unhappy, both as men and writers, because they lacked silence and reverence. They could plunge daggers through constitutions and stab a king through the heart with a single sharp word but they were incapable of articulating life's deepest secret, which is the miraculous sense of being here at all, the delight of knowing that we are not alone but are cared for by the stars, by women and by our demons, not to mention the happy realization of the extraordinary fact that we must die. Those to whom the pen is just a sword or dagger can never articulate such things, however much power they wield on earth. . . . Such people may influence thrones, human institutions, and individual destinies, but they can do little to suspend our sense of time. . . . And then there are writers like myself. They are the rarest kind," he declared with satisfaction.

"Absolutely," Balbi agreed in awe. "And why are they the rarest, my lord and master?"

His deep, rasping voice bore the impress of prison, alcohol, and disease, as well as wayside hovels and the beds of kitchen maids. Now it was a mixture of curiosity and wariness. He sat with his mouth wide open, still twiddling his thumbs, as if he had blundered into a theater where the actors were performing in some language he only imperfectly understood.

"Because what they write is what they have to lose, which is the text of their own lives," Giacomo's voice was rising. "Do you understand me, you pot-bellied flat-footed fool, you hero of hovel and brothel, do you understand? I am that rare creature, a writer with a life to write about! You asked me how much I have written? . . . Not much, I admit. A few verses . . . a few essays on the magical arts. . . . But none of these was the real thing. I have been envoy, priest, soldier, fiddler, and doctor of civil and canonical law, thanks be to Bettina, who introduced me to knowledge of the physical world when I was fourteen, and thanks, too, to her older brother, Doctor Gozzi, who was my neighbor in Padua, who knew nothing of what Bettina had taught me but introduced me to the world of the fine arts. But that's not the point, it's not the writing, it's what I have done that matters. It is me, my life, that is the important thing. The point, you fool, is that being is much more difficult than doing. Gozzi denies this. Gozzi says only bad writers want to live and good writers find that writing is enough. But I refute Gozzi because there is only one great struggle in life and that is between powerful, justified assertion on the one hand and powerful, justified denial on the other. However Gozzi may dismiss me as a writer now, my being, my life, is the important thing. I want to live. I cannot write until I know the world. And I am only beginning to know it," he said, more quietly, almost in awe. "I am forty. I have hardly begun to live. I can't get enough of life. I have not seen as many dawns as I would wish, there are too many human feelings and sensations that I do not know, I have not yet finished laughing at the arrogance of bureaucrats, dignitaries, and all manner of respectable persons; I have not succeeded as often as I'd like in stuffing the words of fat priests down their throats, I mean those fat priests who count their indulgences in pennies. I have not yet laughed myself sick at human folly; have not rolled into enough ditches in uncontrolled amusement at the world's vanity, ambition, lust, and greed; have still not woken in the arms of a sufficient number of women to know anything worth knowing about them, to have learned some truth that is more sub-stantial than the sad, vulgar truth of what they hide beneath their skirts, which excites the imagination only of poets and adolescents. . . . I have not lived enough, Balbi," he repeated stubbornly, with a genuine tremor in his voice. "I don't want to leave anything out, you see! I am not ambitious for worldly acclaim, I am not ambitious for wealth, for a happy domestic life: there'll be time enough later for strolling about in slippers, for inspecting my vineyard and for hearing the birds singing, for carrying a volume of *De consolatione philosophiae* by the pagan Boethius under my arm, or indeed one of the books of the sage Horace, who teaches that a just man is always accom-panied by two heavenly sisters, Knowledge and Pity. . . . I don't want to give myself over to pity now. I want to live so that, eventually, I might write. This comes at a great cost.

Understand this, my unlucky companion, my fellow in the galleys, understand that I must see everything: I must see the rooms where people sleep, I must hear their whimpers as they enter old age when they can only buy a woman's favors with gold, I must get to know mothers and younger sisters, lovers and spouses who always have something true and encouraging to say about life. I must at least get to shake their hands. I am the kind of writer who needs to live. Gozzi says only bad writers want to live. But Gozzi is not a man, Gozzi is just a timid indolent bookworm who will never write anything of permanent value."

"But when will you have time to write, Giacomo? . . ." asked Balbi. "If you spend it all seeing, hearing, and getting to smell everything you've talked about you will never find enough time for writing. You are right, I don't understand such things. I do, however, know something about the chore of writing, and my experience tells me that even writing a letter takes a long time. Real writing, the work that writers do, would need even more leisure, I imagine. Perhaps a whole lifetime of it."

"I shall write when I have done as much living as I consider necessary," he replied and stared at the ceiling, his lips moving silently as if counting something. "When I have lived, I shall want to write."

Somebody was laughing in the yard beneath the window. It was a warm, youthful, broken laugh and the stranger hurried over to the window and leaned over the balcony. He waved and bowed, and grinning widely, put two fingers to his mouth and blew a kiss.

"Bellissima!" he cried. "My one and only! Tonight! . . ."

He turned around, his voice somber.

"I have to do everything now for the sake of writing later. I have to experience life and everything life offers. Writing demands serious commitment. . . . I must see everything so I may describe habits and habitations, the places where I was once happy or miserable or simply indifferent. I don't yet have time for writing. And those people," he cried with a sudden fury, so angrily that for a moment the whites of his eyes looked enormous, "had the nerve to lock me up in jail! Venice denied me. They denied a man who, even in the galleys, was as true a Venetian as any dignitary painted by Titian! They dared deprive me of my right to be an author, a real author who dedicates each day of his life to gathering material for his work! They dared stand in judgment on me, on a writer, and a Venetian writer, at that! The bigwigs of Venice took it on themselves to shut me away from life, from sunlight and moonlight; they stole an important part of my time, of my life, a life that is nothing more than a form of service undertaken for the community. . . . Yes, that, in my fashion, is the service I perform! I serve the community! . . . And they dared take sixteen months of life from me! A plague on them!" he declared lightly but firmly. "A pestilence and plague on Venice! Let the Moors come, let the pagan Turks come with their topknots and cut the senators into delicate little pieces, all except Signor Bragadin, of course, who was a father to me when I had no father and who gave me money. I'm glad I remembered him. In fact I must write to him immediately. May shame and desolation be the lot of Venice who threw me, the truest son of Venice, into a rat-infested cell! I will make it the mission of my life to revenge myself on Venice!"

"Bravo!" cried Balbi enthusiastically, his fat face, yellow and warty as a marrow, beginning to glisten. "You are right, Giacomo, I understand you. I feel the same. I might not be a Venetian when it comes down to it, but I, too, know how to write. Well said: a plague on Venice. I'm with you there, believe me."

But he could not finish what he was saying as the stranger suddenly seized him by the neck and set about strangling him.

"How Dare You Curse Venice"

"*H*ow dare you curse Venice?" he gasped. "That's for me to do! Do you understand? . . . I will take care of Venice!" His voice was terrifying. He struck his breast with his left hand and his face was strangely twisted in the heat of the moment, scarcely human, like the half-comic, half-horrific masks worn by Venetians at the wildest peak of the carnival. His right hand was gripping the friar's shirt collar and lapel while his left hand hung in the air like a bird of prey, blindly seeking the dagger he had just deposited on the mantelpiece. And so they retreated together toward the fireplace, Giacomo dragging the friar, whose face slowly changed from its customary marrow color to a bright puce as the grip tightened. His hand located the dagger on the marble shelf, seized it, and raised it high in the air. "How dare you curse Venice?" he repeated, calmly this time, the point of the dagger raised, his victim pressed against the wall. "No one except me is allowed to curse Venice! No one else has the right! You understand? No one!" He spat the words out, not simply in a figurative sense but quite physically, his lips swollen, the boiling white-hot saliva issuing from his yellow gums and spraying the friar's face as he spoke: it was as if something in the excited human cauldron within him had suddenly boiled over and the contents of his entire life were bubbling and spitting, and had started to overflow. He was pale, a grayish-yellow, all passion and fury. "I'll curse her myself!" he reiterated, whispering the words into the ears of the terrified, silent, and by now perfectly blue friar as if they were a seductive promise of pleasures to come. "I alone! Only a Venetian is allowed to do that! What do you know, how could you know?! . . . How would you know, you loafers, vagrants, wastrels, and layabouts? You might as well claim to know the courts of heaven as to know the least thing about Venice! You sit in the taverns in the alleys of the Merceria, sipping sour wine, and think you are in Venice! You stuff your guts with fish, flesh, and fowl, with pâté and long strings of pasta, with *dolce latte* and other smelly cheeses, and think you know Venice! You lurk in cheap bordellos, tickling the fancy of some Cypriot whore on a rotten mattress, and because you can hear the bells of St. Mark's in the distance you make believe you are part of Venice! You stop by the balcony of the Doge's Palace, cheering with the crowd, anticipating a handout, or looking around with an eye to a bargain, and you imagine yourselves to be Venetians! Leave Venice alone, do you hear! You are not to lay a finger on her! What can you possibly know of her, what can you see of her, what can you hear of her? Do not dare to speak of Venice, you have nothing to say about her. Worms will be feeding on your fat belly, which is the legacy of Venetian bakeries and Venetian pots and pans, before you are ready to say anything on the subject! You will keep your mouth shut about Venice as the Jews of the Diaspora do about their God. You will keep silent if you value your life and if you ever hope to see Venice again! How could you know Venice? . . . You have seen only the paving stones, the iron feet of the casseroles, the heels of Venetian women, the thighs of Venetian servants and the indifferent sea that carried you to Venice along with all the rest: with the French and their verses, their diseases, and their fine manners; with the Germans, who wander through our squares and gaze at our statues with such anxious looks on their faces, as if it were not life that were the important thing but some lecture they sooner or later had to give; with the English, who prefer warm water to red wine and are capable of staring through their glasses for hours at one or other altarpiece, not noticing that the model for the painting is the marriageable daughter of a nearby innkeeper and that she is praying right next to them on the steps of the altar, recalling her sins, sins that are the talk of all Venice but which Venice has long since forgiven. Because Venice is not the doge or the *messer grande,* not the round bellied canons, nor the senators who, given a bag of gold, are anybody's. Venice is not only the bell ringer in the Piazza San Marco, the doves on the white stones, the wells built by Venetian masons, by the ancestors of my mother and father, and stamped with their genius; Venice is not just the rain glinting in narrow streets or the moonlight falling on the little footbridge, nor is it just the bawds, drovers,

gamblers, and fallen women whose numbers the procura-
tors register in their musty offices: Venice is not simply
what you see. Who knows Venice? . . . You have to be
born there to know her. You have to taste her damp, sour,
stale smell in your mother's milk, smell the noble scent of
decay which is like the breath of the dying or the memory
of happy times without fear of either life or death, when
the spell of the moment, the dizziness of reality, the
enchanted consciousness of living here and now in Venice,
filled each fiber of your body and every nook and cranny
of your intellect. I bless my fate and I go down on my
knees in gratitude to the destiny that decreed I should be
born in Venice. I thank heaven that my first earthly breath
was of the rotten wisdom that lingers in the scent of the
lagoon! I was born a Venetian and that means everything
is mine, that everything that makes life worth living has
been given to me as a gift: the sense of freedom, the sea,
art, manners . . . and, having been born there, I know that
to live is to struggle, and that to struggle is to be a true,
noble Venetian! Venice is happiness!" he cried, letting go
of the friar's purple neck and spreading his arms, staring
about him with a pale face and a glazed expression like a
priest announcing the miraculous news that the light of
heaven was to be found here among us mortals. "It is a
source of pride and delight to me that Venice exists, that
over and above reality, which is flat and dull, there floats
something whose stones are suspended between the sky
and the water, that is supported not only on columns but
on the souls of my forefathers. It delights me that the
streets and squares where the nations of the world remove

their shoes and go about on bare feet, their faces purple with devotion, were simply places where I played as a child, where I took the part of policeman or criminal, of Turk or Moor, in games with the children of street sweepers and patricians! Venice is a city of miracles where everyone, even the street waif larking among pigeon droppings by the campanile, can aspire to be an aristocrat. Mark my words, Balbi: every Venetian is indeed an aristocrat, and you should address me with due reverence! The milk that a Venetian sucks with the first hungry movement of his lips from his mother's breast tastes of the sea and the lagoon: it tastes and smells of Venice, that is to say it is a touch salty, lukewarm and terrifyingly familiar. Wherever I go and smell the sea it is always Venice that comes to mind, Venice and my mother. Things were always best in Venice. I was three years old when I learned to walk on water like the Savior. We were filthy and ragged, and everything belonged to us. The marble palaces, the gateways with their stone arches that looked like fine lace, and the harbor, where, from morning to night, they were loading and unloading cargoes, ferrying gold and ivory and silver and amber and pearls and rose oil and cloth and silk and velvet and canvas, everything that could be bought in the bazaars of Constantinople or was manufactured by the studios of Crete, by the fashion houses of France or by English armament factories: everything was disgorged here, in the harbor in Venice, and everything was ours and, because I was a Venetian, it was mine too. Even when I was a child at play I was aware that I was a Venetian. And when I grew up, stood on the Rialto, and watched the world's nations bringing their wares and throwing them at Venice's feet, I saw that the gold, frankincense, and myrrh they were bringing was in adoration of Venice. His Merciful Highness, the first secretary, that bureaucratic bloodhound of the Inquisition, accused me of the false use of a noble surname! But who in the world is more properly entitled to be aware of his nobility than I, who am Venetian born? . . . Show me the pope, the emperor, the king, or the princeling who is better fitted to bestow nobility on a man than the Queen of all the World, my birthplace, Venice? . . . My mother and father were both Venetians, I and my siblings were all born there: could there be a more genuine *grandezza* or nobility than ours? . . . Are you beginning to understand? You will not curse Venice!"

He stood pale, with circles round his eyes: he looked to be in a kind of trance. Balbi kept feeling his neck and breathed with difficulty after the fright he had suffered. He mumbled through his cracked and gritted teeth.

"I understand, Giacomo. I understand now, the devil take you. I recognize the fact that you are a Venetian. But if you lay your hands on my neck again I'll bite your nose off."

"I wasn't going to hurt you," replied Giacomo, laughing. "You can run and play now if you want. We shall spend a few days in Bolzano because I have things to do here: first, I must write a letter to Bragadin and wait for his answer, and while we are waiting we should get some new clothes because, without finery, even a Venetian nobleman looks like a beggar. Yes, there are things to do here in Bolzano, but by the end of the week we can be on the road again. I shall take you to Munich, so you may visit the order of which you are, alas, no longer a member. My destiny as a writer calls me further afield. Revenge can wait. The thought of it is deep in my heart, though, and will never fade. You must nurture revenge as you would a captive lion, by feeding it daily with a little raw flesh, the bloody remnants of your remembered insults, so as not to blunt its taste for blood. Because I will return to Venice one day! But in the meantime, no one but me will be allowed to curse her. The fires of revenge will continue burning, but that is a matter between the two of us: between myself and the Inquisition, between myself and the first secretary, myself and the Venetians. If you value your life at all, you'll not raise a finger against Venice. I will take care of her in due course, don't you worry. And, mark my words, Balbi, by Venice I do not mean the Venetians. No one knows them better than I who was born among them, who is blood of their blood, the blood of those who humiliated me and cast me out. Who should know them better than the man who introduced the male prostitute to the cardinal? The man who obtained a state loan for the senator responsible for artistic affairs by raiding the state funds reserved for the orphans of the republic? The man who introduced the castrato singer to the gracious head of the supervisory committee? The man who saw the exalted, the high-minded, and the pious, masked and with their collars turned up, sneaking through the notorious doorways of Madame Ricci's house after sunset? The man who knows that, in Venice, the price of a man's life is five gold pieces? The man who knows the precise addresses of hired assassins who spend their days hanging about the taverns in the side streets by the fishmarket and who are just as openly eager to place their poisons and daggers at the disposal of the exalted, the high-minded and the pious as the religious-goods vendors are their candles and icons? Who else knows what happened to Lucia, the adopted daughter and secret lover of his grace, the papal delegate? How did she vanish? Who is in a better position to know from whom, and from where, they bought the needle, the thread, and the sacking with which, on Michaelmas night, they stitched up the body of Paolo, the wild son of His Most High Excellency? . . . Who is in a position to reveal what still lies rotting in the cellars of certain Venetian houses and which head belongs to which torso as they both drift down the Grand Canal on the day after the Carnival? These are the people! . . ." he cried and grabbed the table whose great oak top shook as he touched it. "These are the people who judged me! Patricides, murderers of their own sons, usurers, gluttons, parasites, living off orphans' tears and sucking the blood of widows with their taxes—and these are the people who dared pass judgment on me! Murderers! Thieves! Exploiters! Mark my words, Balbi! One day I shall return to Venice."

"Yes," agreed the friar and crossed himself. "But I wouldn't like to be traveling with you when you do, Giacomo!"

They glared at each other. Then, still staring into each other's eyes, they started to laugh and were soon shaking with uncontrollable hilarity.

"Send for the barber," said Giacomo. "And for a cup of

chocolate. And ink, a finely-cut pen, and some paper to write on. I must write to Signor Bragadin, who was father to me when I had none. I might be able to squeeze a hundred or so gold pieces out of him. Look sharp, Balbi: don't forget you are my secretary and manservant. We might have to spend a few more brief days in Bolzano. Go carefully, keep your eyes open, don't spend all your time sniffing round the skirts of kitchen-maids because, for a plump pigeon like you, there is always a cage like the Leads, ready and waiting. And I won't pull you out through the bars again. Get a move on. There is a banker in the town, a man called Mensch, a well-known moneylender. Find out his address."

Using a gesture he had learned from the pope—the extending of the hand for a kiss on its ringed fingers—he dismissed his traveling companion. He went over to the mirror and, with careful, precise movements, began to comb his hair.

Francesca

Teresa brought in the chocolate and announced that Giuseppe, the pretty, rosy-cheeked, blond, blue-eyed boy, had arrived and was even now waiting for his instructions. Giacomo gave the girl money, had some white stockings brought over from the nearby fashionable haberdasher, then—on credit—ordered two pairs of lace gloves and a pair of clasped shoes as an extra. While the barber lathered him, the various servants proceeded round him on tiptoe, changing the bed, pouring hot water into basins, and ironing his clothes, for he had taken considerable pains to impress upon Teresa the importance of carefully starching the ruffles on the front of his shirt. The barber's soft hand moved over his face, rubbing the lather in, then, like a conductor, wove and teased each curl of his locks into place.

"Talk to me," said the guest, his eyes closed, stretching his limbs out in the armchair. "What news in town?"

"Town news?" the pretty barber began in a singing, slightly effeminate voice, lisping a little. "You, sir, are the news. No other news in Bolzano since sunset last night. You alone. May I?" he asked, and with the ends of his scissors he began to snip at the hair sprouting from the guest's wide nostrils.

"What are they saying?" came the question, along with a sigh of satisfaction. "You are allowed to tell me the worst as well as the best."

"There is only the best, sir," the barber answered, snapping his scissors in the air, then taking the heated curling tongs, breathing on them, and turning them about. "This morning, as usual, I was up at the crack of dawn with His Excellency. I'm there every morning. You should know, sir, that His Excellency does us the honor of affording our company his patronage. It is my privilege to shave him and to prepare his peruke for him, since His Excellency—and I tell you this in confidence—is perfectly bald now. My boss, the renowned Barbaruccia—they say there is no one, not even in Florence, who possesses his skill in cutting veins or restoring potency with a special herbal preparation—is both doctor and barber to His Excellency. My job, as I have explained, is to shave him. And Signor Barbaruccia's wife massages him twice a week, but at other times, too, whenever he feels in need of it."

"Surely not!" he replied coldly. "His Excellency requires both massage and restoratives? . . ."

"Only since he got married, sir," answered the barber, and began to curl his thick hair with the hot tongs.

He only half heard the news, stretched out as he was in the exquisite minutes of self-indulgence afforded by the submission of one's head to the soft fingers of a barber.

Giuseppe's fingers were nimble but he was even nimbler in his talk. His voice was light and gentle, like the sound of a spring, full of lisping, eyeball-rolling scandal; he spoke in the manner peculiar to barbers, who are at once friends, experts, counselors and confidants for whom the town holds no secrets, for they know about aging bodies, about the cooling of the blood, about scalps that are losing their former glories, about the slackening of the muscles, about the delicate creaking of frail bones, about toothless gums and bad breath, about the crow's-feet gathering on smooth temples, and who listened with attention to everything that the bloodless lips of their customers had to say. "Chatter away!" thought Giacomo and stretched his body again, yielding himself to the effeminate voice, to the fine scent of the burned alcoholic tincture being rubbed into his brow and the rice powder being sprinkled on his wig. He enjoyed this half hour in this distant town, as he did in every distant town, these moments when, after rising, he would welcome the appearance of the barber, the official traitor to the municipality, who snapped his scissors and whispered the secrets of the living and the dead. He encouraged the nimble youth with the odd blink or brief aside—"Really? Completely bald?"—in mock astonishment, as though it were the most important thing in the world, as though he had his own suspicions as to the condition of the gracious gentleman who required feeding and massage now that he was married. "But surely there remain a few stray locks on his nape at least?" he asked confidentially, narrowing his eyes.

"Yes," Giuseppe brightly replied with the unselfish volubility of one prepared to divulge still darker and more melancholy information. "But how thin those locks are, exceedingly thin. His Excellency is a great patron of ours. My master, Signor Barbaruccia, is among his favorites, as am I. It does us no harm, that sort of thing. We order him roe from Grado for the increasing of his desire, and Signor Barbaruccia's wife prepares a brew of beetroot, horse-radish, and spring onions for him to ward off apoplexy should he then be assailed by particularly carnal thoughts. His Excellency has mentioned you, sir."

"What did he say?" he asked, his eyes wide with amazement.

"Only that he would like to meet you," answered the barber in his best obedient-schoolboy manner. "His Excellency, the duke of Parma, would like to meet you. That's all."

"I am very much obliged," he responded carelessly. "I will pay my respects to His excellency, if time allows."

So they chattered on. The barber completed his task and left.

"The duke of Parma!" he muttered, then washed himself, drew on the white stockings that Teresa had left at the side of the bed for him, drank his chocolate, licked his fingers and smoothed his bushy eyebrows before the mirror, trimmed his nails with a sharp blade, pulled on his shirt, and adjusted the hard-ironed pleats with the tips of his fingers while occasionally touching his neck with the index and ring fingers of his right hand, as if testing his collar size or wishing to ascertain that his head was still there. "The duke of Parma!" he grumbled. "So he wishes to see me." The possibility hadn't occurred to him when he escaped and hired the trap to drive him to Bolzano. He whistled quietly, lit the candles in front of the mirror because the early afternoon had already filtered into the room with its brownish blue shadows, sat down at the spindle-legged table, arranged paper, ink, and sand for blotting, and with goosequill held high above his head, his upper body slightly reclined, his eyebrows suspiciously raised, he peered attentively and curiously into the mirror. It was a long time since he had seen himself like this, in circumstances so fitting for a writer. It was a long time since he had sat like this, in a room with fine furniture, before a fire, in a freshly starched shirt, in long white pearlescent stockings, with a real quill in his hand, ready for literary production in the hour most apt for solitude and meditation, for complete immersion in the task before him, which, at this precise moment, was neither more nor less than the composition of a begging letter to Signor Bragadin. "What a letter this will be!" he thought with satisfaction, the way a poet might contemplate a sonnet the first few rhymes of which are already jangling in his ears. "The duke of Parma!" he reflected once more, compelled by an association of ideas he could not dismiss. "Can he still be alive? . . ." Pursing his lips, he began to count aloud.

"Four," he counted, then stared thoughtfully at the ceiling, adding and subtracting. "No, five!" he declared, precise as any tradesman. He gazed into the candle flame, fascinated and round mouthed. "I am a poet about to write a poem," he thought, quill in hand, leaning back in the armchair, facing the writing desk and the fireplace, his hair lightly combed, his clothes washed and starched. He was enjoying the situation. "Five," he considered again, this time a little anxiously, and raised the five fingers of his hand, as if showing or proving something to someone, like a child claiming, "It wasn't me!"

"Five," he grumbled, and bit hard on his lower lip, wagging his head. Screwing up his eyes, he gazed into the flame, then into the deep shadows of the room, then finally into the far distance, into the past, into life itself. And suddenly he gave a low whistle, as if he had found something he had been looking for. He pronounced the name, "Francesca."

He raised the quill and with a gesture of amazement wrote the name in the air, as if to say, "The devil take it! But what can I do?" He stretched his legs in the scarlet light of the fire, breathed in the scented warmth, threw away the quill, and watched the flames. "That's the one," he thought. "Francesca!" And once again: "The duke of Parma! Bolzano! What a coincidence!" But he knew there was no such thing as coincidence, and that this was no coincidence, either. Suddenly, it was as though a hundred candles had been lit in the room: he saw everything clearly. He heard a voice and was aware of the familiar scent of verbena mingling with the sane, cheerful smell of freshly ironed women's underwear. Yes, it had been five years, he thought, mildly horrified. For these last five years had swept away everything in their filthy hot torrent, everything including Francesca, nor had he once reached out to save what had vanished in it. Yes, it had been five years:

and he wondered whether they recalled the story in Pistoia, in the palazzo from which the aged countess would ride out in a black baldachin-covered coach into Florence at noon when the gilded youth and little lordlings of the city went promenading before the exquisite stores of the Via Tornabuoni? Would they still recall the midnight duel in Pistoia where the bald and elderly aristocrat waited for him, sword in hand, where they fought in the square before the palazzo, in the presence of the silent Francesca and the old count who kept rubbing his hands? They had fought silently, for a long time, their swords glittering in the moonlight, in a genuine fury that transcended the very reason for which they were fighting, so there was no more yearning for revenge or satisfaction but simply a desire to fight, because two mortal men in pursuit of one Francesca was one too many. "The old man fought well!" he acknowledged under his breath. "He didn't need Signor Barbaruccia's wife's aphrodisiacs then: he could vie for Francesca's affections without such things." He covered his eyes to see more clearly, unable, not even willing, to shut out the images that now grew clearer and assumed ever more life-size proportions behind his closed eyelids.

There stood Francesca in the dawn breeze, in front of the crumbling stone wall of the count's garden, slender, wearing a nightgown, fifteen years old, her dark hair falling across her brow, one hand clutching a white silk shawl across her breast, her eyes wide, staring at the sky. Had it been five years? No, it was only the swish of swords that had happened five years ago; the moment in which he had first seen Francesca was stored away in a deeper, more secret crevice of time. There she stood before the garden wall in the shadows of the cypresses, and the sky above them was a clear and gentle blue, as if every human passion had dissolved and gentled in that clear, all-pervading blue. The wind is embracing Francesca, the soft folds of the nightgown are hugging her girlish body like a swimming costume. Francesca seems to have stepped from a bathing pool compounded of night and dreams, her body shimmering, dew-drenched, and in the corner of her eyes there is some sparkling liquid whose precise nature is hard to define, a teardrop, perhaps, or a drop of dew that has deserted its usual habitat in the depths of the flower cup to settle on a young girl's lashes. . . . And he stands opposite the girl and listens. Only desire can listen with such intensity, he now thinks. I tend to talk a lot, far too much, in fact, but I listened then, in Pistoia, by the crumbling castle wall, in the garden, where the olives ran riot and the cypresses stood about as somber as you could wish, as somber as the halberdiers of a king in exile. Francesca has stolen from her bed in the castle, out of the night, out of childhood and out of a sheltered life into the garden on the morning of the day that he exchanges dueling cards with the duke of Parma. He saw and felt everything now. He caught the scent of the morning, and it stirred up jealousy and other intense feelings in him, memories of moments experienced only by those who are no longer young. Because Francesca represented youth and so did those silent gardens: perhaps it was the last minute of his own youth passing in the impoverished count's garden in Pistoia; perhaps these were the somber, tattered, grandiose theatrical props of his own decaying memory, a memory that was disintegrating under the pressure of years; maybe this scene represented his youth as it was many years ago in a garden in Tuscany when the sky was blue and Francesca stood by the garden wall, her hair and clothes fluttering in the wind, her eyes closed; when they were both listening, confused and intoxicated by a feeling, that even now sank its claws into him and tortured him. "How extraordinary she was!" he thought, and pressed his fists even tighter into his eyes. It was as if she were saturated with light, so intensely did that sweet yet disturbing energy flow from her to touch the man standing opposite her. Yes, she was filled with light. It was the rarest of all sensations, he reflected approvingly, like a connoisseur. There was light in her, and when a man looked into her eyes it was as if lamps were being lit all over the world; everything around him was brighter, more real, more substantially true. Francesca herself stood as if entranced and he did not speak as the old suitor stepped through the garden gate, offered his arm to Francesca, and led her back into the house. That was all. And a year later, in the very same place, in a corner of the yard before the castle gate, quite possibly at the same precise hour, two men fought each other.

The old man fought well, he thought again, curling his lip in homage, and smiled bitterly. Was that all? . . . Perhaps the adventure was simply about youth, the last year of real youth, that mysterious but exciting interval when even the nervous traveler lets the reins of his horse go, relaxes into the gallop, looks round, wipes his brow, and sees that the road waiting for him ahead is steep, that far off, beyond the woods and the hills, the sun is already beginning to set. When he first met Francesca it was still bright, still high noon. They stood in a valley in the foothills of Tuscany. He had just arrived from Rome, his pockets bulging with the cardinal's gold and with letters of introduction. Travel was different then, he thought with satisfaction and a touch of envy. Few could travel the way I did, he proudly reflected. He had a shameless self-confidence born of genius, of an artist at the top of his form: "The sound I can get out of that flute! Remarkable! Can anyone compare with me? . . . Let him try!" There were indeed few who could travel like him and even fewer who could arrive in the style he did, in the good old days, five years ago! For there's a trick, a manner of carrying things off on the stage of human endeavor, and he knew all the theatrical tricks; that there's a way of choosing the horses, the equipment, the dimensions of the coach, and, yes, even the coachman's uniform; that one must master the art of arriving at the palazzo of one's host or at an inn of good reputation, as well as the art of driving through the gates of a foreign city and of leaning back in one's seat in one's lilac-edged gray traveling cloak, or of raising one's gilt-handled lorgnette in one's gloved hand and crossing one's legs in a careless, faintly interested manner, the way Phoebus himself might have traveled at dawn in his fiery chariot drawn by four prancing horses above a world that, to tell the truth, he mildly despised. These were the tricks you had to master; this was the best way to travel and to arrive! How few people knew such tricks! There were remarkably few people who were capable of understanding that it was vital that, within half an hour of arriving at the inn or at your host's palazzo, the whole serving staff of the establishment should be buzzing around you! This was the way he arrived one day at Pistoia, at the home of the old impoverished count who was related to the cardinal who now, in turn, was sending his blessing to the family, to the fat countess and to Francesca, his godchild. He proceeded to stay a month, entertained the family, made over a gift of two hundred ducats and golden caskets to the count, returning twice the next year, and at the end of that year, one moonlit night, fought a duel with the ancient suitor, the duke of Parma. He opened his shirt and examined the wound on his chest.

He touched the scars with his fingertips, itemizing and remembering them. There was a line of three scars on his left, all three just above the heart, as if his enemies had unconsciously yet somehow deliberately, instinctively, aimed precisely at his heart. The central scar, the deepest and roughest of them, was the one he owed to His Excellency of Parma and to Francesca. He put his index finger to the now painless wound. The duel had been fought with rapiers. The Duke's blade had made a treacherous incursion above his heart, so the surgeon had had to spend weeks draining the blood and the suppuration off the deep wound; and there had also been some internal bleeding, as a result of which the victim, after fever fits, bouts of semiconscious delirium, and stretches of screaming and groaning insensibility, finally bade farewell to adventure. He lay in Florence in the hospital of the Sisters of Mercy where he had had himself conveyed in the duke's coach on the night of his wounding. He had not seen Francesca since that moment, and he learned of the engagement only some three years later in Venice, at a masked ball, from the French ambassador, who regretfully let fall that the cousin of the grand duke, a Parmesan kinsman of His Most Christian Majesty, forgetting his rank and high connections, had, in the idiotic thoughtlessness of his declining years, married some little village goose from Tuscany, a rural demi-countess of some kind. . . . He had smiled and held his peace. The wound no longer gave him any pain, and only when the weather was damp did he feel the slightest pang. So life went on and no one ever mentioned Francesca's name.

Why is it, he wondered, that I have remained aware of her all these years? And later, too, when I received the second wound, that long jagged one above the little carte de visite left me by the duke of Parma, that long brute across the chest, administered with a sword at dawn by the hired assassin of Orly the cardsharp as I was leaving the gambling den at Murano, my greatcoat stuffed with hard-earned gold prized from the pockets of a cheating banker and various other rogues, gold earned through the judicious use of quick wits and even quicker fingers; why was it that, in those days after the assault, as I lay in a state between life and death, this image of Francesca by the garden wall under the blue Tuscan sky kept coming to mind? And the third scar, that odd scratch where the Greek woman went at him with her sharp fingernails, and which hurt more than other cuts and thrusts received at the hands of men, that mysterious wound through which the toxins of death seeped into his body, which was less than a pinprick yet so dangerous that Signor Bragadin and the finest doctors of the council fussed around his bed for weeks, torturing the poor patient with enemas and cuppings until one day he grew weary of dying and, asking for orange juice and hot broth, simply recovered—why was it that, in the delirium caused by this deadly female weapon, he kept seeing Francesca and calling on her? "Is it possible that I loved her? . . ." he mused with a sincere, almost childlike sense of wonder, and stared into the mirror above the fireplace. "Heaven knows, I might have! . . ." he thought, and looked about him with pious stupefaction.

But life proved more resilient, more resilient than even the memory of Francesca, and every day brought something miraculous to a man providing he was healthy and did not go in fear of anything. Who was Francesca, what was she, in the years when gold coins spilled from his fingers at gaming tables, into women's palms, into the pockets of fashionable tailors, into the fists of layabout acquaintances, into the hands of whoever happened to be about when he needed medicine to cure the terrible pox or to save him from a frightening, secret boredom? "I am a writer," he thought, "but I don't like being alone." He considered this peculiar phenomenon. This might be why life dealt him such a cruel hand in the enforced solitude of the penitentiary; perhaps the sapient and subtle masters of the Inquisition knew about his secret terror; perhaps they suspected that boredom and loneliness were as much a form of torture to him as the Spanish boot, the red-hot pincers, or being broken on the wheel was to others? What was the point of life if one were removed from the busy commerce of the world? However one dreamed or imagined, thought and recalled, or meditated on sensations that life had burned up and reduced to ashes, it was no compensation for the loss of the most humble, most idiotic detail of a life experienced directly! Anything but solitude! he thought and shuddered. Better to be abject and poor, better to be mocked and despised yet able to slink over to the light and crouch there where lamps are burning and music is being played, where people crowd together and enjoy the greasy, foul-smelling yet cheeringly sweet, bestial sense of community that constitutes human life. Life was company for him, nothing more: he was always in company, always carelessly taking his wares to market because the market was where he wanted to be. He loved the racket, the proximity of other bodies, the sheer buccaneering adventure of it. Sometimes the bargaining was rough and crude, at other times sophisticated and sly, but most of the time it was like a game, a competition in which one took on all comers much as one did one's own destiny. The marketplace was the only place for him, for the writer in him. It was life itself. He scratched his ears and felt a cold thrill run down his spine.

And that was why his clever, superior torturers had punished him with solitude, a fate worse than death, he thought with disgust. Four hundred and eighty-eight days! And the memories! Each memory just one more condemned soul. And sometimes the image, that shining blue-and-white moment in the Tuscan garden: Francesca!

For hers was the only face, the one and only face he had not gazed at with the brazen curiosity he usually directed at women's faces. Her face persisted more obstinately and with greater force than reality itself, even in his underworld prison where living men groaned and wept. It was a banal enough occasion when their paths first crossed. The cardinal's kinsman was entertaining him in a coat with ragged elbows, in a room full of clouded mirrors and broken-legged Florentine furniture while the Apennine wind whistled through the cracked windows. As in all houses where not only plaster but discipline itself has begun to crumble, the servant had been confidential, pushy, chatty, and fat. The countess no longer wished to know about anything except occasional excursions to Florence in her threadbare coach, excursions that might take in a mass and a promenade down the corso where she might glimpse the ghost of her much-admired younger self. The count bred doves and, like the pitiful old man he was, regretfully and fearfully awaited the arrival of the messenger from Rome who on the third day of every month would bring him papal gold in a lilac-colored silk purse, this being the modest pension provided for him by the cardinal. The house was dense with dreams, spiders, and bats. Francesca's first words to him were, "What is it like in Rome? . . ." She stared at the stranger with wide eyes and an expression of terror on her face. For a long time after that she said nothing at all.

This love matured slowly, for like the best fruit it needed time, a change of seasons, the blessing of sunlight and the scent of rain, a series of dawns in which they would walk through the dewy garden among bushes of flowering may, conversations where a single word might suddenly light up the landscape locked in her tender, cloistered heart, when it would be like looking into the past and seeing ruined castles, vanished festivals where traps with gilded wheels rolled down the paths of neat, properly tended gardens past people in brightly colored clothes with harsh, powerful, and wicked profiles. There was in Francesca something of the past. She was fifteen but it was as if she had stepped out of a different century, as if the Sun King had seen her one morning on the lawn at Versailles playing with a hoop covered in colored paper, and had summoned her to him. There was a kind of radiance in her eyes that suggested women of long ago, women who would risk their lives for love. But it was he that had risked his life, he the suitor, the soldier of misfortune, when his old, terrifyingly rich, and disturbingly aristocratic rival pierced his bare chest just above the heart. Francesca watched the duel from an upstairs window. She stood calmly, her unbound hair hanging in black tendrils over her soft youthful shoulders, wearing the nightgown that the duke of Parma had ordered for her from Lyon a few days earlier, for he had personally taken charge of his future fiancée's trousseau, stuffing heaps of lace, silk, and linen garments into individual boxes. Calmly she stood in the moonlight in a window on the second story, her arms folded across her chest, watching the two men, the old one and the younger one, who were prepared to shed their blood for her. But why? she might have wondered in that moment. Neither had received any favors, neither was taking anything away from the other, but there they were, leaping about in the silvery light, their bodies bare from the waist up, the moonlight flashing off the blades of their swords, the steel chiming like crystal goblets, and the duke's wig slightly askew in the heat of the contest so that Francesca was genuinely afraid that this noble encounter might result in His Excellency of Parma losing his artificial mane. Later she saw the younger man fall. She watched carefully to see if the loser would rise. She tightened the silk scarf above her breasts. She waited a little longer. Then she married the duke of Parma.

"He wants to see me!" muttered Giacomo. "What does he want of me?" He vaguely remembered a rumor he had once heard that His Excellency had inherited some lands near Bolzano and a house in the hills. He felt no anger thinking about the duke. The man had fought well. There was something lordly and absolute about the way he had whisked Francesca away from the house of dreams, spiders, and bats, and Giacomo could not help but admire his aristocratic hauteur, even now, when he could no longer recollect the precise color of Francesca's eyes. "The seduction was a failure," he noted and stared into the fire. "The seduction was a failure, but the failure may also have been my greatest triumph. Francesca never became my lover. It might have been stupid and oversensitive of me but I felt only pity for her. She was the first and the last of those for whom I felt such pity. It might have been a great mistake, maybe even an unforgivable mistake, there's no denying or forgetting that, but there was something exceptional about Francesca. It would have been good to have lived with her, to drink our morning chocolate together in bed, to visit Paris and show her the king and the flea-circus in the market at St. Germain, to warm a bedpan for her when her stomach ached, to buy her skirts, stockings, jewels, and fashionable hats and to grow old with her as the light fades over cities, landscapes, adventures, and life itself. I think I felt that when she stood before me in the garden under the blue sky. That is why I fled from her!" The thought had only just occurred to him, but he took it calmly. He had to face the laws of his own life. "That's not the kind of thing I do," he said to himself, but he threw aside the pen, stood up, and felt the restless pounding of his heart.

Perhaps it pounded only because he was now reminded that the gossip had been right, that Francesca and the duke of Parma were living nearby. For all he knew they might have been his very neighbors or occupying some palazzo in the main square, since it was likely, after all, that in winter they would leave their country house and move into town. And now that he recalled his ridiculous failure and remembered the melancholy lingering sense of triumph that accompanied it, he couldn't help feeling that the morning that Francesca saw him lying wounded on the lawn of the garden of the Tuscan palazzo did not signify the end of the affair, that it hadn't actually settled anything. You cannot after all settle things with a duel and a little bloodshed. The duke, having wounded him, was courteous, generous, and noble in bearing, and had personally lifted him into the coach. Even half-conscious as he was, he was amazed at the old man's strength when he picked him up! It was the duke in person who had driven the horses that bore the invalid to Florence, driving carefully, stopping at every crossroads, dabbing with a silk handkerchief at the blood issuing from him, and all this without saying anything, confident in the knowledge that actions spoke louder than words. It was a long ride by night from Pistoia to Florence. The journey was tiring and he was bleeding badly, the stars twinkling distantly above him with a peculiar brightness. He was half sitting, half lying in the back seat and, in his fevered condition, could see the sky in a faint and foggy fashion. All he could see in fact was the sky full of stars against the dark carpet of the firmament, and the slim straight figure of the duke keeping the horses on a short rein. "There," said the duke once they had arrived at the gates of Florence in the early dawn. "I shall take you to the best surgeon. You will have everything you need. Once you are well you will leave the region. Nor will you ever come back. Should you ever return," he added, a little more loudly, without moving, the reins still in his hand, "I will either kill you myself or have you killed, make no mistake about it." He spoke in an easy, friendly, perfectly natural manner. Then they drove into the city. The duke of Parma required no reply.

Theatrics

*F*inally he got down to it and wrote the letter to
Signor Bragadin. It was a fine letter, the kind a writer
would write, beginning "Father!" and ending "I kiss your
feet," and, over six pages, he related everything in considerable detail: the escape, the journey, Bolzano, the duke of
Parma, his plans, and he mentioned Mensch, too, the secretary, money changer, and usurer, to whom money might
be sent. He needed more than usual, if possible, or, better
still, a letter of credit he could take to Munich and Paris,
because his journey would lead him far afield now and it
would be a great adventure that would test him to the
limit, so it was possible that this letter might be the last
opportunity to say goodbye to his friend and father, for
who knew when the hearts of the Venetian authorities
would soften and forgive their faithless, fugitive son? The
question was rhetorical, so he labored to blend bombastic
phrases with hard practical content. What could I, the
exiled fugitive, offer Venice, that proud, powerful, and
ruthless city? he asked, and immediately answered: "I offer

my pen, my sword, my blood, and my life." Then, as if realizing that this did not amount to much, he referred to his understanding of places and human affairs and to his store of ready information on everything and everybody that the Holy Inquisition might wish to know. Being a true Venetian, he knew that the republic had no need either of his pen or of his sword, but that it could always use sharp ears, smooth tongues, and well-trained eyes; that what it required was clever, well-born agents who were capable of observing and betraying Venetians' secrets.

He had no desire to return to Venice for the time being. The insults he had borne still glowed fiercely in his heart and gave off a dense smoke that clouded every dear and charming memory that might gently have reminded him of the city. For the time being he was content to hate and to travel. Surely Signor Bragadin, that wise, good, noble, and pure soul, understood that. The senator, who to this very day believed that the half-conscious Venetian fiddle player he had laid gently in his boat in the lagoon one dawn had later saved his life with an extraordinary combination of spells and potions, snatching his rapidly cooling and decaying body from the grasp of doctors and even death; that noble member of the Venetian Council, Signor Bragadin, was perhaps the only friend he had in this world, most certainly the only friend in Venice. It was as impossible to explain this friendship as it was to explain human feelings generally. The truth was that from the very first he had cheated, gulled, and laughed at the noble gentleman. Signor Bragadin was selflessly good to him in a way no one else had been; so good, he suspected, that he would never, in all his insecure rough patchwork of a life, meet his like again. His goodness did not fail or tire: it was silent and patient. Giacomo observed this human phenomenon for a long time, keeping a suspicious, uncomprehending eye on it; there are, after all, certain colors a color-blind man is unable to distinguish. He scrutinized goodness from under lowered lids, his eyes flicking to and fro, wondering when that goodness would exhaust itself and be revealed in its true colors, when it would be time to pay for all the fatherly tenderheartedness with which the old man overwhelmed him, when the doting old gentleman would remove his mask and show his true and terrifying visage. The time could not be delayed for long. But months and years flew by and Signor Bragadin's patience did not tire. He occasionally admonished him for the gold he squandered, refused the odd wild and impudent demand, warned him of the value of money, preached the joys of honest work, pressed on him the significance of honor in human conduct, but he did all this without any apparent ulterior motive, with a tact and patience born of good breeding, expecting no gratitude, in the knowledge that gratitude is ever the mother of revenge and hatred. For a long time Giacomo failed to understand Signor Bragadin. The old man with his silk waistcoat, aquiline nose, thin gray hair, smooth, ivory-colored brow, and calm and gentle blue eyes, might have stepped out of a Venetian altarpiece: a minor dignitary, a martyr-cum-witness in a toga, a pillar in the earthquake of life. "He must want something!" thought Giacomo impatiently. There were times he loathed this all-comprehending goodness and the almost inhuman patience. "Who could possibly love me without desire or thought of advantage?" he wondered.

Such people were extremely rare, much rarer than friends or lovers, and this one inhabited a different world from his own, a place to which, he instinctively felt, he would never gain true access. He could only stand on the threshold and gape at Signor Bragadin's calm, patient, and upright world from there. "What does he know about me?" he puzzled every so often, at dawn, on his way back to the palazzo across the lagoon, passing the sleepy houses, his gondola swaying through the dreamy leaden water in the heartbreaking silence of first light, disturbed only by the splashing of oars which Venice alone offers by way of greeting to the nocturnal traveler as he emerges into dawn, moving down the Lethean current into the mysterious heart of the city. Signor Bragadin's household was still asleep and only the old man's window at his balcony showed the flickering of a night light. He crept up the marble stairs on tiptoe, into his room, the adopted child and prodigal son of this noble residence, opened the window to the Venetian sky, collapsed on the bed, and felt ashamed. He had spent the night at the card table as usual, living on promissory notes and on the credit of his patron, then made the rounds of the dives near the docks in the company of his drunken friends and the giggling, silk-frocked inhabitants of Venetian nightlife, and, now that it was dawn, had arrived here, in this quiet house where this lonely soul kept vigil for him and received him without reproach. . . . "Why?" he asked ever more impatiently of himself. "Why does he tolerate me? Why does he forgive my misdemeanors? Why does he not hand me over to the authorities, knowing, as he does, all there is to be known about me, such terrible things that the merest whiff of them would be enough to set the eyes of the Venetian magistrates rolling and have me sent to the galleys? . . ." Signor Bragadin was the sort of man you don't read about in books, the sort who made sacrifices without expecting gratitude or reward, and unlikely as it was, he could look kindly and with almost superhuman forbearance on every variety of human passion and weakness. He was one of the powers behind Venice, but one that exercised his power with care, knowing that it was better to govern with intelligence and understanding than with terror.

He wrote the letter to Signor Bragadin, smiling as he did so. "Maybe it was precisely why he did forgive me," he thought and stared into the fluttering candle flame. "Maybe it was precisely because I lack everything that the tablets of the law, both human and divine, demand of me, except the laws of desire." He read over the lines with close attention, carefully struck out an epithet, and gave a sigh, his breathing shallow and light. The wisdom of Signor Bragadin was so noble, so mature, it was as if he had become a distant accomplice to all that was errant, lustful, and human in him. "He's like the Pope," he reflected with satisfaction. "And like Voltaire, and the cardinal. There are a few such people in Italy, in the domain of his Most Christian Majesty. They exist; not many of them, though. . . . For what I know by instinct, through my sense of destiny, in my bones, such people know with their hearts and minds; they know that the law under which I was born is the law of wounds and scars, not the law of virtue. They realize that there is another law, itself a kind of virtue, one loathed by the guardians of morality but understood by the Almighty: the law of the truth to one's nature, one's fate, and one's desire." The articulation of this perception sent a shiver through him from the ends of his hair down to his toes; he trembled lightly as though feeling a sudden chill. "Perhaps that is why Signor Bragadin has stood by me," he thought. "He has sat in the council with the others, hearing secret reports, dispensing rewards and punishments, but deep in his soul he has realized that under the letter of the law there is another, unwritten, law, and that one must do justice to that, too." He felt delightfully moved. He watched the flickering candle flame with shining eyes. "You should send the money to Bolzano, care of Signor Mensch," he added with true feeling, in clear firm letters.

"I shouldn't have sold the emerald ring, though," he reflected as an afterthought. His fatherly friend had chosen the emerald ring for him from among his family treasures, lending it to him for one night only as he was setting out to some glittering occasion, on one of those dangerous but enchanting Venetian Carnival nights, dressed as an Eastern potentate. The emerald ring was a memento, an item favored by the late wife of his generous friend. "It was a mistake to pawn it that night while the banker was dealing. It couldn't be redeemed later. . . . I even passed the ticket on. Well, people make mistakes," he thought, generously excusing himself. And when he was offered it for redemption by a man introduced to the noble gentleman after Giacomo himself had been incarcerated in the Leads, he redeemed it! Redeeming such slips of paper might have had an alienating effect on his father and friend, but he never mentioned it. "He paid the price and redeemed it," he thought, and shrugged his shoulders. He paid up without any song and dance, his one and only Signor Bragadin, he who sent him parcels at Christmas and for New Year's while he was imprisoned, his old heart full of impotent rage, for it was plain that he could not live without loving somebody, even in his old age, even if the object of love was unworthy of such noble feelings, even if that object had gambled away his most highly prized emerald ring and managed, with passable ingenuity, to forge his signature on documents commonly circulated in commercial transactions. None of this counted for much with him. There were times he almost envied Signor Bragadin this selfless impulse, whose true meaning he could comprehend only through the intellect, not through his emotions. For a while he suspected that the noble gentleman's love for him was of a perverted kind that he might not be able to admit, even to himself. But the old man's life was an open book, for never once, in all the time since he was born, had he left his birthplace: he had lived his life in the morass that was Venice, surviving it the way a pure and healthy plant continues to thrive in the fumes of a marsh. All the same, he could not bring himself to believe that a person could love somebody without an ulterior motive or a sensual impulse: the concept simply did not fit into his intellectual framework. For a long time he thought that there must be something wrong with him.

There were too many secret ties of affection and attraction, and he had encountered them all in the Venetian docks, where desires of East and West mingled. You could tell what was going on by the way people looked at each other. He hated this other, perverted love: for though he was happy to plumb the depths of depravity himself, those depths always yawned between the opposing shores of men and women; this was how it was, how it had always been, and how it would be in the future. Venice provided a market stall where castrati, Orientals, and other slaves to lust could be bought and sold like meat at a butcher's shop; and it was precisely here, in Venice, that he, of all people, never once strayed from the beaten path of desire. He trawled the sexual bazaar with a wrinkled nose and a contemptuous smile that spoke of mockery and disgust in equal proportions, observing the sick unfortunates who sought the favors of Eros on shores beyond the world of women. "Ah women," he reflected with a calm, dark rapture, as if pronouncing the words "Ah, life!"

But because he lived in Venice he regarded even Signor Bragadin with suspicion for a while. The Venetian market offered too much variety, too much clatter, too great a range of color. Yet not even the foul mouths of Venetian pimps could find a single aspersion to cast at the good name of Signor Bragadin. No one in St. Mark's Square could boast of having sold favors for cash or privilege to the honorable senator. The senator was as much a child of Venice as he was, but he was not a product of the filthy and narrow alleys of the theater: he was the scion of a prominent, aristocratic marriage bed, had always lived in

Venice, was married and widowed here, and even in great old age continued to mourn the early death of his beloved. He lived a lonely life, without relatives, with only a few wise, sophisticated friends and his old servants for company. His house, which was among the most private, most respected in the republic, would open its doors only to a handful of choice spirits, on the occasions when he organized supper for friends: to be invited to one of them was a mark of distinction that few could boast. And this fastidious, private nobleman, this pure fine being, had raised him from the shadows of his murky existence, fished him out of the muddy swirls of the lagoon, him of all people, at the very moment that every star in his firmament had more or less gone out. And why? Not because of secret lusts or passions but out of sheer compassion and a decency that never once tired.

True, not even Signor Bragadin could save him from a cell in the Leads; not from the cell, nor from exile, either, not even in his office as senator when it came to the powers of the Inquisition. The charge the Merciful Ones had brought against Giacomo was laughable. He knew that it had nothing to do with practicing the black arts, nor with orgies, nor debauchery, nor even so much with the diligence of the passion with which he turned the heads of Venetian ladies and maidens. "Not much turning required," he recalled. "People never understand this. It was never I who made the first move." Not that this was something he could discuss with the first secretary. People were apt to lie about such matters as they were about everything that really counted in life. So he was referred to as the notorious "seducer," the officially branded "faithless" lover, the model of inconstancy, the skirt lifter: he was a clear and present danger and labeled as such by the authorities . . . if only they knew! He was not in a position to tell them that it was not he that picked his victims but they that picked him; there was no way of putting into writing the fact that women's views on virtue and the way they actually went about things did not entirely accord with what was proclaimed in public offices or promoted from the pulpits of churches. There was no one he could tell: indeed, there were only rare moments of solitude when he himself could face the fact that when it came to the high combat of love it was he who was the exploited party, the abandoned one, the victim. . . . But this was not the point. The redeeming of pawn tickets, the episode with the emerald ring, the orgies, the days and nights of gambling, the broken promises, the strutting posture, the obstinate bearing: none of these were genuine charges. This was simply what life was like in Venice. . . . What they couldn't forgive, the reason they threw him into jail where even the mighty Signor Bragadin could not save him, was that the danger and corruption he represented for them referred to something else, something other than any crime or indiscretion he might have committed: it referred to his entire manner of being, his soul, the face he presented to the world. "That is what they couldn't forgive," he realized, and shrugged. For what the world demands is hierarchy and obedience, the painful act of self-surrender, the unconditional acceptance of mortal and divine order. Deep inside him burned the threatening flame of resistance to such things, and that was unforgivable.

There was nothing anyone could do about this: even Signor Bragadin was helpless to change it. At Christmas he had sent a fur-lined coat, a purse full of gold, and something to read in prison. That was all he could practically do. There is no saving a man from the world; one day it will break in on him and force him to his knees. But that day, his personal day of judgment, had not yet arrived. He had escaped from prison, escaped from them, and now he had to fight like a soldier, to choose his weapons and prepare for combat. So he wrote the letter, got dressed, and set out to seek appropriate ammunition in Bolzano.

He thought he would make a quick, anonymous survey of the town, so he turned up the collar of his coat and walked as fast as he could. Night was already drawing in, flakes of snow drifted across the street. No one recognized him. He fairly swept along, examining things intensely as he went, surveying the terrain. There was nothing particularly attractive to tempt him. It was as if the place were living not only in the shadow of the mountains but of its own prejudices: the houses were pretty enough but there was a suspicious look in people's eyes. He found this uncomfortable. Like all the great artist-raconteurs, he was only truly relaxed in the company of receptive kindred spirits. "Not much of a place," he thought with fierce antipathy, crossing the grand central square and entering the back streets. Everything was precisely halfway between high and low: it was a mode of being out of his normal range. The town existed precisely in the no-man's-land between all he loved and all he avoided in life. It was sober and well ordered, which is to say it frightened him. He hurried along the street with his handkerchief to his mouth because he feared the strange air might give him a sore throat and he pulled his hat down over his brow because he feared the gaze of the local people, though his own half-closed eyes flickered into life every time he crossed glances with a passing man or woman. He kept casting anxious looks at doorways and peering through lit windows trying to guess which of these gabled houses might be the residence of the duke of Parma. "It's a nice town," he thought bitterly when he had done his tour. "A clean town. A foreign place, too foreign." Foreign to him, was what he meant: there was no tempting familiar complicity in its air, no joie de vivre, no passion, no pomp, none of the mysterious radiance that emanates from the desire for pleasure, a radiance he could detect as readily in cities as in people. It was a solemn, virtuous town, he thought, and felt the goose pimples rising on his flesh.

He began counting the days. According to his calculations, it would be five days before he could expect an answer from Signor Bragadin. Nevertheless he entered the vaulted shops and set about shopping. He needed a great many things, indeed he did, if he meant to establish himself and stand on his own two feet again. "I must rise from my ashes like the phoenix," he thought, mockingly adopting a literary turn of phrase, and "What do phoenixes need?" he asked himself in the next breath. He stopped on a street corner below an oil lamp whose low, flickering flame was being snuffed out by the north wind. Throwing his coat over one shoulder, half-hiding his face with it, he gazed at passersby, his eyes flickering and sputtering with light, like the windblown flame of the oil lamp. More than anything he needed some lace-embroidered shirts, say a dozen, some white Parisian stockings, lace cuffs, two frock coats, one green with gold edging and one lilac with gray epaulettes; he needed some lacquered shoes with silver buckles, crocheted gloves for evening wear, and a thin pair of kid gloves for the day; one heavy winter coat with fur collar, a white silk Venetian mask, lorgnettes—without which he felt defenseless—a three-cornered hat, and a silver-handled cane. He totted them up silently. He had to have all this by the next night. Without the right clothes, without appropriate outfits and accessories, he felt naked, positively abject. It was imperative that he be dressed as only he knew how. Seeing a lottery shop opposite he quickly stepped inside and invested in three numbers that corresponded to his birthdate, the day of his imprisonment, and the day of his escape. He also bought two sets of playing cards.

Carefully concealing the cards in his pockets, he sought out Signor Mensch. He found him behind the church, in a single-story house, in a dark room that overlooked the courtyard, surrounded with caskets and balances. At first glance it seemed that despite the literal meaning of his name, there was little that was human about him. A short, scrawny creature, he was sitting in a dressing gown at a long narrow table, the fingernails of his delicate, yellow hands grown sharp and curling, so that he appeared to grasp things the way a bird of prey seizes its quarry, his lank gray locks hanging over his brow, and his small, bright, intelligent eyes, eyes that glowed from beneath deep, wrinkled lids, staring with burning curiosity at the stranger. He greeted Giacomo in his dirty kaftan, lisping and bowing stiffly without rising from his chair, mixing French, Italian, and German words in his speech but mumbling all the while, as if not quite taking him seriously but thinking of something else, not really listening to his guest. "Ah!" he said, once the visitor had given his name, and raised his eyebrows until they met the dirty locks above them. He blinked rapidly, like a monkey hunting for fleas. "Have these old ears heard correctly? Is an invalid to trust these poor ears of his?" He spoke of himself in the third person, with a kind of tender intimacy, as if he were his own nephew. "Mensch is a very old man," he lisped ingratiatingly. "No one visits him nowadays, old and poor as he is," he mumbled. "But here is a stranger come to call," he concluded and fell silent.

"As a matter of fact you are the first person I have called on," the stranger replied courteously.

They spoke quietly about money, the way lovers speak of their feelings. There was no preamble: they got straight to the point, passionate, full of curiosity, like two professionals meeting each other at a party, like guests who isolate themselves in some alcove so they may discuss the marvelous secrets of their common trade while the hostess is busy playing the piano or someone is reciting verses, to argue a point about masonry or the physiology of the emu. Money was the subject they talked about, their speech plain but littered with technical terms, and there was no need for a glossary since both were entirely at home in the matter. "Security," said Mensch, and the word fizzed in his mouth like an oath. "Credit," declared the other with some heat, convincing and natural, certain that nothing could be simpler, as if the sound of the word and its firm enunciation were sure to touch the old man's heart. They discussed the two concepts readily and at some length. If anyone had been watching them from a distance he might have thought he was witnessing an abstruse argument between two scholars. Both of them were articulating deeply held beliefs, beliefs that corresponded to the essential inner truths and realities of their beings, beliefs so fervently adhered to they would have staked their lives on them. Because what "security" represented for the one represented "credit" for the other, and not just at this precise moment, at the specific dusk of this one evening, but at other times, too, in every circumstance of life. That which one could conceive of only in terms of security and guarantee, the other demanded in terms of credit from the world, his demand consistent and passionate beyond the material business of the present, itself an item of faith. One could experience the world only insofar as he could accept it as security, the other wanted all life on credit: happiness, beauty, youth, but above all, money, possession of which was the essential condition of life. It was ideas, not amounts, that they were discussing.

Signor Bragadin's name clearly impressed the money-lender. "A most honorable gentleman," he said, blinking even more rapidly than before. "A sound name. Worth its weight in gold!" There was a certain suspicion in his voice, for he was sure that the stranger was wanting to cheat him, to sell him something of dubious value, something that didn't exist, or even that, ultimately, he wanted to sell Signor Bragadin's own person. "A ring, perhaps!" he ventured, and raised his little finger with its long, black fingernail, crooking it to indicate that almost anything was better, more valuable, more apt for commercial purposes than a human being. "A little ring," he wheedled in a singing, pleading voice, like a child asking for marzipan. "A little ring, with a precious stone," he added grinning, and winked, rubbing the thumb and forefinger of his right hand together to demonstrate what a pretty, fascinating object a little ring could be, especially one with a precious stone, a ring on which one could offer some security. His myopic eyes filled with tiny teardrops thinking of it, but he kept a careful watch on his visitor, busily blinking all the time, anxious, yet striving to give an impression of cheerfulness, like a duelist who, however unwillingly, recognizes that the man he has taken on is a genuine adversary, worthy of his attentions. He would like to have been over the contest but his fingers and toes were tingling with excitement: the feeling was hot and arousing, it resembled desire. It was the excitement of knowing that the moment had arrived, that rare moment when he found himself pitched against a real opponent, a fit adversary who knew the secret ceremonies and strategies of conduct, who was, in effect, part of the meaning of his own life, the kind of opponent for whom he had always most earnestly yearned. He drew the sleeves of his kaftan further up his skeletal arms as if to say: "So now it is the two of us! Let battle commence!" They eyed each other in admiration.

Mensch knew that he would eventually give the man money because there was no alternative, and the visitor knew he would eventually receive money even in the unlikely event that Signor Bragadin failed to send him the gold he had pleaded for in such convincing literary manner. "Mensch will give me money," he had thought even in the Leads when he was planning the details of his escape, when the name itself had been enough to rouse his imagination, so that he could almost see him, as in a vision; and now that he stood face to face with the usurer he noted with satisfaction that the vision was pretty close to the truth, that reality did not disappoint him. It was this same mysterious instinct that had whispered to him that Mensch, whose name he had heard but once from a Dutch trader in raw cloth, would be a proper adversary and an appropriate business partner, that their fates were linked, and that, one day, he would have to appear before him, and that however Mensch might snigger and squeal, he would do him no real harm. Here's his address, people said, there you are, take it down; but what value did an address have? What did it mean? . . . A great deal, as he well knew: an address was practically a person, an event, an action, you only had to breathe on it, warm it, bring it to life with the breath of imagination and desire, and the address would tentatively assume independent existence, become a reality, and finally take a form that, however it ground its teeth, would eventually hand over the money.

He knew of such addresses in Lyon, in Paris, in Vienna, and in Manchester, too. Such addresses were passed on by oral tradition, like the legends that animate a nation's life: in Naples, for instance, there lived a moneylender to whom all you had to say was, "May Charon come knocking for you!" and he'd immediately begin to weep and agree to the deal. So he regarded Mensch calmly, marveling only that reality and fantasy could so completely agree: he was so calm that the calm was verging on tenderness. And Mensch looked at him in the same way, blinking and blinking in the frightening yet exciting consciousness that fate had brought this man to him.

So Mensch finally gave him some money—not a lot, but just enough to cut a proper figure in Bolzano, where, Giacomo felt, his audience must be waiting impatiently for him to appear. Mensch gave him thirty ducats, which he counted out in gold at the lacquered table, his hands trembling with astonishment, without ring or forfeit, as advance against nothing more than a piece of paper assuring him of the credit of Signor Bragadin, a gentleman who might have lived on the moon as far as he was concerned, or at least a considerable distance off, as did all money that did not actually lie on the table in front of him. When he had wrapped the gold in parchment and handed it over he rose from the table, and bowing with the religious reverence of a high priest, ushered his guest to the door. He watched him for some time from the threshold until his customer disappeared in the fog.

The man to whom he had so trustingly advanced the money hastened down the twilit street while Mensch continued bowing and mumbling Italian, German, and French words under his breath. By now he was racing, practically running toward the lights of the main square. He arrived near the church just in time to see a carriage with two lackeys in the backseat holding torches. Behind the glass he caught sight of a pale face he recognized.

"Francesca!" he cried.

Suddenly it began to snow. He stood alone in the square, under the snow, as the carriage drove by him. He was stricken with the pain one always feels when desire becomes reality. Then he returned to The Stag, his hands clasped behind him, his head bowed, his body weighed down by his thoughts. He felt lonelier here and now than he had in the underworld, under the Leads.

The Consultation

*T*hat evening he sat in the restaurant of The Stag drinking mulled wine, waiting for the card party to arrive. They appeared cautiously: the chemist whom Balbi brought along, the dean who had visited Naples, a veteran actor, and an army officer who had deserted the day before at Bologna. They played for low stakes, going through the motions, getting to know one another. The chemist was caught cheating and was asked to leave. The soldier pursued the fat, foolish-looking man to the door and threw him out into the street where the snow was still falling. By midnight Giacomo was bored. He and Balbi went upstairs to his room where they lit candles and, with elbows propped on the table, set about marking the pack of cards he had bought that afternoon and which the engraver and printer had decorated with the legend STAMPATORI DE NAIBI immediately below an image of Death and The Hanged Man. The friar was surprisingly skilled at the work: they labored in silence, waxing the corners of the most important cards and using their nails to carve identifying symbols into the wax.

"Are you not worried this might get us into trouble?" asked the friar in passing, absorbed in his task.

"No," he replied, holding an ace of diamonds up to the light and examining it through half-closed eyes before winking and painstakingly marking it. "What is there to be worried about? A gentleman is never worried."

"A gentleman?" queried Balbi, sticking his tongue through his pursed lips, as he tended to do when expressing astonishment. "And which gentleman might that be?"

"I," he said and touched the marked card gently with his fingertip. "Who else could I mean?" he stiffly remarked. "There are only two of us in the room, and it is certainly not you."

"Do gentlemen cheat?" asked the friar and yawned.

"Of course," he replied, throwing the cards away and stretching his limbs so his bones cracked. "It is very difficult to win otherwise. It is the nature of cards to be fickle. There are very few people who can win without the aid of some device. In any case," he went on in a matter-of-fact voice, "everyone cheats. At Versailles the most respectable people cheat: even generals and priests."

"Does the king cheat too?" asked Balbi, somewhat awestruck.

"No," he answered solemnly. "He simply gets cross when he loses."

They considered the nature of the king's anger. Soon enough Giacomo was alone, and eventually he, too, sighed, yawned, and went to bed. For three days he continued in this deeply solitary fashion with only Balbi, Giuseppe, and little Teresa for company. He played faro with messenger boys and oil salesmen in the bar of The Stag, frequently winning, thanks to the waxed cards which certainly helped, though he occasionally lost because everyone else cheated at the time, especially in the taverns of London, Rome, Vienna, and Paris, where professional itinerant gamblers offered *banque ouverte* to all and sundry. He remembered one occasion when he had fought a Greek whose remarkable dexterity enabled him to produce ace after ace from his sleeve, but he felt no anger at the time, it was only to keep in practice.

He didn't see Francesca nor did he make any special effort to look for her just yet.

It was as if life itself were slumbering in thin air below mountain peaks.

Then there came three days of raging winds when the windows of The Stag were plastered over in snow. The sky was thick with gray woolly clouds as dirty as the cotton in Mensch's ears. The suits, the shirts, the coats, the shoes, the white silk Venetian mask, the walking stick, and the lorgnette were delivered, and he had a coat for Balbi too, if only for the sake of cleanliness and respectability, because the friar was running round town in a robe that might have been worn by a corpse freshly cut down at a public hanging. But most of the time he just sat in his room alone in front of the fire, in the apathetic, melancholy frame of mind that, despite a lively curiosity and an acquaintance with music, action, lights, and the thrill of the chase, he, of all people, had been ever more frequently afflicted by these last few years. It was as if everything he had planned and dreamed about in jail—life, pleasure, and entertainment—now that he was back in the world and had only to stretch out his hand to grab it, had lost something of its attraction. He was seriously considering returning to Rome, going down on his knees to his generous friend, the cardinal, and asking for forgiveness: he would beg to join the priesthood or plead for a position as a librarian in the papal offices. He thought of towns where nothing awaited him but inns, cold beds, women's arms from which he would sleepily have to disentangle himself, the corridors of theaters where he'd hang about and tell lies, and salons and bars where his carefully prepared cards might provide him with a modest haul of gold: he thought of all this and yawned. He was acquainted with this mood of his and was afraid of it. "It'll end in flight and a bloody nose," he thought and drew together the nightgown covering his chest because he was shivering. This condition had begun in childhood and it was accompanied by a fear and disgust that, without warning, would suddenly come over him and end in nosebleeds that only Nonna, his strong, virtuous grandmother, could cure with herbs and lint. He thought of Nonna a lot these days, never of his mother or his siblings, but of this strong woman who had brought up three generations in Venice and had been particularly fond of Giacomo; she kept appearing in his sad and somewhat disturbing dreams. Nonna used to place an icy piece of lint on his neck and cook him beetroots because she believed that beetroots were effective against all sorts of bleeding, and eventually both the bleeding and the sadness would pass away. "Nonna!" he thought now, with an intense yearning that was keener than anything he had felt for other women.

Francesca lived nearby: by now he knew which house, knew the Swiss guard with his silver-tipped stick and bearskin cloak, had seen the lackeys, the hunters, and the postilions who escorted the duke of Parma on his journeys into town, and, in the evening, he would walk past the palazzo whose upper windows glimmered overhead—the duke enjoyed a busy social life, receiving guests, giving parties—and in the light that streamed from the window across the street he would imagine the magnificence of the reception halls. Balbi, who had talked to the servants, told him that every evening they replenished the golden branches of the chandeliers with three dozen candles, candles of the finest sort, made of goat fat, which the chandlers of Salzburg provided specially for the duke. "Francesca lives in the light," he acknowledged with a shrug of his shoulder, but he didn't talk about her to Balbi. Yes, Francesca lived in the light, in a palace, attended by lackeys, and on one or two evenings he could even hear the stamping and neighing of the bishop's horses as he drew up at the coach entrance and imagined the horses glittering in silver and dressed with a variety of official insignia. For the duke of Parma kept a busy house in the winter months, as befitted his rank, and perhaps the dignity of his young wife, too. And yet there would have been nothing easier than to enter the house and pay his respects to Francesca; the duke would no longer complain of his attentions, and had, in any case, intimated that he wanted to see him—or that, at least, was what Giuseppe had said. It was true that he mentioned it only once, on his very first visit and not since then, for he came every day to run his delicate pink fingers along Giacomo's jowls, to rub his temples and reset his curls, and, every morning, he would recount in considerable detail the events of the previous night: the manner of the reception, the nature of the party games, the gaiety of the dancing at midnight, and the ins and outs of the card sessions conducted into the early hours of dawn. Giacomo noted them all. Every evening there was dancing, cards, reciting of verses, and playing of party games; every evening there was feasting and drinking at the duke of Parma's. "Does the duke not get tired?" he occasionally asked in his most arch manner. "What I mean is, does he not tire of so many parties, every night? He stays up late each time; don't you think this might be tiring for a man of his age? . . ." Giuseppe shrugged but refused to say any more.

The barber had mentioned the invitation only once, on the first day, and having mentioned it once remained eloquently silent on the subject, skirting the guest's ingenuous questions. "Is the duke tired? . . ." he echoed and, lisping fastidiously, chose his words with care. "He would have every reason to be tired, I suppose. His Excellency always rises early and goes to hunt at dawn, however late he retired the previous night, then he takes his breakfast in his wife's bedroom, where they receive guests at the morning levee. Is the duke tired?" he repeated the question and shrugged. The tiredness of the privileged was quite different from the exhaustion of the poor. The wellborn eat a lot of meat and that is what makes them tired. He, Giuseppe, would only say that, as far as he personally was concerned, he was never tired of dancing, flirtation, or of cards, but thinking, fine manners, and the general standards of behavior required by high society had often exhausted him. "The duke is given to thinking!" he whispered confidentially. And he winked and fluttered his eyelashes as if he were betraying some secret passion of the duke's, a major vice or a tendency to a peculiar form of depravity; he winked as if to suggest that he could say more if he chose, but would not, because he was a careful man and knew the ways of the world. The stranger heard the news and bowed. "Given to thinking, eh!" he asked in a low voice indicating intimacy. They understood each other perfectly. The language they spoke was their mother tongue in the full meaning of the word, the language of people who, without knowing it, share certain tastes, certain traits of character: it was an underworld language that the inhabitants of a superior world can never quite understand. However, Giuseppe made no further mention of the duke's invitation to the visitor: it was something he passed on, that first day as a matter of minor courtesy, then kept his peace, a peace that, in its own way, said as much as his loquaciousness.

"Is the duchess beautiful?" asked the visitor one day, in a disinterested, airy sort of way, as if the question were of no importance. The barber composed himself to answer. He put the tongs, the scissors, and the comb down on the mantelpiece, raised his epicene, long-fingered hand like a priest bestowing a blessing during mass, cleared his throat, then quietly embarked on a singsong, pleasantly lilting speech. "The duchess has dark eyes. On the left side of her face, near her downy pitted jaw, there is a tiny little wart which the chemist once treated with vitriol, but it has grown back again. The duchess artfully covers up this wart." He recited all this, and a wealth of other minor detail, as though he were a priest delivering a sermon or an apprentice painter discussing the graces and shortcomings of a masterpiece. The coolness of his judgment signified an appreciation far surpassing mere enthusiasm. For Giuseppe was every day in the presence of the duchess, before the lesser and the greater levee, when the maids were depilating Francesca's shins with red-hot walnut shells, polishing her toenails with syrup, smearing her splendid body with oils, and scenting her hair with the steam of ambergris before combing it. "The duchess is beautiful!" he sternly declared, the solemn expression ludicrous on a face as childish and effeminate as his, a face so chubby it was not quite human, the kind of face some highly respectable artist might have painted on the walls of an aristocratic woman's bedchamber at Versailles as the face of a shepherd in a naïve, sentimental, wholly unselfconscious, and charmingly corrupt pastoral. The visitor waited while the long, delicate fingers finished with his face and hair and, having learned that the duke was given to thinking and that the duchess was beautiful despite the fact that a tiny wart had grown on her face again, he listened to various other interesting items of news. He remained silent while the other talked. They might have shared a common language but now they were speaking of different things. The fact remained that the duke had not repeated his desire to see the visitor.

So he stayed in town, that foreign, somewhat alien town, even after Signor Bragadin had sent the requested gold, along with a wise and virtuous letter full of noble, practical advice that was perfectly impossible to follow. Mensch was delighted that Signor Bragadin had obliged, and enthusiastically counted out the money with trembling, assured fingers, using a blend of German, French, and Italian expressions, separating interest and capital, with much mention of the terms "credit" and "security." Signor Bragadin had in fact sent more money than his adopted son had asked for, not a lot more, just a little extra to show that an official loan was being topped up by the affections of the heart. "A noble heart," thought the moved fugitive, and Mensch nodded: "A sound name! Fine gold!" As to Signor Bragadin's letter, it contained all that a lonely, aged man could or might say while exploring such unconventional feelings, for all feeling is a form of exploration, and Signor Bragadin knew that this relationship would do nothing to enhance his whiter-than-white reputation and spotless respectability. No gossip or suspicion dared attach itself to the senator's name but, when it came down to it, how far would Venice understand the deep morality underlying his affection? An ordinary Venetian would wonder whether this feeling, even in such irreproachable form, were all it seemed to be, and would not understand why a nobleman, a senator of Venice no less, should squander the affections of his old and none too healthy heart on a notorious playboy. "Why should he?" asked the Venetian public, and the more vulgar of them put their hands to their mouth, gave a wink, and whispered, "What's in it for him?" But Signor Bragadin's knowledge was deeper than theirs: he knew humanity's most painful obligation is not to be ashamed of true feeling even when it is wasted on unworthy subjects. And so he sent money, more than his fugitive friend had requested, and wrote his long, wise letter. *"You have made a new start in life, dear son,"* he wrote in firm, angular characters, *"and you will not be returning to your birthplace for some time. Think of your home with affection."* He wrote a great deal on the subject of his homeland, a page and a half. He advised Giacomo to forgive his birthplace because, in some mysterious way, one's birthplace was always right. And a fugitive, more than anyone, especially he, who was now to be swept to the four corners of the world, should continually reflect on the fact that his birthplace remained his birthplace in perpetuity, even when it was in error. He wrote gracefully, with the certainty that only very old people with highly refined feelings can write, people who are fully aware of the meaning of every word they use, who know that it is impossible to escape our memories and that it is pointless hoping that we might pass our experiences on to others; who realize that we live alone, make mistakes alone, and die alone, and that whatever advice or wisdom we get from others is of little use. He wrote about his birthplace as he might of a relative who was part tyrant and part fairy godmother, stressing that, whatever the strains, we should never break off relations with our family. Then he wrote about money and, much more briefly and practically, about a friend in Munich who was prepared to help a traveler at certain times, up to certain amounts; he wrote of the Inquisition which was greater than the great ones of the world, or as he put it, how the *"powers of Church and State were fully united in the hands of the leaders of this incomparable institution."* But he had to write this, for as the addressee recognized, a sentence to this effect could not be omitted from any Venetian letter, for even the letters of Signor Bragadin were open to the inspection of the *messer grande.* Then he gave his blessing for the journey, and for life itself, which he said was an adventure. Giacomo read the letter twice then tore it up and threw it on the fire. He took Mensch's gold pieces and could have set out for Munich or elsewhere immediately. But he didn't. It was his fifth day in Bolzano and he had got to know everyone, including the captain of police, who called on him to ask most courteously how long he intended remaining in town. He avoided answering and cursed the place after the official left. He paid off debts and gambled away the rest in the bar of The Stag and in the private apartments of the chemist whom they had earlier ejected from The Stag but who was now hosting sessions of faro at home. Without money, and with the address of Signor Bragadin's acquaintance in Munich in his pocket, he had every reason for moving on. But now that he had paid the innkeeper and the shops, had bought a present for Teresa, and offered a handsome tip to Giuseppe; now that the gold had allowed him a few moments of Venetian brilliance, he could afford to stay. He enjoyed credit, not only with Mensch, whom he had sought out again in the last few days, not just with the shops who had been paid off once, but with a more problematic company, the gamblers. An English gentleman—who, when he wasn't gambling, was studying the geology of the surrounding mountains—accepted his IOU address in Paris. Given such losses and gains achieved by dint of experience and light fingers, having paid off old debts and piled up new ones, the natural ties of his new situation, based on interest and a general relaxation in his circumstances, slowly established themselves. Everyone was happy to extend credit to the stranger now because they knew him, because they recognized that the odds on him winning or losing were impossible to calculate: they accepted him because the town quickly got used to him and tolerated his presence behind its walls the way any man tolerates a degree of danger.

And is that why he stayed? No, it was because of Francesca, of course, and because the duke had said he'd like to see him. He waited for the call the way a peasant youth waits at the bar of his native village when someone challenges him. He stands there with his hands on his hips, as if to say: "Here I am, come and get me!" Giacomo struck the same attitude: he waited silently. What did he want of Francesca? Her very name was disturbing, full of the regret of unfinished business. He could of course have decamped, penniless, to Munich, where the elector of Saxony had just arrived and the weeks ahead promised splendor and amusement with pageantry, first-rate theater, Europe's most brilliant gamblers, and mounds of snow. He could have left at any time, not sneaking off at night or when it was foggy, but in broad daylight, in a fancy carriage, his head held high, because he had paid his debts to innkeeper and shopkeeper at least once and because Mensch was still sufficiently under the spell of Signor Bragadin's credit to service him. But instead of going, he stayed because he was waiting for a message from the duke. He knew the message would come eventually, that the palazzo guarded by the solemn Swiss guard with his silver-tipped staff would send for him. He understood that the lack of communication was itself part of a secret dialogue, that there was a purpose in his arrival in Bolzano, that he had things to do. So every day had a meaning: he was waiting for something to happen. Because to live is, in some respects, to wait.

One afternoon, when the main square was full of blue-gray shadows and the wind was hooting and screeching like an owl through the flues of the fireplaces in The Stag, he was sitting idly in the fireside chair, his skin covered in goose pimples, leafing through a volume of Boethius in his lap, when the door opened and Balbi stumbled in, waving his arms.

"They're here! . . ." he declared triumphantly.

Giacomo turned pale. He leaped from his chair, smoothed his rice-powdered hair with all ten fingers, and whispered hoarsely, his voice a faint squeak.

"Get me my lilac coat!"

"Don't bother," said Balbi, tottering closer. "You can greet this lot in shirtsleeves if you like. Only don't undersell yourself!" And when he saw the look of fear and incomprehension on his fellow fugitive's face, he stopped, leaned back against the wall, and clasped his hands across his belly. His speech was a little slurred and he giggled with embarrassment, his full stomach shaking. He was enjoying the secret delight of knowing that he was the begetter and abetter of a wonderfully clever piece of mischief.

"There are only three of them this time," he said, "but all three are rich. One of them, the baker, is quite old; he is first in line. He is old and deaf, so you must be careful to address his more intimate problems in sign language or the whole of Bolzano will hear of his shame. He will be followed by one Petruccio, a captain who considers himself a gallant. He is not quite the gallant now. He is waiting quietly with his arms folded, leaning on the banisters and gazing into the deep. He looks so miserable that he might be contemplating murder or suicide. He's a stupid man: easy game. The third client, the priest's secretary, arrived precisely at the hour I told him to. He's young and looks as if he might burst into tears. And there'll be more of them coming. Allow me to inform you, dear master, that your reputation both frightens and attracts people. Ever since you arrived they have been bombarding me with questions in private, in bars, in doorways, and later in shops and warehouses, but also in the street, anywhere they could confidentially take me aside, press a few pieces of silver into my palm, and invite me for a drink or a roast goose. They are begging to be introduced to you. Whether your name attracts or frightens them it seems they can't forget it."

"What do they want?" he asked mournfully.

"Advice!" said Balbi. He put two fingers to his lips then raised them into the air, rolling his eyes, his belly shaking with silent laughter.

"I see," said Giacomo and gave a sour smile.

"Now be careful," Balbi warned him. "Mind you don't set too low a price on your services. How long do you want to stay here? A day? A week? I'll make sure you have visitors and clients every afternoon: I'll have them lining up on the stairs as they do for famous doctors when someone's dying or coming down with the plague. But remember not to set your price too low: demand at least two gold pieces for each item of advice, and if it's potions they want, ask for even more. I learned a lot in Venice, you know. During the period of my retreat"—this was how Balbi delicately referred to his time in prison—"I came to the conclusion that a thought can be as sharp as a file and worth its weight in gold. You are a clever man, Giacomo. There are purses out there overflowing with gold. Let them weigh your wisdom by the pound. What do you say? . . . Shall I send in the baker?"

And so they began to arrive in patient, sheeplike manner, Balbi herding them in each afternoon, from noon to dusk. His new profession amused Giacomo. He had never played this game before. People came to him with wasted bodies and troubled souls and stood in a line at his door exactly as Balbi had said they would, much as they did outside surgeons' apartments in big cities, but instead of arms in slings and broken ankles they brought broken hearts and wounded self-respect for treatment. What did they want? Miracles. Everywhere people wanted miracles:

they wanted love that would cater to their vanities, power without effort, self-sacrifice that wouldn't cost more than a gold piece or two, tenderness and understanding providing they wouldn't have to work too hard to earn them. . . . People wanted love, and wanted it free, without obligations, if possible. They stood in line at his door, in the corridor of The Stag, the crippled and the humiliated, the weak and the cowardly, those who thirsted for revenge and those who wanted to learn forgiveness. The range of their desires was diverting enough. And there was an art to the handling of the private consultation that offered a glimpse into the mysteries of love, a mystery he himself had never had to learn. Venetians were born knowing the ways of love, they knew them down to their fingertips and their traditional wisdom coursed like an electric current through his every nerve. The art he inherited was ancient too, and once he got over his initial surprise and recognized the ailments the sick brought to him, once he had learned to explore the hidden places and the secret scars, he gave himself willingly and passionately to the project of quackery. His fame soon spread and it quickly became known that he was holding surgeries every afternoon until dusk. Balbi dealt efficiently with the business side of things and kept a strict eye on the waiting patients.

Everyone came to see him, not only from the town but from outlying districts, too. The first to arrive was the deaf baker, who in his seventieth year had become a victim of passion. He hobbled in, a bent figure leaning on his stick, his stomach so fat it hung over his knees, and his brown felt cloak hardly covered it. "Let me tell you what happened," the baker began, panting, and stopped still in the middle of the room to draw a ring in the air with his short rough stick. Then he went on to describe what had happened, as they all did eventually, though only after an initial period of stubborn silence or a sulky shrug of the shoulders. Then they blushed and the first few words came stumbling out, a stuttering confession or two, after which their entire manner changed: they no longer felt ashamed and told him everything. The baker was angry and spoke very loudly the way a deaf man does when he is furious and full of suspicion; he had to be calmed with tactful, fluttering gestures. In a voice that was as deep as it was loud, he informed Giacomo that he could not cope with Lucia, and the only question was whether he should hand her over to the Inquisition or strangle her with his own bare hands then cremate her in his large oven where the lads would bake their long, crumbly loaves each morning. It was a straightforward choice, and it was in such simple terms that Grilli the baker, the seventy-year-old president of the master bakers' guild, saw matters relating to Lucia. The person to whom these questions were addressed, whose advice and professional opinion was being sought, sat and listened. He stroked his chin with two fingers, as scientists were supposed to do, crossed his arms, and from under knitted brows darted sharp, quizzical glances at the angry old man, hearing his complaints with some amazement. "It is a tricky problem!" he exclaimed in a loud stage whisper so that the baker should hear him. "Damned tricky!" Suddenly he grabbed the old man by the arm, dragged the scared, resisting body to the window, took the warty wrinkled face in the palms of his hands, turned it to the light, and spent a long time peering into his rheumy eyes. The consultation took some time. The baker wept. His weeping and snuffling was a little theatrical, not altogether sincere, perhaps, but it was involuntary, if only because he didn't know what else to do. Some terrible intimate disaster had occurred and he could not reconcile himself to the disgrace that would now follow him to the grave. "I have a recommendation," the stranger ventured after careful consideration. "You should buy her rings. I saw a few over at Mensch's, quite attractive ones, with sapphires and rubies." The baker grunted. He had already bought rings and a gold chain and a little cross with diamonds and a silver figurine of the saint of Padua, with enamel inlay. But none of it helped. "Buy her enough silk for three skirts," he advised. "It will be Carnival soon." But the baker waved the advice away and wiped a few tears from his face. The cupboards at home were full of silk, cotton, felt, and brocade. They thought a while in silence.

"Send her to me," said Giacomo generously, with a new firmness.

The baker hummed and hawed, then slowly began to back away towards the door.

"That will be two gold pieces," said the stranger, accepting the fee, flinging the finely minted coins on his desk, and courteously escorting his guest out. "Send her tomorrow morning!" he added as an afterthought, as if doing him a considerable favor. "After mass. I shall have more time then. I'll speak to her. Please don't kill her just yet." He opened the door and waited while the old man, careworn and somewhat terrified by both the advice and his own helplessness, crossed the threshold. "Next please!" he cried to the dark staircase and pretended not to see the shadows huddled in the half-light. "Ah yes, the captain! This way, my valiant fellow!" he warbled cheerily, ushering the grim figure through the door.

And so he conducted his surgery. The varieties of sickness did not surprise him; he knew them and understood that it was the same old disease, only under various guises. What was the disease? He thought about it, and once he was alone in the room, he pronounced its name: selfishness. It was the grinning mask of selfishness that lay behind every problem, stinting what it could and demanding everything one person could demand of another, ideally without having to give anything in return, nothing real or substantial in any case. It was selfishness that bought its darling a palazzo, a coach-and-four, and jewels, and believed that by presenting her with such gifts it had parted with something secret and more precious without the exchange of which there can be no true attraction or peace in one's heart. It was selfishness that wanted everything and believed it had given everything when it devoted time, money, passion, and tenderness to the male or female object of its affections, while withholding the final sacrifice consisting of a simple, almost incidental, readiness to leave everything and devote its life and soul to the other without expecting anything in return. For this is what lovers, those peculiar tyrants, actually wanted. They were happy enough to give money, time, rings, ornaments, even their names and hands, but in all this welter of gift giving, there was one thing they were all determined to keep back, and that something was themselves, whether that self was Lucia or Giuseppe or the gallant captain, Petruccio, now standing in the middle of the room, grasping his sword with both hands and looking as grim as he might at his own execution.

"What is the problem, dear captain?" he asked in his friendliest, most charming manner. But the captain was warily turning his head about, like a wild animal examining his cage. Then he bent to the stranger's ear and whispered the secret. He stood there with burning eyes, gripping his sword, his warrior heart wildly beating, and whispered it. No, this was not a matter he could advise him on. He shook his head in complete understanding and tutted indignantly. "Perhaps," he said in a low voice, "you should leave her. You are a man. A soldier." But the captain did not answer. He was like the dead who realize that nothing will ever change again, that they are stuck in this uncomfortable position in the grave, under the earth, under the stars. He was not a man who took readily to advice, preferring to treat his injuries as lower ranks: a senior officer does not consort with lower ranks. "Leave her!" Giacomo repeated, warmly, with genuine sympathy. "Even if you can't bear it, it's better than your current suffering." The captain groaned. His understanding was that there was no advice, no consolation, no remedy for his grief. That groan, that wounded, hopeless grunt of his, was a declaration. "Even this suffering is better than not seeing her; it is better to live like this than to leave her," it said. Some people just can't be helped.

Many more people came, usually arriving near dusk. The priest's secretary, a spotty-faced boy who read Petrarch and could not bring himself to write a letter to the lady of his heart's desire, received his advice at the cost of one gold piece. The stranger wrote the letter for him, solemnly escorted him out, then shut the door and laughed till his sides split, throwing the gold into the air, before passing it over to Balbi, who took his hands as they shook each other in delight. "Doctor Mirabilis!" cried Balbi, his cracked voice whinnying with laughter. "They're even coming in from the countryside now!" Snow was falling thickly, but they kept arriving despite the drifts and showers, not only men, but women, too, with veils over their faces, promising cash in hand, tearing the jeweled brooches from their bosoms, casting their veils aside. "Work your wonders, Giacomo, talk to him, brew me a magic potion, tell me your opinion, is there any hope for me? . . ." they begged.

One day there arrived a woman, no longer young, a solid, respectable figure, her dark fiery eyes ablaze with passion and hurt. "I came in the snow," she told him, her voice raw with feeling, as she stood by the fire, opened her fur stole, shook her head, and waited for the sparkling snowdrops caught on her veil and scarf to melt. "One horse died. We almost froze as the evening closed in. But here I am because they say that you give advice, understand magic, and know people's hearts and souls. So get on with it." She spoke indignantly, as though smarting from an insult. He offered the lady a chair and paid close attention to her. He had known women in every state and condition of life, and having found reason enough to be wary of them, kept his eyes open for changes of mood. She ignored his offer. She was past forty, tall, red-faced, and healthily plump, the kind of woman happy enough to stand in the kitchen and watch the pork roast, who washes her face in rainwater and whose linen cupboard smells pleasant without the use of scents, the kind of woman who would happily administer even an enema to the man she loved. He regarded her with respect. There was enough passion smoldering under the furs and in those flashing eyes to set a forest on fire. She was used to giving orders and probably kept her household on a tight rein. Servants, guests, relatives, and admirers would all listen devotedly to whatever she had to say and would be sent scattering by her fury. Even her tenderness would smolder with a sharp aroma, like the brushwood fire in a forest when herdsmen forget to put it out after preparing game. She was a woman strong in anger through whom the tide of feelings ran most powerfully, and she stood now in commanding fashion, ready to deal the world several sharp blows, after which, with a single passionate movement of her firm arms, she would sweep some chosen loved one to her breasts in a deathly embrace. The snow, the cold fields of Lombardy, and the smell of the River Adige all emanated from her presence. "Here I am," said the woman, puffing slightly, her even voice barely under control. "I have come to you. I have come, though the laundry has piled up at home, though they are smoking salami, and though they say that in November, in the hills round here, a traveler is likely to be eaten by wolves. I am a Tuscan," she said quietly but firmly.

The stranger bowed. "And I am Venetian, madam," he said, and, for the first time, gazed more deeply into his guest's eyes.

"I know," the woman replied and took a gulp. "That's why I am here. Listen, Giacomo. You have escaped from prison and know the secrets of love, so they say. Look at me. Am I the sort of woman who should humbly beseech a man to love her? Who is it who looks after the house? Who works in the fields in July at harvest time? Who shops for new furniture in Florence when we have to present an imposing face to the world? Who takes care of the horses and their equipment? Who mends the socks and underwear of her fastidious master? Who makes sure that there are flowers on the table at noon and that musicians with flageolets are playing in the next room when it is somebody's birthday? Who keeps all the drawers in order? Who washes in cold water every morning and every night? Who has linen brought over from Rumburg so that the bed in which the man of the house embraces her should smell as fresh as the fields of Tuscany in April? Who keeps an eye on the kitchen so that every requirement of his delicate stomach and demanding palate should be satisfied? Who tests the flesh of the young cockerel before it is slaughtered so it should be as plump and tender as he likes it? Who checks the smell of the calf's leg brought over from the butcher in town? Who goes down to the cellar, down those dangerous steep stairs, to sulphur the wine casks they have rolled in barrels from the vineyard? Who makes sure that the glass of water they have left on the small table by his bed at night should contain a spoonful of sugar because after his carousings and lecheries, his weak heart needs a drop of sugar before he can sleep? Who stops him eating too much ginger and pepper? Who turns a blind eye to his lustful moods when ropes and chains can't keep him at home? Who keeps her peace when she can smell the rotten perfume of other women on his coat and linen? . . . Who puts up with it all? Who works and says nothing? Look at me, Giacomo. They say you are wise in the ways of women, a brilliant doctor of love. Look at me. I have borne two children and lost three, no matter that I groveled on my knees before the image of the Virgin, begging her to keep them alive. Look at me. I know time has had its way with me, that there are those who are younger, who smile more obligingly, and are better at wiggling their hips; nevertheless, here I am. Am I the kind of woman whose kisses are to be rejected? Just look at me!" she cried in a hoarse, powerful voice, and opened her fur coat. She was wearing a dress of lilac-colored silk, her dark brown hair covered by a headscarf of Venetian lace, a golden clasp holding together the shawl across her mature, pleasantly full bosom, her build tall and muscular without a trace of excess fat, firm of flesh and sound of blood, a solid forty-year-old woman with white arms, her head thrown proudly back. She stood before him and he bowed to her with a natural male courtesy, in genuine admiration. "There's no need to bow," she said, lowering her voice, a little embarrassed. "I haven't left the estate in a snowstorm and traveled all the way to Bolzano just so that I should be bowed to by a stranger. It's not consolation I am seeking. I know what I know. I am a woman. I can sense when a man is looking at me. I can recognize genuine desire in an impudent, unrespectful stare but can also feel the circumspect passion in a mere glance. I know I have a few years left in which to make the man who loves me completely happy."

She drew the fur across her chest once more, as if cold or embarrassed, hesitated, then continued in a fainter, more tremulous voice. "Why can't I have what I want? . . ." she asked. Her voice was perfectly quiet now, and she was taking deep gulps in an attempt to hold back her tears, speaking humbly, without a trace of Tuscan pride. "What should I have done? . . . I gave him everything a woman can give a man, passion and patience, children, excitement, peace, security, tenderness, freedom from care . . . everything. People tell me that you understand love the way a goldsmith understands gold and silver: question me then, stranger, examine my heart, make your judgment, and give me your advice! What should I have done? I have humbled myself. I was my husband's lover and accomplice. I understood that there had to be other women in his life, because such was his nature. I know he desired in secret and that he came running back to me to escape the pressures of the world, to escape his own passions and adventures, and that he still escapes because he is frightened, because he is no longer young, because death is breathing down his neck. Sometimes I have willed him to grow old and to be plagued by gout, so that he should be mine again, so I could bathe his aching feet. . . . Yes, I have longed for old age and for sickness, may Our Lady forgive me and may God pardon my sins. I gave everything. Tell me what else I should have given. . . ."

She was abjectly begging for an answer, her voice faint, her eyes full of tears. The man thought about it. He stood before her, his arms crossed over his chest, and his verdict was courteous but final.

"You should have given happiness, signora."

The woman bent her head and raised her handkerchief to her eyes. She stood dumbly weeping. Then she gave a great sigh and answered subserviently in a cracked voice.

"Yes, you are right. It was only happiness I couldn't give him."

She stood, head bowed, fondling the gold brooch with her delicate fingers, as if distracted. Still staring at the floor, she added, "Don't you think, stranger, that there are certain men to whom you cannot give happiness? There is a kind of man whose whole attraction, every virtue, every charm, emanates from his incapacity for happiness. The entire faculty for happiness is absent; he is stone deaf to happiness, and, just as the deaf cannot hear the sweet sound of music, so he is insensible to the sweet sound of happiness. . . . Because you are right, he never was happy. But, you see, this is the man that heaven and earth have chosen for me, and it was not as if he found happiness anywhere else, either, however he looked for it, in over fifty years. He is like the man who buries his treasure in a field then forgets where he has buried it. He digs up everything in sight, he turns his whole life over. . . . I sold my rings and pendants so that he could travel further afield to seek it, because, believe me, there was nothing I wanted more than to see him happy. Let him seek happiness on voyages across seas, in strange cities, in the arms of black women and yellow women, if that is his fate. . . . But he always came back to me, sat down beside me, called for wine or read his books, then spent a week with some slut with dyed hair, usually an actress. That's the kind of man he is. What should I do? Throw him out? Kill him? Should I go away myself? Should I kill myself? . . . Every morning after mass I have knelt before the Savior in our small church, and, believe me, I searched my heart carefully before coming to you with my grief and wounded pride. Now I will go home and my pride will no longer be wounded. You are right: I did not give him happiness. From now on I shall only want to serve him. But please tell me, for I am desperate to know: seeing that there are men incapable of happiness, do you think the fault is entirely mine? He is restless and melancholy and seeks happiness at every turn: in the arms of women, in ambition, in worldly affairs, in murderous affrays, in the clinking of gold coins; he seeks it everywhere, all the while knowing that life can give him everything but happiness. Is there anyone else like this? . . ."

She spoke the last words challengingly, as if she were demanding something or accusing him. Now it was he who bowed his head.

"Yes," he said. "Take comfort. I do know such a man. He stands before you."

He spread his arms and bowed deeply, as if to signal that the consultation was over. The woman gazed at him for some time. Her fingers trembling, she clasped her fur coat together and the two of them moved toward the door. Then as if talking to herself, by way of good-bye, she said:

"Yes, I felt that. . . . I felt as soon as I stepped into the room, that you too were that kind of man. Perhaps I felt it even before I set off in the snow. But he is so terribly lonely and sad. . . . There is a kind of sadness that may not be consoled: it is as if someone had missed some divine appointment, and had found nothing to interest him since. You have more self-knowledge than he does, I can tell that from your voice, see it in your eyes, feel it in your very being. What is the trouble with these people? Is it because God has punished them with too much intelligence, so they experience every feeling, every human passion, with the mind rather than the heart? . . . The thought had occurred to me. I am a simple woman, Giacomo, and there is no need for you to shake your head or to be polite. I know why I say these things. I make no apology for my simplicity. I know there are forms of intelligence beyond those admired by the vainly intellectual, that the heart has its own knowledge, and that it too is important, very important. . . . You see, I came to you for advice, but now that it is time to go it is I who am feeling sorry for you. How much do I owe you?"

She drew a silver-crocheted purse from the lining of the coat and extended it nervously toward him.

"From you, signora," said the man, bowing once more

as at the end of a dance, his knee slightly bent, his arms spread wide, "I will not accept any money."

He declared this in a spirit of generosity, humbly enough but with just enough hauteur in his voice for the woman to turn around at the threshold.

"Why?" she asked over her shoulder. "It is what you live on, after all."

He shrugged.

"You, dear lady, have already paid a great price. I would like you to be able to say that you met with a man who gave you something for nothing."

He escorted her as far as the stairs, where they looked at each other once more in the gloom with serious and somewhat suspicious expressions on their faces. He raised the candle high to light his guest's way, for it was already dark and the bats were beginning to flitter through the stairwell of The Stag.

The Contract

It was dark. They were ringing the bells of Santa Maria, and down in the shadows the bar and restaurant of The Stag were tinkling with silver and glass as they spread the tables, when he heard sleigh bells. He stood still a moment, leaning over the banisters, listening. He, too, was a bat, suspended upside down over the world, the kind of creature who comes to life only when the dull lights and sounds of evening awaken him. The sleigh stopped by the doors of The Stag, someone shouted, servants came running with lanterns and fixed them to the ends of long pointed poles, settling silence on the intimate noises of restaurant and bar, the kind of noises he loved to hear down the corridors of inns in foreign towns, when he would emerge from his room on tiptoe, his black gold-buckled half soles on his feet, his white cotton stockings stretched tight over his full legs, wearing a violet-colored frock coat and a narrow, gilt-handled sword strapped to his waist under the black silk cloak that came down to his ankles, his hair carefully sprinkled with rice powder, his fingers bright with rings, a purse made of fish bladder containing gold coins hanging at his side, and a packet of marked cards in his pocket; and, thus prepared for the evening, he would be ready to face the world, impatient for adventure, his heart expectant and melancholy, expectancy and melancholia being much the same thing, then patter down the stairs, eyes darting here and there, knowing that in various rooms in the same town there would be women sitting next to candles from which the smoke gently billowed while they looked into the mirror, quickly tying a bow in a bodice, pinning flowers in their hair, anointing themselves with rice powder and perfume, adjusting the beauty patch on their faces, knowing that musicians would already be tuning up in the theaters, the stage and auditorium rich with the sour-bitter smoke of oil lamps, and that everyone was preparing for life, for the evening, which would be festive, secretive, and intimate: it was the time at which he loved to stop on the stairs of strange inns and listen to the faint brushing noises of waiters and servants and the clinking and chinking of the cutlery, the glass, the silver, and the china. There was nothing finer in life for him, anywhere in the world, than observing preparations for festivities: the prelude, the fuss, every detail infused with the sense of anticipation of all that was unpredictable and surprising. What delight it was to dress at about eight o'clock, when the church bells had stopped ringing, and when pale hands, their movements sensitive and mysterious, reached from windows to fasten the shutters, thereby closing out the world and safeguarding the house which always represents some mutuality, some turning away from worldly affairs; to put on one's clothes and prepare for the evening with the pleasant quickening of the heart that tells us we are capable of anything, of both happiness and of despair; to stride with sure, light steps past houses, toward the dim shores of the darkening evening. It was this part of the day he loved best: his walk changed, his hearing grew keener, his eyes glittered and he could see in the dark. At such times he felt wholly human, but also, in the complex but not at all shameful sense of the word, like a creature of the wild that, after sunset, when tamer beasts have retired to shallows and watering holes, stands like a great predator, still and silent in the brush, listening to the sounds of twilight, his head raised in rapt attention. So it was now when they were laying tables that he heard the shuffling, tinkling noises rising from the restaurant, and in that instant the whole world seemed festive. Was there any feeling to compare with it, he wondered, a feeling that so quickened the heart and made it pound with apprehension as that of waiting for festivities to begin?

The clatter had stopped now. The shuffling of feet was followed by the sounds of a lighter, younger pattering movement, then he heard the knocking of shoes with wooden soles breaking into a run. "An important guest!" he thought as he stuck his tongue out and licked his dry lower lip in quick, thirsty anticipation. The agitation of the house coursed through him. To his highly developed ear, the word "guest" was one of the most magical sounds in the world, along with other words like "prize," "prey," "suddenly," and "luck": it was, in short, among the finest sounds a man could wish to hear. "A substantial guest!" he thought in approval, with a pleasant excitement. The light of the torches moved about the upper floor. The voices below were barking short, hard words: the guest must have been at the very door, the host of The Stag bowing before him, issuing stern orders and promising who-knows-what earthly and divine delights. "A difficult guest!" he thought, like a fellow professional, for he himself was just such a "difficult" guest who liked to make his host squirm with a long series of testing questions, to visit the kitchen and examine the size of the salmon, capon, or saddle of venison for himself, to try its quality, to have a much-praised vintage brought up from the cellar then take his time sniffing the cork after the bottle was opened, to wave away the offered wine with contempt and ask for a new bottle and, when it arrived, solemnly and with utmost concentration, to taste the thick, oily, blood-red drops of the French or South Italian grape, then, graciously, with a slightly sour expression, finally agree on the potential of some specific wine, and to turn round at the top of the cellar stairs, or at the door of the kitchen, with a finger half-raised to remind his host in harsh, admonitory tones that he should take care that the chestnuts, with which they were to stuff the breast of the turkey, be boiled in milk and vanilla first, and that the Burgundy be warmed in its straw carafe precisely forty minutes before serving; and it was only after all this that he would take his place at the table and haughtily survey the hall, rubbing his eyes to signify a slight weariness and satisfaction, taking in the furniture and the paintings, whose arrangement and whose local or international character did not truly interest the "difficult" guest, since the most difficult part was over, and one only had to watch that the serving staff always stood at a distance of two paces, far enough not to hear any whispered conversation, but close enough to leap to the table at the lowering of an eyelid and attend to any business immediately. "They are negotiating something!" he thought, for the hard voice of the guest and the humble, fawning voice of the host were still engaged in conversation. "A guest from out of town!" he thought. He remembered that there was a ball tonight at Francesca's, a masked ball, to which the local nobility had been invited. There had been a lot of talk in town about the ball in the last few days, and all the tailors, cobblers, haberdashers, ribbon makers, seamstresses, and hairdressers were proudly complaining that they couldn't keep up with demand, as a result of which he himself had spent three useless days vainly demanding his two frilly evening shirts from the washerwoman, who was too busy starching, washing, and ironing the finest linen for Francesca's ball, and the whole town was filling up with guests preparing for wonderful games and high festivities, all caught up in the kind of exciting, intense, and, to all purposes, good-natured activity that in its own twisted and mysterious manner touches even those who are not directly involved in the affair. . . . I expect a lot of people will be spending the night after the ball at The Stag, he thought. The weather is dreadful, the Tuscan woman was almost eaten by wolves, and the local gentry and their ladies are hardly likely to set straight off after the event across snow-covered roads, at dawn, in their sleighs and foot muffs. And this "difficult" guest, he too must be bound for the ball, he thought, and felt a sharp stab of envy, as people do when they suddenly discover that they are barred from attending a desirable occasion. The feeling surprised him. It reminded him of his childhood when he learned that adults were planning something strange and wonderful without him. He shrugged, listened a moment longer to the discussion between guest and host, then turned back to his room.

"In other words, nobody!" the harsh commanding voice declared at the foot of the stairs, down in the depths. The answer must have been silent: he could imagine the obliging landlord, his hand crossed over his heart, his upper body bowed, and his eyes cast heavenward to indicate that everything would be as the guest demanded. But something about the voice stopped him as he was about to enter his room. It was a familiar voice, an intimately and frighteningly familiar voice, the kind a man recognizes because there has already been unavoidable and close contact between it and him. This instinctive recognition was an important force in his life: he had set his compass by it. He raised his head, listening intently, like an animal on the scent. The voice was unmistakable! He stood at the door with a serious, almost respectful look on his face, his fingers on the handle, his whole body tense, some instinct telling him that he was on the verge of a fateful encounter. He knew by now that the footsteps slowly, laboriously ascending the stairs with such even tread were a vital component of his own life, that the anonymous voice rising from the depths was bringing him a personal message. The "difficult" guest was looking for him. The astrological chart of his life was, in a few moments, once again, and not for the last time, about to undergo a dramatic readjustment. He took a deep breath and straightened up. A nervous shudder ran through him, and as always in such situations, his instinct momentarily overcame his reason, and he felt the urge to run into his room, climb through the window, shimmy down the storm drain of The Stag, and disappear in the accustomed manner, into the evening and the blizzard. It was, after all, the only voice he was afraid of, this "resonant" voice already drawing closer in the half-light on the stairs. He recognized the same unavoidable "resonance" when it radiated from women or from men who belonged to women. He had been happy enough to fight a duel in Tuscany, bare-chested in the moonlight, with only a narrow sword in his hand, against an old man maddened by jealousy who was skillful and dangerous with swords; he had been quite prepared to leap from rooftops and to tangle with vagrant scoundrels on the floor of a dive in a pub brawl; he was, in short, afraid of nothing but this "resonance," which he associated with a specific feeling, for he sensed that every feeling, but this one above all, was woven to bind him. It was this that really frightened him. That was why he thought he should shut the door now, seize his dagger, and leave by the window. At the same time he knew that, in the end, there was no escape from this particular kind of resonance, that it was a trap from which one could not escape unscathed. So he waited at the threshold, his hair standing on end, with fear and anticipation, gripping the handle of the door, staring over his shoulder, scanning the dim space with sharp, suspicious eyes, seeking the man who would shortly address him in that familiar voice. It was past eight o'clock. The steps hesitated, apparently tired, resting at a turn of the stair. There was no more clattering of cutlery in the bar and the silence was such that you could hear the snow fall; it was as if the mountains, the snow-covered street, the river, and the stars, the whole of Bolzano, were holding its breath. "There is always this moment of silence at a vital turn in a man's life," he found himself reflecting, and smiled with satisfaction at the phrase, because he was, after all, a writer.

Then they came into view, the landlord first, stooping and turning as he ascended, muttering, explaining, assuring, a smoking taper in his hand and a soft satchel-shaped hat of red material on his head, the kind of hat that used to be worn by Phrygian shepherds and more recently by publicans and freethinkers in the cellars of Paris and out in the provinces. The innkeeper's ballooning stomach was covered with a leather apron that he must have been wearing in the cellar where he was probably tampering with the sugar content and temperature of the wine, a foul habit he could not bring himself to abandon, and over the apron, a blue jerkin whose splendor exceeded that of the ceremonial vestments of guilds and connoisseurs and suggested a long-standing religious ritual such as might be conducted by a lower grade priest of an ancient, pagan cult whose devotees were crowned with rings of onions. It was he who came first. He looked over his shoulder, muttering and assuring with a great show of humility and concern, like any hotelier with an important client, for it is the duty of the hotelier to be solicitous in his attentions, to see his guest rise and set off in the morning, leaving behind a messy room, the bed his noble body had vacated, the basin with its dirty water, the vessel containing human effluent, and things even the most exquisitely refined of human beings leaves as evidence of his presence in the room of a hotel. And so the innkeeper bowed and scraped with remarkable zeal, his every gesture speaking of five decades of experience as landlord and jack-of-all-trades to all and sundry. He kept three steps ahead of his guest, much as a postilion does at night when the king, the prince de Condé, or, as it may be, the duke of Parma, happens to be passing through. And in his wake there followed the procession of four men ranged about a fifth, two in front, two behind, each member of the escort equipped with a five-branched silver candelabrum raised high above his head, each clad in his lackey's uniform of black silk jerkin, knee breeches, and white wig, with silver chains about his neck and a flat-cocked hat on his head; the heavy calfskin pelisses around their shoulders billowed like enormous wings as they walked stiffly on, looking neither behind nor ahead, their pace as mechanical and jerky as those of marionettes at an open-air performance in the market-place. The guest proceeded slowly in the cage of light they made for him. He gauged each step of the stair with caution before moving on, his body shrouded in a plain, violet-colored traveling cloak that flapped about his ankles, a cloak brightened only at the neck and narrow shoulders by a wide, beaver-skin collar; and so, leaning on a silver-handled stick, he made his way gradually upstairs, carefully fixing the point of the stick on the edge of the next step, as if each tread required careful consideration, not just as an intellectual proposition but as a physical problem occasioned by the condition of his heart, for his heart was finding the burden of stairs ever more difficult. The procession therefore wound on extremely slowly with the ornate and rigorous ritual of a man who has all but lost his freedom of movement but remains enslaved by his own rank, the trappings and obligations imposed on him by his station in life. "It's not hard to see," thought Giacomo, wide-mouthed, his contempt tempered by a grudging respect as he stood at the half-open door of his room, "that he is related to Louis Le Gros!" And so thinking, he took a step back into the shadows of the room, on the far side of the threshold, and waited there with both hands on the door frame, carefully flattening himself against the wall in the darkness while the duke of Parma made his way upstairs.

By now the procession had reached the landing, and had arrived just where the corridor curved away, so he could see a complete line of faces where the attendants formed a double guard with their raised candles, waiting for their master to get his breath. Of course he had recognized the duke of Parma before he got to the top of the stairs, even before hearing his voice; he recognized him because the duke was intensely resonant, a man of whose presence he would immediately be aware, a man with a pivotal role in his life. He knew he was nearby long before he even saw him: he was aware of it when the Tuscan woman left his room to return to her shadowy, joyless servitude, to life with her melancholy, much-traveled husband; he felt his presence when the sleigh stopped by the door and the landlord began his wheedling and assuring. Few people knew how to arrive like this, and he contemplated the arrival with a certain professional satisfaction, as if he himself were a landlord, porter, or waiter or, better still, the perennial guest accustomed to grand entrances; he studied the duke's manner of entering, from the point of view of a fellow craftsman, with a peculiar mixture of mild contempt and involuntary respect, for the manner was formal, meticulous, and appropriate to the company that automatically accommodated itself to the rituals of the duke's person and role, even now, even here, in this bat-infested provincial inn of somewhat dubious reputation, as if he had drawn up outside at his palace in Bologna, his sleigh dripping with dead foxes, wolves, and wild boars bagged along the way, or had marched into Monsieur Voisin's or the Silver Tower Restaurant in Paris, or alighted from his carriage at Versailles, at the entrance of the Trianon, where His Celestial Host was entertaining a bevy of beauties at the royal court with a game of pin the tail on the donkey. . . . The duke of Parma did not simply "turn up" at The Stag but "made an entrance"; he didn't simply go upstairs but was escorted there as part of a procession; he didn't just stop when he reached the upper floor but made a ceremonial appearance. The entire progress was dreamlike: it was like a vision of the final judgment.

Now the guest drew himself up and ran his eye severely

down the length of the shadowy corridor, across deep pools of tremulous darkness, while the servants raised their elaborately embroidered arms to light his way with their blazing scarlet candelabras.

The duke of Parma, the kinsman of Louis, was this year completing his seventy-second year. "Seventy-two," calculated the stranger quite calmly as he caught his first glimpse of the visitor. He did not move from the doorway but stood clutching the doorpost, nonchalant yet watchful, exuding the indifference of someone accidentally coming upon an ordinary guest of no particular importance in a dark and none too salubrious inn, a silent, disinterested witness to a rather overelaborate procession. "It's the only way he knows how to conduct himself," he thought, and shrugged, but then another thought occurred to him. "He wants to intimidate me!" The idea struck him with irresistible force, flattering his self-esteem. "No one takes a room at The Stag in such a manner!" His hunches were correct as far as they went, though they did not go far enough, he suspected, and even as he watched the duke of Parma surveying the corridor, his head thrown back and his eyes screwed up until he discovered the man he had been seeking in the doorway, the tingling in his toes and stomach confirmed the suspicion. One casual glance assured him that the duke's escort was unarmed, and, as far as he could see, the duke himself carried no weapon. His appearance, movement, and progress seemed dignified rather than threatening. At this hour of the late afternoon—or was it early evening? a stranger could not go by what usually happened at such hours in more metropolitan, glittering places—when the palazzo would have been getting ready for the ball, an especially brilliant ball, a champagne occasion that the whole district had been talking about for days, the host would not have sallied forth without good cause, not with such a splendid escort, certainly not so that he could take up rooms in a dubious inn just two steps from his own home. "It is I he has come to see, of course!" thought the stranger, and was deeply flattered, above all by the ceremonial manner of the visit. At the same time, however, he knew that this procession was only the most general of homages to him; that he was merely an itinerant, someone with whom the duke of Parma had exchanged a few valedictory words some years ago on a misty sea-colored morning at the gates of Florence; that the ceremoniousness had to be interpreted as a permanent and natural feature of the guest's mode of existence, the pomp an organic part of his being; that the procession was the equivalent of the brilliantly colored tail the male peacock permanently drags behind him, something the peacock, when he becomes aware of being watched, opens as casually as one might a fan. This was the way the duke of Parma had traveled everywhere for a good long time now. Now he waved the lackeys aside. He recognized the straight figure standing in the doorway, carelessly raised to his eyes with a well practiced movement the lorgnette that had been dangling on a golden chain at his breast, and, slightly blinking, as if unsure that he had found what he had been looking for, gazed steadily at the stranger.

"It is him," he pronounced at last, terse and satisfied.

"Yes, Your Excellency," the innkeeper enthusiastically agreed.

They were talking about him in his presence as if he were an object. He was amused by the neutrality of their tone. He remained where he was, making no haste to welcome his visitor, nor did he go down on his knees, for why should he? . . . He felt a deep indifference, a blend of contempt and impassivity in the face of every worldly danger and even more so now. "What's the point?" he thought and shrugged. "The old man has come to warn me off, perhaps to threaten me; he'll try a little blackmail then call on me to leave town or else have me transported back to Venice. And what's it all for? . . . For Francesca? He does have a point, of course. Why haven't I already left this rotten town to which nothing ties me? I have sucked Mensch dry, can expect no further assistance here from papa Bragadin, there's nobody in town with whom I could discuss the finer points of literature, I am fully acquainted with the enticing, walnut-flavored kisses of little Teresa, Balbi is pursued every night by jealous butcher's boys wielding cudgels and machetes, and playing cards with the locals is like taking on a pack of wild boars. Why am I still here after six, or is it eight, days now? I could have been in Munich days ago. The elector of Saxony has already arrived there and will be blowing a fortune at faro. Why am I still here?" And so he pondered in stillness and silence while the duke, the innkeeper, and the lackeys carefully examined him like an object that someone had temporarily mislaid but had eventually found after a not particularly thorough, half-hearted search, an object not especially desirable or even clean, about which the only remaining question was how to handle it, whether to grasp it or hold it at arm's length with one's fingertips, and whether to dust it down with a rag before throwing it out of the window. . . . He considered the various possibilities. Then, perfectly naturally, his mind turned to Francesca. "Of course!" he thought. And in that instant he understood how all this was the result of a logical and necessary chain of events that had not begun yesterday nor would be certain to end this coming night; how once, in the dim and distant past, a process had begun whereby his own fate and the fates of Francesca and the duke of Parma were tied together. The present situation was merely the continuation of a conversation begun a long time ago, and this was why he had not moved on, why he was standing here, facing the duke of Parma, who even now was staring at him, lightly puffing and somewhat out of breath, standing at the head of his lackeys like a general preparing to charge: yes, he thought, a general with his troops. "Hello!" Giacomo exclaimed in a very loud voice and took a step toward the ornately costumed group. "Anyone there?"

The tone was sharp and it rang like a sword. There was undoubtedly a "someone" out there in the corridor, a person large as life and plain as a mountain, a river, or a fortress: you couldn't miss him. That "someone" stood leaning on a silver-handled cane, his gray head, cocked to one side, boldly and gracefully balanced on the broad shoulders surmounting the slender figure like a miraculously carved ivory globe at the tip of a fashionable ebony walking stick. It was as if the balding, perfectly rounded skull, fringed at temple and nape by a sheen of thin, silky, metallic hair, had been turned on a lathe. Granted this, Giacomo's voice sounded arrogant, almost insolent, for even a blind man could feel, if not see, that the person of the "someone" who had arrived at The Stag was not a person to be snubbed or taken in with a sidelong glance, that a man making a call like this, with his complete retinue, was not to be ignored, shouted at, or addressed in terms such as "Hello! Anyone there?" Aware of the potential outrage, the lackeys shrank back in terror and the innkeeper covered his mouth and crossed himself. Only the duke himself remained unruffled. He took a step forward in the direction of the voice, and the light of the candles illuminated the bloodless, ruthless, narrow mouth that appeared to be smiling in surprise at both question and tone. The question must have pleased him. "Yes, it is I," he replied, his voice faint and dry, yet refined. He spoke quietly in the knowledge that every word of his, even the quietest, had weight and power behind it. "I have something to say to you, Giacomo."

He advanced once more, ahead of the innkeeper and the lackeys who formed an effective guard of honor and, with a wave of his hand, instructed them to leave. "Tell the sleigh to wait," he said and stared stonily ahead of him without catching the eyes of those he commanded. "You people wait in the stairwell. No one is to move. You," he gestured, without so much as a flicker of his eyelids, though everyone knew he meant the innkeeper, "you will see to it that no one interrupts us. I'll let you know when we have finished." The lackeys set off silently according to command, disappearing along with the light to the bottom of the stairs: it was as if dusk had settled in. The innkeeper followed them with nervous stumbling steps. "May I impose on you?" asked the duke with the utmost courtesy once everyone had gone, bowing slightly, as if he were addressing a close confidant or a member of the family. "Would you be kind enough to receive me for a short while in your room? I will not take up too much of your time." The request was made in the most elegant and aristocratic manner but there was something in the tone that sounded less like a request than a strict order. Hearing that tone, his host immediately regretted using terms like "Hello" and "anyone." Like any host, assured that his visitor was a man of some importance and that conversation was by no means to be avoided, he bowed silently and indicated the way with a motion of his outstretched arm, allowing his guest to precede him into the room, then closed the door behind them.

"I am most grateful," said the guest once he had taken his position by the fireplace in the armchair his host silently offered him. He stretched his two thin, pale hands—the anemic but commendably muscular hands of an old man—toward the flickering fire and for a while bathed himself in its gentle glow. "Those stairs, you know," he confided. "I find stairs hard nowadays. Seventy-two is a substantial age and little by little one learns to count both years and stairs. I am relieved that I did not climb them in vain. I am glad to find you at home." He gently folded his hands in front of him. "A stroke of luck," muttered his host. "It is not luck," he answered politely but with some finality. "I have had you watched these past eight days, and have been aware of your every movement. I even know that you were at home this afternoon, receiving visitors, halfwits who come to you for advice. Though it is not for advice that I come to you, my boy."

He said this tenderly, like an old and trusted friend who understands human frailty and is anxious to help. Only the expression "my boy" rang a little ominously in the dimly lit room: it hung there like a highly delicate, hidden threat. Giacomo scented danger and drew himself up, casting an instinctive and well-practiced glance at his dagger and at the window.

He leaned against the fireplace and crossed his arms across his chest. "And what gives the duke of Parma the right to have me observed?" he asked.

"The right of self-defense," came the simple, almost gracious answer. "You know perfectly well, Giacomo, you above all people, who are well versed in such matters, that there is a power in the world beyond that of ordinary authorities. Both the age in which I live and my own decrepitude, which has turned my hair white as snow and robbed me of my strength, justify me in defending myself. This is the age of travel. People pass through towns, handing keys to one another, and the police can't keep up: Paris informs Munich of the setting forth of some personage who intends to try his luck there. Venice informs Bolzano that one of her most talented sons intends to room there on his travels. I cannot trust authorities alone. My position, age, and rank compel me to be careful in the face of every danger. My people are observant and reliable: the best informers of the region answer to me not the chief of police. It was they who told me earlier that you had arrived. I would have found out anyway, since your reputation precedes you and makes people uneasy. Did you know that since you arrived, life beneath these snow-covered roofs has become more fraught? . . . It seems you carry the world's passions about with you in your baggage, much as traveling salesmen carry their samples of canvas and silk. One house has burned down, one vineyard owner has killed his wife in a fit of jealousy, one woman has run away from her husband—all in the last few days. These things are nothing directly to do with you. But you carry this restlessness with you, the way a cloud carries its load of lightning. Wherever you go you stir tempers and passions. As I said, your reputation precedes you. You have become a famous man, my boy," he sincerely acknowledged.

"Your Excellency exaggerates," Giacomo replied without moving.

"Nonsense!" answered his guest with some force. "I will accept no false modesty, you have no right to assume it. You are a famous man, your arrival has touched people's souls, and they announced your arrival to me the way they would have announced a guest performance of the Paris opera: you are here and people find an ironic delight in the fact. You arrived eight days ago, strapped for cash. News of your escape caught people's imagination and set it alight. Even I was filled with curiosity to see you, and thought of contacting you the day you arrived, of giving you some sign. But then I hesitated. Why has he come here? I asked myself. Our agreement was final and binding, the agreement we made at the gates of Florence just before I gave your wounded body up to the surgeons, to the world. After all, I thought, he knows very well who I am, and that my orders are never revoked. I don't have much faith in human oaths and promises: promises flow from human mouths more easily than spittle from a cow in season. But I do believe in actions, and, I argued, he knows that my words are as good as my deeds, and that I have promised to kill him if he once so much as looks at Francesca ever again. That's what I said to myself in my heart, for the less time we have left to live the more we have to remember and recall. And now here he is! He knows he is risking his life. Why is he here? With what purpose? I asked myself. Is he still in love with the duchess? Did he ever love her? . . . It is not an easy question, not one he can answer, I told myself, because he knows nothing of love: he knows a great deal about other realms of experience, about feelings that resemble love; he knows the anxious, agonizing temptations of passion and desire, but about love he is perfectly ignorant. Francesca was never his. He knows it, I know it. There have been times down the years when I was extremely lonely, when I almost regretted the fact. Are you surprised? . . . I am surprised that you should be. There is a time of life, and I, through the ineffable wisdom of time and fate, have now arrived at that time, a time when everything—vanity, selfishness, false ambition, and false fear—drops away from us, and we want nothing but the truth, and would give anything for it. That is why I sometimes thought it was a pity she had never been yours. Because if

Francesca had ever at any time been his, I reasoned, my vanity and selfishness would have suffered, and perhaps Francesca might have suffered, too, but he would have been miles away by now, nor would he ever have returned to Bolzano as his first stop from prison, and I could be certain that something that had begun a long time ago had come full circle in human terms and ended. Because what man learns in his dotage, the total sum of all he understands and learns, is that human affairs need to run their full course and cannot be terminated before they do so: the course cannot be left unfinished, because there is a kind of order in human affairs that people obey as they would a law, one from which there is no escape. Yes, my boy, it is far harder to escape from unfinished business than it is from a lead-roofed prison, even at night, even by rope! You cannot know this yet: your soul, your nervous system, and your mind are all different from mine. I don't even care whether you believe me or not. All you need to know is that I promised that I would kill you if you ever returned and tried to gain access to us or if you so much as glanced at the duchess. Do you believe me when I say I am pleased to see you? Do you understand, wise counselor, who for the tinkle of a few gold coins dispenses advice all day long to the simpleminded and vulnerable, how, in view of all that has happened between us or, more precisely, not happened, given the news of your impending arrival, I was confirmed in my own belief that you have been drawn into the vicinity of our premises and lives involuntarily, without design or subterfuge, by a fateful attraction, in simple obedience to a law as fixed as the law that dictates the course of the moon about the earth, and that I am therefore delighted to find that your first instinct has brought you to Bolzano. Do you believe me when I say I am delighted? . . . Yes, Giacomo, it is a delight and relief to me that you are here. Can you understand that?"

"I don't understand," he replied, intrigued.

"I will do everything in my power to explain," came the ready, courteous, slightly sinister response. "I was not being quite precise enough when I referred to my feeling as delight. This miraculous language of ours that the great lover, Dante, made potent with his kisses is occasionally clumsy when articulating ideas. Delight is a common word, with a commonplace ring: it suggests a man rubbing his hands and grinning. I did not in fact rub my hands on hearing of your arrival, and I certainly did not grin: my heart simply beat a little faster and I felt the blood accelerate through my veins in a way that distantly reminded me of delight, to which the feeling I am seeking to name is undoubtedly related, for the same deep well feeds all human emotions, whether these appear as stormy seas or gentle ripples on the surface. *J'étais touché,* might be the best way of putting it, to adapt a precise expression from fencing terminology, a terminology imbued with human feelings, for fencing is an analogous language that you will be as familiar with as I am. The fact is that something touched me and the expression struck me as an accurate one, one that you as a writer—for that is what I hear you are, according to the rumors spread round town by your accomplice and familiar—would certainly understand and approve. I should say that the notion of your being a writer—Bolzano is a small town where no human frailty can be hidden for long—pleasantly surprised me; I have never doubted you had some special vocation, and indeed believed that you had been entrusted with a kind of mission among your fellow human beings, but I must confess I had never, until now, associated you with this particular vocation or role; somehow I always imagined that you were the sort of person whose fate and character was part of life's raw material, the sort of man who wrote in blood not ink. Because your true medium is indeed blood rather than ink, Giacomo; I trust you know that? . . ."

"Your Excellency is quick to judgment," he haughtily replied. "Artists take time and pains to discover the material with which they most prefer to work."

"Of course," the duke answered with surprising readiness and almost too much enthusiasm. "Pardon me! What am I thinking! You see how age afflicts me! I had forgotten that the artist is merely the personal embodiment of the creative genius that drives him, that he cannot choose, for his genius will press a pen, a chisel, a brush, or even, occasionally, a sword into his hand, whether he will or no. You will be thinking that the great Buonarroti and the versatile Leonardo—products of our cities, like you—wielded pen, chisel, and brush in turn; and yes, Leonardo, with his remarkable and frightening sense of adventure, even employed a scalpel, so that under the cover of night he might edge a little closer to the hidden secrets of the human body, as well as designing brothels and fortresses; just as Buonarroti, that tetchy and monstrous demigod, scribbled sonnets and plastered domes, and, my dear Giacomo, what plastering, what domes! And he designed arches, funerary monuments, and in the meanwhile, because he had time to spare, he painted *The Last Judgment*! There's an artist for you! The human spirit swells, the heart throbs, when it contemplates the enormous scope of such geniuses; ordinary people grow faint when faced with such far horizons. Is that what you mean, when you say you are a writer? I understand, I really do. I am delighted to recognize the fact, my boy, for it explains a great deal to me. We have a very high regard for writers where I come from, and you, in your fashion, are a fine example of the species, as indeed you told your secretary, who faithfully repeats and disseminates all you say; you are a writer who dips his pen, now in blood, now in ink, though for the time being, to judge by your completed works, the uninitiated observer would be inclined to the opinion that so far you have written them entirely in blood, at the point of a dagger! Don't deny it! Who is in a better position to understand this than I, who have written several bloody masterpieces with my ancestral sword? The last time, when we faced each other with swords in our hands, we must have been engaged in an as yet unwritten but perfect dialogue, a dialogue that, at that particular moonlit moment, we considered finished, with its own full stop or period to mark the end. But now I understand that you truly are a writer," he declared with the same ambiguous air of satisfaction, "a writer who travels the world collecting material for his books!" He nodded vigorously in enthusiastic approval, his eyes shining with rapture. He was like an old man in his second child-hood finally comprehending a complex web of relation-ships: it was as if he fully believed that the person he had sought out was indeed a writer and that the belief filled him with astonishment and delight. "So now you are coming to an end of your years of wandering! Vital years they are, too, ah yes . . . there was a time when I myself . . . but of course I have no right to compare myself to you, because I have composed no great work, no, not even in my own fashion: my work was my life and nothing more, a life that I had to live according to rules, customs, and laws, and in that enterprise, alas, I fear I have almost succeeded. Almost, I said, dear boy, and I beg you not to split hairs in your desire for exactitude, for I too have learned enough to know that we should be as precise in our use of words as possible if we want them to be of any value or help in life. Almost, I said, for you see, I, who am not a writer, find every expression difficult and am simul-taneously aware of both my difficulty and of my inability to solve it. Indeed, there is nothing more difficult than expressing oneself without ambiguity, especially when the speaker knows that his words are absolute, that behind each sentence stands the specter of death. And I really do mean death, you know, yours or mine," he added, his voice quiet and calm.

Receiving no answer, he stared at the scarlet and black embers in the fire, his head tipped to one side, gently wag-ging, as if he were dreaming and remembering at once.

"I am not threatening you, Giacomo," he started again in a slightly deeper voice, but still very friendly in manner.

"We are no longer at the stage when threats are appropriate. It's just that I would like you to understand me. That is why I used the word, 'almost.' It was death I was talking about, pure and simple, nor was it my aim merely to admire the formal beauty of a frequently discussed philosophical concept while exploring its darker significance. The death I am talking about is direct and personal, a death that is timely and fully to be expected should we be unable to come to some agreement in an ingenious, wholly human way. For, you see, I no longer feel like fighting, if only for the simple reason that fighting never solves anything. We discover everything too late. Assaulting someone is not a conclusive way of ending any business, and defending oneself only settles things if our defense is just and reasonable: in other words, we must employ not just arms and fury, however delightful the exercise of both may be, but the wiser, leveling power of the active intellect. How old are you now? Forty next birthday . . . ? It's a good age for a writer. Yes, Giacomo, it's the time of one's life, and I can remember that time without envy, for it is not true to say that the more quickly life vanishes the more we thirst for what is gone—though the time is indeed gone, isn't it? Do help me out if I express myself inadequately: you are after all a writer! Have we in fact lost what we had before? Are we in danger of suffering what those people who are prey to easy and false sentiments label, wholly imprecisely, 'loss,' meaning loss of youth, youth that bounds away from us into the distance like a hare in the meadow, and loss of manhood, manhood over which one day the sun begins to set, in other words the loss of the time we have enjoyed, the time in which we acted, that we once owned as we own objects, as a form of personal property? No, the time that is gone is a self-contained reality and there's no reason to bewail its passing; it is only the future that I view with anxiety, with a certain intensity that may be appropriate to regret; yes, the future, however strange and comical it may seem at my time of life. As to lost time, I have no wish to recover it: that time is well-stocked and complete in itself. I do not mourn for my youth, which was full of false perceptions and fancy words, with all those touching, tender, lofty, confused, patchy, and immature errors of heart and mind. I view with equal satisfaction the vanished gilded landscape of my adult self. I have no desire to reclaim anything of the past. There is nothing as dangerous as false, unconscious self-pity, the wellspring of all man's misery, sickness, and ignorance: self-pity is the common well of all human distress. What has happened has happened, nor is it lost, preserved as it is by the miraculous rituals of life itself, which are more complex than those dreamed up by the early priests and more mysterious than the activities of contemporary entomologists who preserve the organs of the dead for posterity. As far as I am concerned the past has its own life and it stinks of power and plenty. I am interested in the future, my boy," he repeated very loudly, almost shouting. "Being a writer, you should understand that."

He clearly required no answer. And there was no mockery in his voice when he stubbornly repeated the word "writer." With great sympathy he described the exiled writer who must now be reaching the end of his wanderings, having gathered material—such as his adventures here in Bolzano, where the duke of Parma lived with his duchess for example—material that he would, one day, use for his books; he spoke as if he fully and enthusiastically approved the writer's calling and the manner of behavior it entailed, as if he were addressing a fellow reveler at a masked ball with a courteous wink, as if to say: "I have recognized you, but I won't tell. Keep talking." But his host remained silent: it was only the visitor that spoke. After a short silence, he continued:

"The future concerns me, because my life isn't quite over yet. It is not just writers like yourself who like a story to be properly finished, the world, too, likes it that way: it is only human nature that both writer and reader should demand that a tale should reach a genuine conclusion and end appropriately, according to the rules of the craft and in line with the soul's inner imperatives. We want the well-placed period, the full stop, all *t*'s crossed and all *i*'s dotted. That's how it has to be. That is why I repeat the word 'almost' once more, thinking it might be of some help in bringing our mutual history to a conclusion. Something remains to say, something to settle, before the story can end, though it is only one story among many hundreds of millions of such human stories, a story so common that, should you ever get to write your book, having collected enough material for it, you might even leave it out. But for the two, or should I say three, of us, it is of overwhelming importance, more important than any previous story composed either with pen or sword; to us it is more important than the visit the great poet of heaven once made to hell. And we must conclude it here on earth, because for us it is more interesting than either heaven or hell. Whatever may yet happen to round off the sentence and allow us to dot our *i*'s and cross our *t*'s; whatever arranging and winding-up of our affairs is required to conclude the history of the two, or rather, the three, of us, and whether that arrangement turns out to be somber and funereal or cheerful and sensible, depends on you alone, you the writer. You can see that I am visiting you at a bad time of life, when I am plagued by gout, when, by the time evening comes round, I prefer to remain in my room with my old habits and a warm fire to console me. Nor would I have come now if I did not have to, for believe me, as we enter our dotage, our bones creaking with age, our spirits exhausted by wicked words and harsh experience, our sense of time grows keener and we develop an intelligent, economical orderliness of manner, a kind of perceptiveness or sensitivity that tells us how long to wait and when, alas, to act. I have come because the time is right. I have come at the hour when everyone in the house is preparing for festivities, when the servants are setting the tables, the orchestra is tuning up, the guests are trying on their masks, and everything is being done properly, according to the rules of the game that brings a certain delight to living, and it certainly delights me, for there is nothing I like more than observing the idiotic and chaotic rout from my corner, wearing my mask. I shall have to start home to get changed soon. Would you like to see my mask, Giacomo? . . . If you come along tonight—as I hope you will, please take these words as a belated invitation—you will certainly know me by my mask, which will be the only one of its sort there, though the idea itself is admittedly unoriginal, something I borrowed from a book, a verse play written not in our sweet familiar tongue but in the language used by our ruder, more powerful northern cousins, the English. I discovered the book a year ago when visiting the library of my royal cousin in Marly, and I must admit the story fascinated me, though I have forgotten the author's name; all I know is that he was a comedian and buffoon a while ago in London, in the land of our distant, provincial cousin, that ugly, half-man, half-witch, Elizabeth. The long and short of it is that I shall be wearing an ass's head tonight and you will recognize me by it if you come and keep your eyes peeled. You probably know that in the play it is one of the main characters who wears the ass's head, he whom the heroine clutches to her bosom, she being a certain Titania, the queen of youth, and that she does so with the blind unseeing passion that is the very essence of love. That is why I shall wear the donkey's head tonight—and perhaps for another reason, too, because I want to be anonymous in my mask and hear the world laugh at me; I want to hear, for the first time in my life, through donkey's ears, the laughter of the world in its fancy dress, in my own palazzo, at the climax of my life, before we finish the sentence and dot the *i*. There will be quite a noise don't you think?" He was talking loudly now, politely, but with razor-sharp edge to his voice: it was like the clashing of swords after the first few strokes in a duel. "I really do want to hear them laughing at me, at the man with the ass's head, in my own palace. Why? because the time is ripe: the hour, Giacomo, has finally arrived, not a moment too soon, at its own pace and in its own good time, at the point when I could bring myself to knock at your door, at the point when I am ready to put on the ass's head that befits a lover like me, the ass's head I shall wear tonight because, in my situation, if I must go as an animal, this is the most congenial and the least ridiculous such creature, bearing in mind that it is entirely possible that come the morning I might be wearing something else, the horns of the stag for example, in accordance with a humorously mocking popular expression I have never entirely understood. Really, why is it that cheated, unloved husbands are thought to be horned? . . . Do you think you, as a linguist and writer, might be able to explain that to me?"

He waited patiently, his hands clasped, blinking, slightly tipped forward in the armchair, as if it were a very important matter, as if the etymology of a humorous and mocking popular expression really interested him. The host shrugged.

"I don't know," he answered indifferently. "It's just a saying. I will ask Monsieur Voltaire should I happen to be passing his house in Ferney, and, if he lets me, I shall send you his answer."

"Voltaire!" cried the rapt visitor. "What a marvelous idea! Yes, do ask him why language presents the cuckold with ornamental horns. Do let me know! But do you think that Voltaire, who is so well versed in language, has direct experience of the phenomenon, there in Ferney? . . . He is a cold man and his intellectual fire is like a carbuncle that glows but cannot warm. To tell you the truth, I would prefer your opinion, since I feel reasonably hopeful that your explanation might comprehend some of its power to burn. . . ."

"Your Excellency is joking," the host replied. "It is a joke that honors me and appeals to me. At the same time I feel I should answer a different question which has not yet been asked."

"Really, Giacomo? Is there a question I have failed to ask?" the visitor exclaimed in astonishment. "Could I be so far wrong? . . . Do you really not understand why I am here, and what I want to ask you? Not after all that has and has not happened between us—for as you see, the deed is not everything, indeed it is so far from being all that I would not be sitting here at this late hour, which is in any case bad for me as well as inconvenient, if you had acted rather than spoken? Now, having said that, I have all but asked the question that you can no longer answer in words. I repeat, Giacomo, I had to come now, not a moment too soon: the time for my visit is absolutely right, for the affair I need to settle with you can no longer be postponed. It urgently requires your attention. I have brought you a letter—its author may not have thought to have it delivered by my hand, and, I must confess, it is not a particularly rewarding role I find myself playing nor a fitting one, since only once in my life have I delivered a billet-doux, and that was written by a queen to a king. I am not an official *postillon d'amour,* I despise the go-between's skill and low cunning, all those qualities learned by servicing the underworld of human feeling. Nevertheless I have brought you the letter, the letter of the duchess, naturally, the one she wrote at noon, shortly after the levee when I left her to study my books. It's not a long letter: as you must know, women in love, like great writers, write brief notes using only the most necessary words. No, the duchess could not have imagined that I would be her messenger, and even now probably thinks that the letter that she—like all lovers who share an extraordinary, blind belief in the power of the will to hurry time—was so impatient to have answered, has been lost. Lovers sometimes think they have dominion over eternal things, over life and death! There may, in fact, be reasons for believing this, because now, as I turn my eyes from the time that has vanished and concentrate entirely on the time that still remains to me, a time that, as the hourglass reminds me, is shorter than the time that preceded it, I see that the time to come may offer more than it has ever offered me before, for time is the strangest thing: you cannot measure it in its own terms, and your fellow writers, the ancients, have long been telling us that one perfect moment may contain more, infinitely more, than the years and decades that preceded it and were not perfect! Now, when I ask my question, which is also a request, the firmest and clearest of requests, I can no longer shake my head in amazement at lovers' blind confidence in the power of sheer emotion to bring down mountains, to stop time and all the rest. Every lover is a little like Joshua who could stop the sun in its orbit in the sky above the battle, intervene in the world order and await the victory, a victory that, in my case, is also a defeat. Now when I am forced to look ahead, and I don't need to look too far ahead, because even with my poor eyesight I can see how trifling the remaining distance is, trifling, that is, only in earthly terms, for it is timeless and impenetrable to the eyes of love, I find that I do, after all, understand the extraordinary power of a lover's will, and believe that a tiny letter, a pleasantly scented letter, not entirely regular in its orthography—you are a writer so I beg you to excuse its imperfections when you come to glance over it—but intense in its feeling, a feeling that is vague and hilariously childish in some respects, yet is as a coiled spring in the sharpness of its desire, can really suspend the laws of nature, and, for a while, that is to say for a mere second from the perspective of eternity, assert its authority over life and death. Now, when I am constrained to face one of life's great riddles—and both of us are in the position of having to ask and answer questions at once, Giacomo, as in some strange examination where we are both master and pupil!—now, when I should take the rusty flintlock of my life, load it with the live ammunition of the will and take certain aim as I have often done before, with hands that did not shake and eyes that did not easily mist over, when I was not as likely as I am now to miss my mark, I do begin to believe that there is a power, a single omnipotent power, that can transcend not only human laws but time and gravity, too. That power is love. Not lust, Giacomo—forgive me for attempting to correct the essential laws of your existence and to contradict your considerable experience. Not lust, you unhappy hunter, angler, writer, and explorer, you who nightly drag the still-steaming, still-bleeding, excited body of your prize into bed, now here, now there, in every corner of the world; not the grinding hunger that conceals itself and is always seeking its prey wherever lonely and hidden desires are to be found, staring wide-eyed, awaiting liberation; not the gambler's eye for the main chance nor the military strategy that carries a rope ladder and watches the windows of sleeping virtue, preparing to assail it with a few bold words; not the yearning born of sadness and terrible loneliness: it is not these things that prepare one for action. I am talking about love, Giacomo, the love that haunts us all at one time or another, and might have haunted even your melancholy, sharp-toothed, predatory life, for there were reasons for your arrival in Pistoia some years ago and reasons for your escape. You are neither a wholly innocent man nor a wholly guilty one: there was a time when love possessed you too.

"I chased you away at the point of a sword then, the fool that I was! You would have been perfectly entitled to call me an old fool that day. Doting old fool! you might have cried. Do you think that blades sharpened in Venetian ice and fire or scimitars forged and flexed in Damascus can destroy love? . . . They would have been fair questions—a little rhetorical, a little poetic perhaps—but as concerns the practicalities, they would have been fair. That is why this time I have come without sharp swords or hidden daggers. I have another weapon now, Giacomo."

"What kind of weapon?"

"The weapon of reason."

"It is a useless, untrustworthy weapon to use in emotional conflicts, sir."

"Not always. I am surprised at you. It is not the answer

I would have expected from you, Giacomo. Besides, it's the only weapon I have. I speak of true reason, which has no wish to argue, to haggle, or even to convince. I haven't come to beg nor, I repeat, to threaten. I have come to establish facts and to put questions, and in my sorry and precarious situation I am obliged to believe that the cold bright blade of reason is stronger than the wild bluster and bragging of the emotions. You and the duchess are bound together by the power of love, my boy. I state this as a fact that requires no explanation. You know very well that we do not love people for their virtues, indeed, there was a time when I believed that, in love, we prefer the oppressed, the problematic, the quarrelsome to the virtuous, but as I grew older I finally learned that it is neither people's sins and faults nor their beauty, decency, or virtue that make us love them. It may be that a man understands this only at the end of his life, when he realizes that wisdom and experience are worth less than he thought. It is a hard lesson, alas, and offers nothing by way of consolation. We simply have to accept the fact that we do not love people for their qualities; not because they are beautiful and, however strange it seems, not even because they are ugly, hunchbacked, or poor: we love them simply because there is in the world a kind of purpose whose true working lies beyond our wit, which desires to articulate itself much as an idea does, so that though the world has been going around a long time it should appear ever new and, according to certain mystics, touch our souls and nervous systems with terrifying power, set glands working, and even cloud the judgment of brilliant minds. You and the duchess are in love, and though you make an extraordinary and baffling enough pair, only a novice in love would be amazed at the fact, because, where people are concerned, nothing is impossible. Animals keep to their kind and there is no instance, as far as I am aware, of an affair between a giraffe and a puma or any other beast: animals remain within the strict precincts of their species. I trust you will forgive me, for I do not mean to insult you by the comparison! If anyone should be insulted by it, it is I! No, animals are straightforward creatures, whereas we human beings are complex and remarkable even at our lowest ebb, because we try to understand the nature of love's secret power even when we remain ignorant of its purposes, so that eventually we have to accept facts that cannot be explained. The duchess loves you, and, to me, this seems as extraordinary a liaison as an affair between the sun at dawn and a storm at night. Forgive me if I abandon the animal images that seem to be haunting me with a peculiar force tonight, probably because we are preparing for the ball where I shall be wearing an ass's head. But however extraordinary the love of the duchess for you, it is still more extraordinary that you should love the duchess: it is as if you were breaking the very laws of your existence. You will be aware that the feeling of any deep emotion whatsoever represents a revolt against those laws. There is nothing that frightens you so much, that sends you scuttling away so fast, as a confrontation with emotion. You were hungry and thirsty in jail, you beat at the iron door with your fists, you shook the bars of your window, and threw yourself on the rotten straw of your bed, helpless with bitterness, you cursed the world that deprived you of your fascinating life, while knowing that behind your solitude, behind the filthy straw, behind bars and iron gates, behind your memories, there was another prison, worse than the cells of the Holy Inquisition, that jail was, in its way, a form of escape, because it was only the fires of lust that burned you there, because you were not condemned to the terrifying inferno of love. Jail was a shelter from the only feeling that might trip you up and destroy you, for feeling is a kind of death for people like you: it stifles you with responsibility, as it does all insubstantial, so-called free spirits. . . . But love touched you briefly when you met the duchess, who at that time was plain Francesca, and it is love that has brought you close to her again, not the memory of an affair that never quite got started. What is this love of yours like, really? I have long pondered that. I had time enough . . . from the encounter in Pistoia, through the period in Venice, and after that, when you were in jail, by which time Francesca had become the duchess of Parma, long after we fought for her. In all that time you continued, amusingly enough, to believe that she was just another brief fling like all the rest, a conquest which did not quite succeed, an adventure in which you were not fully your ruthless self. But charity is a problematic virtue. You are not naturally one of the merciful, Giacomo: you are perfectly capable of sleeping peacefully while, at your door, the woman you deserted is busily knotting the sheets you shared into the noose she is to hang herself with. 'What a shame!' you would sigh, and shake your head. That's the kind of person you are. Your love—the way you follow a woman, the way you note her hand, her shoulder, and her breast at a glance—is a trifle inhuman. I saw you once, many years ago, in the theater in Bologna: we hadn't yet met, nor had you met Francesca, who would have been fourteen at the time, and of whom few had yet heard, though I had heard of her, as a man might hear of some rare plant in a greenhouse, one that grows in an artificial climate, in secret, to flower and become the wonder of the world eventually. . . . You knew nothing of Francesca, nor of me, and you entered the play-house at Bologna where people were whispering your name, and your entrance was splendid, like an actor's solil-oquy. You stopped in the front row with your back to the stage, raised your lorgnette, and looked around. I studied you closely. Your reputation preceded you, your name was on everyone's lips, the boxes were buzzing with you. I want you to take what I am about to say as a compliment. You are not a handsome man. You are not one of those loathsome beaux who flounces around looking ingratiat-ing: your face is unusual and unrefined, rather masculine, I suppose, though not in the normal sense of the word. Please don't be offended, but your face is not quite human. It might, on the other hand, be man's real face, the way the Creator imagined it, true to the original pat-tern which years, dynasties, fashions, and ideals have mod-ified. You have a big nose, your mouth is severe, your figure is stocky, your hands are square and stubby, the whole angle of your jaw is wrong. It is certainly not what is required for a beau. I tell you, Giacomo, out of sheer cour-tesy that there is something inhuman about your face, but

I had to understand your face before I could begin to understand the love between you and Francesca. Please don't misunderstand me: when I say your face is somehow inhuman, or not quite human, I do not mean that it is animal; it is more as if you were some transitional creature, something between man and beast, a being that is neither one thing nor the other. I am sure the angels must have had something in mind when they were blending the elements that made you what you are: a hybrid, a cross between man and beast. I hope you can tell from the tone of my voice that I intend this as a compliment. There you stood in the playhouse, leaning against the walls of the orchestra pit, and you yawned. You looked at the women through your glasses and the women looked back at you with undisguised curiosity. The men, for their part, watched your movements, keeping a wary eye now on you, now on the eyes of the women, and in all this tension, suspense, and excitement, you yawned, showing those thirty-two yellow tusks of yours. You gave a great terrifying yawn. Once, in the orangerie of my Florentine palazzo, I kept some young lions and an aging leopard; your yawn was like that of the old leopard after he finally ate the Arabian keeper. Without a second thought, this noble creature proceeded to demonstrate his indifference to the world that held him captive with a yawn that spoke of infinite boredom and astonishing contempt. I remember thinking that I would have to throw a net over your head and impale you on a spear if I ever found you in the vicinity of a woman whom I too found attractive. And I was not at all surprised when, a year later, you turned up in Pistoia, by the crumbling wall in the garden, together with Francesca, throwing colored hoops with a gilt-tipped wooden stick for her nimble arms to catch. What was it I thought then? Nothing more than: 'Yes, it is natural, how could it be otherwise.' And now I have brought you Francesca's letter."

He drew the narrow, much-folded letter from the inner pocket of his fur-lined cape with a slow, leisurely movement and held it high in the air:

"Please overlook any errors you may find. Have I said that before? It is only recently that she learned to write, from an itinerant poet in Parma, a man who had been castrated by the Moors and whom I had ransomed, his father having been our gardener. I have a fondness for poets. Her hand seems to have shaken a little with excitement and there is something terribly touching about that, for her capital letters have never been good, poor dear; I can see her now, her fevered brow and her chill, trembling fingers as she scratches her message on the blotted parchment— and where in heaven's name did she get that from?—with whatever writing implements she could find, implements probably obtained for her by her companion and accomplice, the aged Veronica, whom we brought with us from Pistoia and whom, it has just occurred to me, we might have been wiser to leave back in Pistoia. But here she is, willing to be of service, and when the moment came, she found some writing paper, a pen, some ink, and some powder, as she was perfectly right to do, for every creature, even one such as Veronica, has some inescapable, traditional part to play. It is not only onstage that nurses have acted as bawds! It is a short letter, so please allow me to read it to you. You can afford to allow it because it is not the first time I have read it; I read it first at about four this afternoon when it was passed to the groom to deliver to you, and again this evening before I set out on my post-masterly, messenger's errand: a man shouldn't leave such tasks to strangers, after all. Are you frowning? . . . Do you think it impertinent of me to read a lady's letter? . . . You wish to remain silent in your disapproval of my curiosity? Well, you are right," he calmly continued, "I don't approve either. I have lived by the rules all my life, as an officer and gentleman, born and bred. Never in all that time did I imagine that I would meet such a woman and find myself in a situation that would lead me to behave in a manner unbefitting my upbringing, abandoning the responsibili-ties of my rank: never before have I opened a woman's let-ter, partly on principle, and partly because I did not think it would be of such overwhelming interest as to tempt me to act against my principles. But this one did interest me," he continued in a matter-of-fact manner, "since Francesca has never written me a letter, indeed could not have writ-ten me a letter even if she had wanted to, because, until a year ago, she didn't know how to write. Then, a year ago, shortly after the castrated poet came to us, she began to show an interest in writing—which, now I come to think of it, was at roughly the same time as the news of your incarceration by the Holy Inquisition arrived from Venice. She learned to write in order to write to you, because as a woman, she likes to undertake truly heroic tasks in the name of love. She learned to use those terrible cryptic cyphers of your profession—the modest, meek, and chubby *e,* the corpulent *s, t* with its lance, *f* with its funny hat—all so that she might offer you comfort by writing down the words that were burning a hole in her heart. She wanted to console you in prison and, for a long time, I thought you corresponded. I believed in the correspondence and looked out for it; I had ears and eyes, dozens of them, at my command, the best ears and sharpest eyes in Lombardy and Tuscany, and those are places where they know about such things. . . . She learned to write because she wanted to send you messages; yet, after all that, she didn't write: I know for certain that she did not write because, to a pure and modest heart like hers, the act of writing is the ultimate immodesty, and I could sooner imagine Francesca as a tightrope dancer, or as a whore cavorting in a brothel with lecherous foreign dandies, than with a pen in her hand describing her feelings to a lover. Because Francesca is, in her way, a modest woman, just as you, in your way, are a writer, and I, in my way, am old and jealous. And that is how we lived, all of us, each in his or her own way, you under the lead roofs of Venice, she and I in Pistoia and Marly, waiting and preparing for something. Of course you are right," he waved his hand dismissively as if his host were about to interrupt, "I quite admit that we lived more comfortably in Pistoia, Bolzano, Marly, and other places, near Naples up in the mountains, in our various castles, than you on your louse-ridden straw bed, under the lead roof. But comfort, too, was a prison, albeit in its own twisted, rather improper way, so please do not judge us too harshly. . . . As I was saying, the castrato taught Francesca to write, and I watched her, thinking 'Aha!' Quite rightly. There are times when Voltaire himself thinks no more than that, particularly when Voltaire is thinking about virtue or power. Each of us is wise at those unexpected moments of illumination when we suddenly notice the changing, surprising aspects of life. That is why I thought 'Aha!' and began to pay close attention, employing the sharpest ears and eyes that Lombardy and Tuscany could offer. But I heard and saw nothing suspicious: Francesca was too shy to write to a writer like you, too embarrassed by the prospect of putting her feelings into words—and isn't it a fact that you writers are a shameless lot, putting the most shameful human thoughts down on paper, without hesitation, sometimes even without thinking? A kiss is always virtuous but a word about a kiss is always shameful. That might be what Francesca, with that delicacy of perception so characteristic of her and of most women in love, actually felt. But she might simply have been shy about her handwriting and about corresponding in general, for, though her heart was troubled by love, it remained pure. And so, when she finally got down to writing to you, I can imagine her agitated, overwrought condition and the shudder of fear that ran through her from top to toe as she sat with fevered brow and trembling fingers, with paper, ink, and sand, to undertake the first shameless act of her life in writing to you. It was a love letter that she was writing, and in giving her all and trusting herself entirely to pen and paper, and thereby to the world and to eternity, which is always the last word in shamelessness, she was venturing into dangerous territory, but she ventured further than that, into yet more dangerous territory, for the point at which someone reveals their true feelings to the world is like making love in a city marketplace in perpetual view of the idiots and gawpers of the future; it is like wrapping one's finest, most secret feelings in a ragged parcel of words; in fact it is like having the dogcatcher tie one's most vital organs up in old sheets of paper! Yes, writing is a terrible thing. The consciousness of this must have permeated her entire being as she wrote, poor darling, for love and pain had driven her to literacy, to the symbolic world of words, to the mastery of letters. But when she did write, she wrote briefly, in a surprisingly correct style, in the most concise fashion, like a blend of Ovid and Dante. Having said that, I shall now read you Francesca's letter." He unfolded the parchment with steady fingers, raised one hand in the air, and, being shortsighted, used the other to adjust the spectacles on his nose, straightening his back and leaning forward a little to peer at the script. "I can't see properly," he sighed. "Would you bring me a light, my boy?" And when his silent and formal host politely picked up a candle from the mantelpiece and stood beside him, he thanked him: "That's better. Now I see perfectly well. Listen carefully. This is what my wife, Francesca, the duchess of Parma, wrote to Giacomo, eight days after hearing that her lover had escaped from the prison where his character and behavior had landed him, and that he had arrived in Bolzano: *I must see you.* To this she has appended the first letter of her name, a large F, with a slight ceremonial flourish, as the castrato had taught her."

He held the letter at arm's length, perhaps in order that he might be able to see the tiny letters more clearly.

"This, then, is the letter," he declared with a peculiar satisfaction, dropping the parchment together with his spectacles into his lap and leaning back in the chair. "What do you think of the style? I am absolutely bowled over by it. Whatever Francesca does is done perfectly: that's how she is, she can do no other. I am bowled over by the letter, and I hope it has had an equally powerful impact on you, that it has shaken you to the core and made its mark on your soul and character the way all true literature marks a complete human being. After years of reading it is only now, this afternoon, when I first read Francesca's letter, that I fully realized the absolute power of words. Like emperors, popes, and everyone else, I discovered in them a power sharper and more ruthless than swords or spears. And now, more than anything I want your opinion, a writer's opinion, of the style, of the expressive talent of this beginner. I should tell you that I felt the same on a second reading—and now, having glanced over Francesca's letter for a third time, my opinion has not changed at all. The style is perfect! Please excuse my shortcomings as a critic, do not dismiss the enthusiasm of a mere family member from your lofty professional height—but I know you will admit that this is not the work of a dilettante. There are four words and one initial only, but consider the conditions that forced these four words onto paper, consider that their author, even a year ago, had no acquaintance with the written word: turn the order of the words over in your mind, see how each follows the other, like links in a chain hammered out on a blacksmith's anvil. Talent must be self-generating. Francesca has not read the works of either Dante or Virgil, she has no concept of subject or predicate, and yet, all by herself, without even thinking about it, she has discovered the essentials of a correct, graceful style. Surely it is impossible to express oneself more concisely, more precisely, than this letter. Shall we analyze it? . . . *'I must see you.'* In the first place I admire the concentrated power of the utterance. This line, which might be carved in stone, contains no superfluous element. Note the prominence of the verb, as is usual in the higher reaches of rhetoric, especially in drama and verse-play, with action to the fore. 'See,' she writes, almost sensuously, for the word does refer to the senses. It is an ancient word, coeval with humanity, the source of every human experience, since recognition begins in seeing, as does desire, and man himself, who before the moment of seeing is merely a blind, mewling, bundle of flesh: the world begins with sight and so, most certainly, does love. It is a spellbinding verb, infinite in its contents, suggesting hankering, secret fires, the hidden meaning of life, for the world only exists insofar as we see it, and you too only exist insofar as Francesca is capable of seeing you—it is, in the terms of this letter at least, through her eyes that you re-enter the world, her world, emerging from the world of the blind that you had inhabited, but only as a shadow, a shade, like a memory or the dead. Above all, she wants to see you. Because the other senses—touch, taste, scent, and hearing—are all as blind gods without the arcana of vision. Nor is Cupid a blind god, Giacomo. Cupid is inquisitive, light-desiring, truth-demanding: yes, above all he wants to see. That's why the word 'see' is so prominent in her discourse. What else might she have said? She might have written 'talk with,' or 'be with,' but both of these are merely consequences of seeing, and her use of that verb confirms the intensity of the desire that drives her to take up the pen; the verb practically screams at us, because a heart smitten by love feels it can no longer stand the dark of blindness, it must see the beloved's face; it must see, it must light a torch in this incomprehensible and blind universe, otherwise nothing makes sense. That's why she chose a word as precise, as deeply expressive as 'see.' I hope my exposition does not bore you? . . . I must admit it is of supreme interest to me, and it is only now, for the first time, that I understand the endeavors of lonely philologists who, with endless patience and anxious care, pore over dusty books and ancient undecipherable texts, spending decades disputing the significance of some obscure verb in a forgotten language. Somehow, through the energy of their looking and the vitality of their breath they succeed in coaxing a long-dead word back to life. I am like them in that I think I can interpret this text, that is to say the text of Francesca's letter. Seeing, as we have said, is the most important aspect of it. Next comes *'must.'* Not 'I would like to,' not 'I desire to,' not 'I want to.' Immediately, in the second word of the text, she declares something with the unalterable force of holy writ—and doesn't it occur to you, Giacomo, that our young author was, in her way, producing a kind of holy writ by writing her first words of love? Don't you think

that the writ of love somehow resembles sacred hiero-
glyphs on a pagan tomb, directly invoking the presence of
the Immortal, even when it speaks of no more than
arrangements for a rendezvous, or of a rope ladder to be
employed in the course of an escape? . . . Naturally, there's
nothing irrelevant in Francesca's discourse: she is far too
fine a poet for that as we may see at a glance. Poet, I said,
and I don't believe that my feelings or my admiration lead
me to exaggerate in the use of the word, which I realize
signifies status, the very highest human status: in China,
as in Versailles, it is poets like Racine, Bossuet, and
Corneille, that follow the king in a procession, sometimes
even those who in life were a little dirty or disreputable
looking, such as La Fontaine: they all take precedence over
Colbert, over even Madame Montespan and Monsieur
Vendôme when the king grants an audience. I know very
well that to be a poet is to belong to an elite, an elite
accorded intimate luster and invisible medals. That may
be why I feel that Francesca is a poet, and in saying that, I
feel the same awe as I would if I were reading the first work
of any true poet, an awe that sends shudders through me
and fills my soul with dizzy admiration, with an extraordinary flood of feelings that unerringly signify the most ele-
vated thoughts about the solemnity of life. That, then, is
why she wrote *must*. What refined power radiates from the
word, my boy! Its tone is commanding, regal: it is more
than a command because it is both explanation and significance at once. If she had written 'want' it would still have
been regal but a little peremptory. No, she chose precisely
the right word, the perfectly calibrated word, the word

that, while it commands some humility: *must,* she says, and thereby confesses that when she commands, she herself is obeying a secret commandment; *must* suggests that the person requesting the meeting stands in need of something, that she can do no other, can no longer wait, that when she addresses you severely and gives you to understand her meaning she is throwing herself on your mercy. There is something touchingly helpless and human about the word. It is as if her desire to meet you were involuntary, Giacomo. Yes, it's true! I cannot tell whether my eyes are capable of reading clearly anymore, whether I can trust these old ears of mine, but there is something in the whole sentence, which might be the first line of a poem, that is helpless and abject, as when a man confronts his destiny under the stars and tells the sad, brilliant truth. And what is that truth? Both more and less than the fact that Francesca *must* see you. The voice is anxious, in need of help; she commands but, at the same time, admits that she is both the issuer and the helpless executor of the command. I *must see:* there is something dangerous about the association of these words; only people who are themselves in danger issue commands like these. Yes, they would prefer to withdraw and defend themselves but there's no alternative, and so they do what they must: they command. The words are perfect. And there follows, naturally enough, a word that is like the lin-lan-lone of bells in the distance: the word *you. You* is a mighty word, Giacomo. I don't know whether anyone can say something that means more to another, or is of greater importance to them. It is a fulfilling word whose reverberation fills the entire human universe, a painful word that forms and names, that enlivens identity and gives it a voice. It is the word God used when He first addressed man at the Creation, at the point that He realized that flesh was not enough, that man needed a name, too, and therefore He named him and addressed him with the familiar *You.* Do you fully understand the word? There are millions upon millions of people in the world but it is *you* she wants to see. There are others nobler, handsomer, younger, wiser, more virtuous, more chivalrous than you, oh indeed there are, and without wishing to offend you, I do think it incumbent on you to consider, however unpleasant it may be, however it may hurt your self-esteem, that there may also exist people more villainous, more artful, more deceitful, more heartless, and more desperate than you are; and yet it is *you* she desires to see. The word elevates you above your fellow mortals, distinguishes you from those whom in part you resemble; it hoists you up and slaps you on the back, it crowns you a king and dubs you a knight. It is a fearsome word. *You,* writes Francesca, my wife, the duchess of Parma, and the instant she writes the word you are ennobled; despite your notoriety as an adventurer, despite hitherto having assumed a false aristocratic name, you are ennobled. *You,* she writes, and with what a certain hand, the letters leaning with full momentum, like arms raised for action, pumping blood and flexing powerful muscles: by now the author knows what she wants to say and is no longer seeking alternatives. She places on paper the only word that can hold the sentence, the syntax, together as though she had addressed the subject of it by its proper name. *You* . . . A mysterious word. Just consider how many people there are in the world, people who are interesting to Francesca, too, people worth seeing even if there is no *must* about it, people who would offer her something more substantial, more true, more of everything than you can, notwithstanding the fact that you are a writer and traveler. For there are men out there who have voyaged to the Indies and the New World, scientists who have explored the secrets of nature and discovered new laws for humanity to wonder at: there are so many other remarkable men alive, and yet it is *you* she wants to see . . . and in so naming you it is as if she were engaged in an act of creation, re-creating you. Because, for example, it is possible that she might want to see me, but there would be nothing out of the ordinary in that, I am her husband after all: but it is *you* that she must see, only *you!* . . .

"Well, there is the text and we have explored its meaning. And now, let us behold it once more with amazement, having examined its parts, seeing the compact, solid whole, admiring the logic of the thought, the momentum of the execution, the terse perfection of the style that, without a hint of superfluity, tells you everything. And finally, let us consider the signature, which is so modest, a mere initial—for true letters and true works of art require nothing more: the work itself identifies the author, is one with her. No one imagines that the *Divine Comedy* required the name of the author below the title . . . not that I wish to invite comparisons, of course. But what need for names when the whole text speaks so clearly, the words, the syntax, the individual letters; when everything is infused with the same character, the same soul, a soul driven by necessity and inspiration to creation, in the recognition that its fate is to see you, nothing more. And having said that," he added carelessly, holding the letter between two fingers and passing it over, "we have done. Here's the letter." And when the host and addressee did not move, he lightly placed the letter on the mantelpiece beside the candlestick.

"You will read it later?" he asked. "Yes, I understand. I think you will often read and reread that letter in the years to come, but later, when you are older. You will understand it then." And he fell silent, breathing heavily, as if he had overexcited himself with all that talking, his heart worn out, his lungs exhausted.

"We have done," he repeated, old and tired now, and leaned against his stick, holding it with both hands. But he continued speaking, still seated, leaning on his stick, not glancing at his host but staring into the fire, frequently blinking and screwing up his eyes, watching the embers.

"I have accomplished one of my missions by giving you the letter. I hope you will look after it properly. I wouldn't like the love letter of the duchess of Parma to be left on the wine-stained table of some inn, nor would I want you to read it out while in bed with a whore, in that boasting and bragging way men have when under the influence of cheap wine and cheap passion. I would not be in a position to prevent that, of course, but it would cause me great pain, and therefore I hope it will not happen. Yet we may be sure that this kind of letter will not remain a secret, and I would not be at all surprised if at some later time, in another, more refined and more generous age, such brief masterpieces were taught in schools as a model of concision. Nor do I doubt that the letter will be imitated, as is every masterpiece, that through the fine capillaries of memory it will enter the general consciousness of our descendants: lovers will copy it and make irreverent use of it without knowing the least thing about the author and its provenance. They will copy it, and not just once, as if they themselves had composed it, committing it to paper, declaring *I must see you*, and signing it with their own names or initials, and by some mysterious process the text will actually have become theirs—like all true texts it will be diffused into the world and be blended with life itself, for that is its nature. All the same, I would prefer it if this process were to follow literary precedent at an appropriate pace, not through your bragging and boasting, or declaiming the text aloud in taverns or in a whore's bed. I would be extremely sorry if that were to happen. But now that I have given you the letter whose true meaning we have, I hope, solved and understood, we must be careful lest our enthusiasm as literary critics, the peculiar and obstinate delight we take in studying it, should divert us from our true obligation: for letters can be as passionate and terrifying as kissing or murder; there is something real and living in them, and we two critics—you the writer and I the reader and connoisseur—have almost forgotten the person behind the letters, she who has committed these perfect lines to paper. It is, after all, she whom we are discussing, and Francesca is inclined to the belief that she must see you. That is the reality to which we must return

now that we have finished admiring the beauties of the letter. And here we must be businesslike, since time is passing and the evening is upon us—isn't it the case that time
never flies so fast as when we lose ourselves in admiration
of the hidden graces of a first-class text?—but our business
is to proceed beyond the eternal literary merits of the text
and to explore the meaning in its practical sense, that
meaning being neither more nor, alas, less than that the
duchess of Parma has fallen in love and must see you. That
is an obligation you cannot avoid, even should you wish
to. I have already said that I have not come to threaten
you, Giacomo: I have simply brought you a letter and all I
want is to understand, articulate, and settle something. I
have not come to threaten: there is no need for you to
stand so rigidly or to twitch like that, there is no question
of us engaging in another armed encounter for the sake of
Francesca, as we once did in such a laughable and yet
admirably masculine manner in Tuscany, our chests bare
in the moonlight! The time for that is gone: and I don't
mean just the time of year, however awful in its effects that
may be, for the cold cuts through me to the bone even
when I am wearing my furs, and heaven knows what it
would do if I presented myself half-naked, no, I mean
another kind of time, the time that has passed. I have
thrown away my sword. I could, of course, buy other
swords, better and finer than the old one, for once upon a
time, as you will recall, I was not altogether hopeless in a
duel. I could buy a sword, one that glittered as I wielded
it, a rapier of ice-cold steel to twist wickedly between your
ribs: I do, after all, hold your life in my hands. But this is

not a threat either, Giacomo: it is a statement, no more. Please don't protest. There is no need to get excited. Your life is in my hands, that's all: in vain did you escape from the republic, in vain did the world look on and chuckle in approval, in vain do local laws protect you with their guarantees of personal and institutional freedom, in vain does tradition underwrite the international rights of refugees. According to laws and customs you are invulnerable here, untouchable. But people are aware, and you in particular have good reason to know, that there exists another law, a more subtle, unwritten law, whose custom and practice underlie the visible, practical, and constitutionally approved sort, a law that is more real and more effective everywhere. It is my kind of law: I dispense it, I and a few others in the world, those who are sufficiently intelligent and powerful to live by such unwritten laws without exploiting them. Believe me, Giacomo, when I say that it really was in vain that you escaped, clever monkey that you are, from the Leads on the roof of the Doge's Palace; in vain that you scuttled like some fugitive water-rat down the filthy and noble waters of the lagoon and reached the far shore in Mestre and later, Valdepiadene; it is in vain that you reside here beyond the perilous border, in a room of The Stag, strutting with confidence, as if you had escaped every danger, for if I wished it you'd be back on the other side of the border in the clutches of the *messer grande* by this time tomorrow, after sunset, you can bet your life on it. And why? . . . Because power does not work precisely as these local boobies believe it works, and you, who are better traveled and more nimble-witted than they are, will be perfectly aware of the fact. You therefore know that there is no nook or cranny in the world where these calloused, exhausted hands, that are no longer up to dueling, would not reach you if I so wished. That is why I am not threatening you. And it's not out of the kindness of my heart, nor out of any false if noble sense of compassion that I allow you to keep running—because run you must, Giacomo, on fleet horses, in covered coaches, or on sleighs with polished runners before the night is through. As soon as you have finished your business in Bolzano and met the duchess, who, as she has commanded both you and me, *must* see you, we will draw a line under the affair and place a full stop at the end of the last sentence. That is why I have no thought of threatening you in revealing to you the vague outline of what might happen behind the scenes, and exposing the real, effective relations of power. I am merely explaining and cautioning. And there is no trace of bitterness in my heart when I say that, no sense of injury, no false male pride, not any more. For you, like me, are merely a cat's-paw, an actor, the tool of the fate that is toying with us both, a fate whose purposes sometimes appear unfathomable. Sometimes it seems the hand it is playing is not entirely above board, that it is playing for its own amusement; a manner of playing that you, who understand not only written slips of paper but those prinked out with spots and numbers too, are in the best position to comprehend. That is why I have come to you. What I want is that you should stay till morning and accommodate yourself to the duchess's desire, which is more command than desire, something neither of us can refuse to obey, for behind it lies the *must* to which the duchess of Parma gives such perfect literary expression. You are, therefore, to remain in Bolzano until the morning. Should I threaten you? Should I reason with you? Should I beg you? Explain things to you? What should I do with you? . . . I could kill you, but then you would be more deadly than before. You would retain your current stocky, fleshy, full-blooded reality, a reality I would have turned into a shade, a memory, a rival impervious to blows, the rotten corpse of a once vigorous presence, an amorous shadow forever lurking in the folds of the curtains of my wife's four-poster bed, taking my place on her pillow after midnight, your voice haunting other men's voices, your eyes looking at her through unknown men's eyes. That is why I will not kill you. Should I send you away? Order you now, this very night, to take to the sledge waiting at the gate, shrouded in the wings of your cloak, so that, under the stewardship and protection of my servants, you should rush over mountain passes, through moonlit forests restless with the shadows of wolves, into a foreign country where you might disappear from the best years of the duchess's life? . . . I could insist on that, too, and you'd have no choice but to obey, because, after all, you want to save your skin, and it is that fact which allows me to exercise a degree of control over you, for you are still careful of your life, solicitous of your esteemed person, your flesh and bones and are not desperately anxious to risk them, while I, on the other hand, no longer fear for my life and am interested only in one thing which, to me, is finer and more valuable. That is why you must obey me.

For this and other reasons of your own. For now I am willing to put my power and strength at the disposal of your own interests and intentions, providing we can come to a friendly, sensible agreement. That is the reason I have come to you tonight. I want to make you an offer. I have thought a great deal about you. I saw before me your face in the theater at Bologna, the way you yawned, and I remembered how, in that moment, without knowing anything much about you, I instinctively understood the nature of your being. And now I know you properly, or as well as anyone can know you, I am sure it would be a mistake to kill you. A man who is loved is a dangerous rival in death: you'd sit with us at table, lie beside the duchess in her bed, precede us into rooms, your light, ghostly footsteps would tread close behind us as we walked through the garden: you would, in short, be omnipresent. You would become funereal, your outlines blurred by ceremony, hidden among the silver and black hangings of feeling and memory. But a fierce scarlet cloud of revenge would trail behind you, its silently smoking fire lighting up the corridors. And I would have become the selfish, cowardly, stupid nonentity who had killed the unique, the miraculous person that Francesca had to see! No, my boy, I will not kill you. I could, of course, simply hand you over into the clutches of the *messer grande* and he wouldn't make the same mistake twice. I could do it because I have influence and influence has long arms and moves in mysterious ways. Do you remember that morning some sixteen months ago when Venetian agents forced their way into your room and you railed at them, spitting with indignation, demanding that you be informed of your crimes? You will certainly recall the next sixteen months, buried away, sprawling on a rotten straw bed, still wondering what it was you were accused of. Do you think it might have been a word in the right ear, a little flexing of muscles that landed you there? It might easily have been my doing. Not that I am saying it was, I only mention it because I think you should consider it as a possibility among others, something you should give some thought to once this night is through. Because, although I am not a writer and am not preparing to embark on any kind of career, and though I am losing my hair and suffer shooting pains in my arms, and though time is certainly not on my side, I am nevertheless possessed of effective means. And, if I wanted to, I could still stretch out my arm and touch a life that considers itself secure in Venice, under the protection of Papa Bragadin. How pale you look! You have taken a step back. Are you looking for your dagger? Is it revenge you want? . . . Control yourself, my boy. I have come unarmed, as you see, and there is nothing to stop you running me through in an act of revenge and then taking to your heels to escape the police of half the world, until you are caught and find yourself on the scaffold. But how pointless that would be! You would lose everything and even your revenge would be tinged with doubt about my part in your imprisonment. Calm down. I haven't said I was responsible for that. I have merely thrown a little light on the faint possibility that I might have been. I have fought too many battles and have lived too full a life to feel any compassion for you. My compassion is not easily earned. Only weak and frightened people shed crocodile tears and hug their enemies to their bosoms with false enthusiasm. I will not take you to my bosom, Giacomo. I will neither kill you nor exile you before your time is due. What course, if any, is there left to me, then? . . . Well, I believe I have found the only acceptable solution. I will strike a bargain with you. I realize that in proposing this bargain, which will be not a whit more crooked or honest than such bargains usually are, I am addressing both your feelings and your intelligence. So let me put it plainly: I want to buy you, my boy. You can name your price, and in case false modesty, false ambition, or any other false feeling prevent you, I will tell you the price, the price I am willing to pay to prevent the reality from becoming a ghostly rival, to ensure that you finally vanish from my life, having completed your business and played your part by allowing the duchess to see you, as she must, as she wishes. . . . I am buying you: these are ugly words, not the words an author or a duchess are likely to use, but they are my words, and they, too, are precise. I have weighed them and chosen them carefully. I know your services will not be cheap, but I am rich and powerful and I shall pay you in gold and clemency, in advice and connections, in documents and cash. Whatever it costs it will be a bargain. Please don't protest. I shall buy you as people buy a donkey for carrying water on the market in Toulon, as they buy a slave on the market at Smyrna: I shall buy you as if I were buying a curio from one of the silversmiths on the Ponte Vecchio. Are you still protesting? Are you staring at the floor and biting your lips? . . . Are you planning some terrible act of revenge, a revenge that might at once wipe out this insult as well as the disgrace of your imprisonment in Venice? . . . Please control yourself. Naturally, I must pay you for those injuries, too, and will offer you the full pleasures of the world, for one has to buy the whole man, with the full complement of his moods and passions, or the bargain is meaningless. I am buying you because you are a mere mortal. Think it over carefully: it is almost a compliment. I used the word 'almost' at the beginning of our conversation and I repeat it now because words bind and their binding power extends to both the past and the future. It is almost a compliment, believe me, for what is man in the daily traffic of the world? . . . A chance combination of character and fate, no more. I know your character and have researched your history, so I know, with absolute certainty, that however pale you grow, however you gasp and stare, you will kill neither me nor yourself. Not because you are a coward!—not at all!—but because it is simply not in your character to do so, because, in your heart of hearts, you are already calculating how much you dare demand of me, because the bargain fundamentally appeals to you, and because there are certain things that you can do nothing about for, after all, how could you? . . . It's how you are. The fact that you are not averse to a bargain might be the one and only fully human feature of your character. Don't worry about how much you can demand of me, Giacomo: I will give you what you ask for. And more on top of that! I may be acting against my business principles in telling you this, but let that be, for I confess that whatever figure you dream up is of no interest to me. Let me offer you a thousand ducats in gold this very evening. Is that too little? Fine. Let us say two thousand, in cash, to see you through Munich and Paris. Not enough? That's all right, my boy, carry on by all means, I understand. Let us therefore say ten thousand ducats, together with a letter of credit for use in Paris. Still not enough? . . . I understand, I really do understand, my boy. Let me throw in a letter of safe passage for use on the road, so you may travel like the prince de Condé, and, in addition, a personal introduction to the elector, who will be happy to hear the story of your escape from your own lips. Is that still not enough? . . . Well, why not? I'm not a petty man. All right, I will trump it all with a letter of introduction to my cousin, Louis himself."

He extended the wasted, aristocratic hand that had until now been held to the fire and turned it over, palm upward, as if he were offering him the world.

"See this?" he asked, almost moved by his own generosity. "Nobody has received as much from me. It is true that the situation is unique in that I have never before played postman, lawyer, and go-between in persuading a man and woman to come together for a common purpose. . . . This evening is indeed unique, since for the first time in my life I shall be wearing in public the mask that befits every aging lover. The ass's head. So it's settled. You will receive that letter, too. Have you any idea of its value? And you will have money on top of that, money in gold and money in the form of credit to be redeemed at the most exquisite address, at any town from any conveyor of your choosing, to the full amount I have promised. I am paying a high price for you, Giacomo, as one must for a gift purchased at the close of one's life, for something one wants to offer a woman by way of farewell, the only woman one loves. That is why I want to strike a bargain with you. I am buying you in a proper, aboveboard fashion, and the letter I shall write to my cousin, Louis, which a trusted servant will give you at dawn, providing everything happens as we have agreed, will be the first and last begging letter I address to His Most Christian Majesty, who will not deny my request. Louis will receive you at Versailles: the letter guarantees that! It is no more than I owe—not to you, nor even to myself—but to the woman on whose behalf I have played postman, the woman I love. It is your price tag. And now that I have settled that price I don't think you can demand more of me. The other letter will open frontiers for you, and you will sleep as comfortably in the inns of foreign towns as your mother once did in the lap of the beautiful diva. The police will no longer bother you, and should clouds of strife or entanglement gather around you and enemies pursue you, it will be enough for you to show that letter and your pursuer will immediately be transformed into an admiring friend. I do this so you may safely find your way through this ugly world. It is the price of our contract. What do I demand in exchange? A great deal, naturally. I demand that you accommodate yourself to the wishes of the duchess of Parma. I demand you spend this night with the duchess of Parma."

He raised the silver-handled stick high in the air with an easy movement, and at the end of the sentence he knocked twice, lightly, on the marble floor with it, as if knocking might put the seal on his words.

"Your Excellency seriously wishes this?" his host asked.

"Do I wish it? . . . No," his guest answered with grave calm. "I command it, my boy."

"I have said," he continued more quietly, more confidentially, "that my contract is intended to appeal both to your feelings and your reason. Listen then. Lean closer. Are we alone? . . . I trust that we are. I have contracted you for one night, Giacomo. I made that decision without deluding myself, without ambition, fear, or confusion. I made the decision because my life is almost over, and that which remains of it I want to freight with the only possible cargo. That cargo is my wife, Francesca. I want to keep this woman for the time that remains, which is not long now, but is not entirely negligible, either: in fact it is precisely as long as fate has ordained for me. I want to keep her: I want not only her physical presence, but her feelings and desires, too, feelings and desires that are currently confused by the fierce intensity of the love she feels for you. I regard this love as a kind of rebellion. It may be a justified rebellion but it runs counter to my interests and I will put it down as I have put down all others. I am not a delicate, oversensitive person. I respect tradition and I respect order, which is far more substantial, far more logical, than the average ninny believes. I believe in order as a source of virtue, though not necessarily the kind of virtue mentioned in the catechism. When the bakers of Parma raised the price of bread I hanged them in their own shop doorways though the law gave me no such right, because I had power and reason enough, and because it kept the order in a manner of speaking, though not in the manner understood by nervous lawyers and august judges. I broke my top general on a wheel outside the gates of Verona because he was insolent and vile to a common soldier, and many found fault with me for this, but real soldiers and real officers understood, because real soldiers and real officers know that to command is to be responsible, and only those who are ruthless in their logic while remaining courteous and responsive are capable of keeping order. I have put down rebellions because I believe in order. There is no happiness, no true feeling, without order, and that is why, throughout my life, I have made use of the sword and the rope to eliminate every kind of sentimental rebellion, whose importunate aim it is to destroy the inner order of things, for without true order there can be no harmony, no growth, nor true revolution, either. This love between you and the duchess, Giacomo, is a form of rebellion, and because I can't break it on the wheel, hang it by the legs at the entrance of the city, or pursue it naked and barefoot at night through the snow, I am buying it instead. I have named the price. It is a good price. Few people have the means to pay such a high price for you. I am buying you as I would a well-known singer, conjuror, or strongman, the way we pay a visiting entertainer who is passing through the city, appears on stage for the lords of the place, and amuses them as best he can for one night. I want you to perform for me in the same way, Giacomo, to make a guest appearance in Bolzano for one night only. I am hiring you to show the customers what you know, and we shall see whether you are applauded or jeered off the stage at the end. Are you still quiet? Do you think it is not enough? Or maybe it's too much? Are you undergoing some significant inner struggle? Enjoy yourself, my boy! Have a good laugh! Let us both laugh, since we are alone, shut away from the world, face-to-face with the facts: let us laugh, for we are intimates after all, parties to a mutual agreement. Is your self-respect troubling you, Giacomo? Ah, Giacomo! I see now I shall have to improve my offer. There must be something else I can offer you, the gallant and gambler, who wants everything and nothing . . . are you shaking your head? Do you mean you have grown up and are no longer an adolescent? So now you know that 'everything' and 'nothing' don't exist in real life: that there are always only gray areas of 'something' between the extremes of 'nothing' and 'everything,' for 'nothing' and 'everything' usually turn out to be rather a lot? Why are you hesitating? Tell me your price, there's nobody else here. Name the sum. Money is of no value to me any-more, so go ahead, you can be as crude as you like, bellow the price that fits with your conscience or whisper it into my ear, tell me how much it will take to persuade you to spend the night with the duchess of Parma. How expensive or how cheap do you estimate your art to be? . . . Speak, my boy," he said and cleared his grating throat. "Speak, because my time is up."

His host stood before him with folded arms. They couldn't see each other's faces in the half light.

"Neither expensive nor cheap, Your Excellency," he

courteously replied. "This night has no price. There's only one way you can buy this night."

"Name the price."

"I will do it for nothing."

The guest stared into the fire again. He did not move, didn't even raise his head, but his bloodless, narrow lips hissed in irritation.

"That is more than I can pay. I fear you have misunderstood me, Giacomo. I cannot pay that much." Giacomo maintained an obstinate silence. "What I mean," continued the duke, "is that the contract is meaningless at that price. It is an impossible sum for me to pay for a service, an art that you foolishly overvalue. You are singing a high tenor, Giacomo, if I may say so. It is not an aria I wanted to hear but the voice of clear calm reason ready to make a good bargain. I thought I was talking to a man, not a singing clown."

"And I thought I was answering a man," replied the other, unruffled, "not Maecenas, the patron of the arts."

"Maecenas is good," replied the duke, shrugging. "A fine answer. Eloquent words. It is an eloquent answer with a precise and respectable literary allusion: but it has nothing to do with reality. It is true that you need eloquence to bargain—a few fine words and some beating of the breast may be necessary—it may in fact be the only way for us to bargain. But we have done with eloquence. Let us descend from the empyrean. I fear you have failed to understand me. You believe this bargain is immoral. By the cowardly standards and timid morals of the world, it may be so. But my time is short and I cannot afford to wait on the morals and judgments of the world. The woman I love loves you, but you cannot truly love a woman, because you are doomed never to be satisfied: you are the sort of man who may drink as much as he likes from a fine crystal goblet or a stone trough but can never quench his thirst and is therefore beyond redemption. Love is a form of addiction for you. It took me a long time to understand that, and I have been trying to understand it from the moment I saw you yawning in the theater at Bologna, to the moment here in Bolzano, when I gave you the duchess's letter. And now that I know your nature, and who you are, I cannot say to Francesca: 'Go! Go with the man you love!' . . . I might be able to say it, Giacomo, if you were not who you are, if I did not wish to protect Francesca from the sad fire that burns within you. And if I pity you for anything, it is for the incapacity, the deafness, that your character and fate have bestowed on you; I pity you because you don't know love, have never heard the voice of love, because you are deaf. Perhaps you, too, if only out of sheer boredom, occasionally give up a woman, or let one go her own way into the flames of her own choosing, because you like the gesture, are playing a game, or because you want to be gallant or generous. But what you cannot know is that love can make a man immoral; you cannot know that a man who loves can let a woman go for one night, indeed for eternity if it comes to that—not for selfish reasons, but because he feels obliged to serve her by sacrificing himself. Because to love is, and always has been, simply to serve. Now, for the first time in my life, I, too, wish to serve.

Even the mighty and the privileged must bow to fate. If you were not who I believe you are, I might even let Francesca with all her youth and her inexperience go with you. But I cannot allow it because all you can give her is a few days and nights while she is with you, a few moments of almost impersonal tenderness, a flame that burns but cannot warm. What can you give her? . . . Only the thrill of seduction. That is your own peculiar art form. It is a high art with a long tradition, and you are certainly a master in your field. But it is the nature of a thrill to be of short duration: that is the kind of art it is and those are its rules and proportions. Now go, and perform miracles, Giacomo!" he said, his voice a little hoarse now, and turned to him, his eyes wide open. They stared at each other a while. "Make this thrill exquisite for her. I insulted you before by offering you cash, freedom, and worldly pleasure in exchange for your art, and you got on your high horse and made a grand speech, with words like 'nothing' and 'Maecenas.' These are only words. The art of which you are a master, the art you understand as truly as a goldsmith understands rings and brooches, the field in which you are a true creative spirit, is that of seduction. So go and create your seductive masterpiece. I know who I am talking to, you see, and I trust you to do a good job. What are the requirements of a seduction? Everything you might need is at your disposal: night, secrecy, a mask, a vow, fine words, sighs, a billet-doux, a covert message, a tryst in the snowdrifts, a tender abduction, the great moment when your captive lies panting in your arms, when she gives herself and cries out, and then the slow

215

descent and conclusion, vows like 'you alone' and 'forever' though by that time you will be keeping half an eye on dawn as it begins to blush through the window, awaiting the moment you may leave in a manner appropriate to your vocation, having completed your work satisfactorily, in private, an artist contemplating his next appearance in some other place. You will not be bought, you said. A laudable sentiment. But I don't believe you because I know that there is nothing in this world that cannot be bought. Perhaps even the fire of love may be purchased. I am striving now to buy what may remain of Francesca's love, the tenderness that is left to comfort my remaining days, because I am weak and must die soon, and I want my last few months and days to be suffused with the wonderful light that radiates from this one body, this one soul. I realize it is a sign of weakness. I want her to get over you as she might get over an illness. It isn't some salacious fantasy that has driven me to this point, now when the musicians are already tuning up in my own palazzo and the ass's head is ready and waiting; no, these are not the pleadings of an ancient lover who can no longer yield his darling amusement and delight. No, Giacomo, you are an illness, the yellow fever, the plague, and the pox combined and we have to get over you. If there is nothing else we can do let us at least survive. That is why I come to you, asking you to spend the night with my wife—an odd enough request on first hearing, but when we take everything into consideration, if we examine our emotions in their true context and use our brains, a most natural one. I see the dangers of the pox, the plague, and the yellow fever and realize that it is vital that we pull through. That is why I need you to work a miracle! There is nothing else you can give her, the poor invalid, but the thrill of seduction—so let us concoct this adventure for her, in the best and most proper manner, with dignity and skill, with the mutual understanding of true accomplices, conjoined in the melancholy complicity that is the unavoidable lot of all men who are in attendance on the same woman. Consult your art and devise one brilliant act of seduction, for it is my wish that in the morning Francesca should return to the palazzo, like a patient recovered from an illness, her heart free, her head held high, not sneaking home down shady alleys, but as proud as I would have her be, for she too has a rank and I am unwilling to see her lose anything of her dignity. This is the way I have contrived in order to keep her with me for the short time that remains to me, now that I understand so much more than I did before, now that my life is almost over. That is why I am addressing my offer not to the man, the ordinary mortal in you, who takes it as an insult, but to the immortal artist and craftsman. All I want is for you to remain true to your art and to create a masterpiece. Ah, now you are looking at me! I think we are beginning to understand each other. . . . Look into my eyes. Good, my boy. We should face each other in the cold light of day, as accomplices. How wonderful it is to have awakened the interest of an artist. The Pope must have felt like this when he persuaded the mighty Michelangelo to raise and complete his dome. Very well, let us construct our dome, in our own fashion, and finish the business properly," he said and gave a sad, twisted smile. "You value your art highly and I am prepared to pay a high price for it, so there's no point in us bandying words, for by dawn tomorrow you will have need of ten thousand golden pieces and of my rare, invaluable letter. Let us not waste any more breath on the subject, nothing could be more natural. I merely mention the details in passing. What is more important is that I finally see the light of under-standing in your eyes. Only a few moments have passed but now I know I have touched the artist in you: I can see the idea interests and excites you. You have a preoccupied look and are probably turning the campaign over in your mind even now, anticipating the problems of execution, wondering how to build momentum at the beginning . . . am I right? I suspect I am. You see, I have calculated care-fully, Giacomo: I know that an artist cannot escape the siren call of his art. I am quite confident that you won't disappoint me and that you will do something wonderful, if only because there is no alternative: you stand or fall by your success. The kind of masterpiece I want you to pro-duce is what they call a miniature: a concentrated form of the art in which that which normally takes a month or a year happens in a few hours. I want the beginning and end to be miraculously apposite and to follow close on each other's heels, and who in all Europe is in a better position to accomplish that than you, you above all people, and precisely at this moment when you are fresh from the prison where time and enforced meditation will have matured your talent and skill? . . . I know your perfor-mance will be perfect, Giacomo! It has to be: that is why I am reasonably, justifiably, paying a high price for you, in words, in gold, in the letter and in blood-curdling threats, all of which you deserve, all of which are in keeping with your person, with my person, and with the person of the woman for whose sake all this is being arranged! I want you to compress and concentrate your art. I realize it is the most difficult thing to do, but I want you for a few hours to suspend the laws of time and to produce a conjuring trick, like the Eastern magi who, in a mere few seconds, can make a bud blossom into a flower that is perfect in scent, color, and form, but dies immediately. The death of the flower is a more melancholy event, but just as spell-binding and mysterious as its blossoming. The miracle of decay, completion, and destruction and the miracle of birth are equally remarkable. How wonderful, how terrify-ing the relationship between awakening, climax, and con-clusion. But I want this to be more than just a conjuring trick, all gold leaf and hollow words: you must give her everything, the true thrill of seduction, a whirlwind affair complete with night, fog, flight, true vows, and real pas-sion, otherwise it is all for nothing. And everything must happen quickly, very quickly, Giacomo, because time presses. I cannot wait long, I don't have weeks to spare for you, not a day or night more than this present one. That is why I have hired you, only you, the one giant among a crowd of fashionable fops who might perform the same service. Because I appreciate and almost—how that word keeps coming back to haunt me!—almost admire your artistry. I know the task requires an impossible blend of intelligence, craft, finesse, and ice-cold strategy on the one hand and fury, passion, tears, ecstasy, madness, the feverish beating of the heart, and even a degree of suicidal torpor on the other, and that what you will do in miniature and in accelerated form in one night would take the average bourgeois lover a long time, perhaps even an entire lifetime to achieve. That is what makes you as much an artist as the man who can engrave an entire battle scene on a tiny piece of stone or paint a crowded city full of people, dogs, and spires on a slip of ivory. Because an artist, and only an artist, can shatter the laws of space and time! And you must shatter them tonight! Tonight you will visit us because Francesca feels that she must see you! You will come in costume, wearing a mask like everyone else. Once you have recognized her, you must call her away, bring her here, and perform the miracle! I can see by the expression in your eyes that you are willing, and I, in my turn am willing to pay the price. What I want, Giacomo, what I demand, is that the duchess be back in the palazzo by dawn. In the meantime I promise you that not a word will ever again pass between us about the events of this night, however it turns out, whatever life brings us in the future. Tonight the duchess will see you, as in her sickness she desires to do, and she will know you, in the precise biblical sense of the word, for love, that contagious fever, is nothing if not a matter of getting to know. Your business as an artist, as a healer, is to ensure that by the time dawn comes round she is free of infection. I am not interested in the secrets of your craft. I want her to recover from you but in such a way that at dawn she returns to me, not surreptitiously but without her mask, as befits a woman of rank, a rank bestowed by me on her, the woman I love. In other words she will not be reliant on the silent, conspiratorial mercies of paid lackeys and procurers but will go about with her head held high. Life is an accident. I don't want the duchess of Parma to break her neck as a result of that accident. I still have need of her. Let her return to me, to her home, at dawn, not creeping but striding, with head held high in the full light of morning, even if all Bolzano happens to be looking on. Do you fully understand me now? I want her to come home completely cured. She is yours to know, Giacomo, but you must make her realize that there is no other life for her but the one I designed for her; let her know that you are an adventure, a fling; that there is no prospect of life with you, not for her; that you are night, the storm, the plague, something that rumbles over the landscape but disappears when the sun rises in the morning and people go about their domestic chores, smoking, plastering, and scouring. That is why I am ordering you to perform a miracle. Within a few hours I want you to reveal your true self to the duchess, and by morning I want that secret self to have become a painless unintrusive memory. Be good to her, but be ruthless and malicious too, as is your way: be tender with her and hurt her, as you always do, as you would if you had a longer time to do it; squeeze everything that can happen between two people into a single night; finish all that can be finished by two people and let it be over by daybreak. Then send her back to me, because I love her and because you have nothing more to do with her."

Having said that he stood up.

"Do we have an agreement, Giacomo?" he asked, leaning on his stick.

His host strode over to the door, his hands behind his back. He opened it, gazed meditatively at the threshold, and asked, "But what happens, Your Excellency, if the performance is unsuccessful? . . . I mean, if I am unable to condense and accelerate everything in such a fortunate manner as Your Excellency requires? What will happen if, come the morning after the night before, the duchess of Parma feels that the night is merely the beginning of something. . . ."

He was unable to finish the sentence. With surprisingly quick and youthful steps the guest hurried past him, hesitated on the threshold, looked him in the eye, and answered in his most cutting manner:

"That would be a big mistake, Giacomo."

They regarded each other for a few long minutes.

"Your Excellency's wish is my command," the other replied and shrugged his shoulder. "I shall serve Your Excellency to the best of my ability, as he wishes and as only I can." He made a deep bow.

The duke turned to him with a last parting shot.

"I told you to be tender with her and to hurt her. Please don't hurt her too much, if that is at all possible."

He went out without closing the door behind him, slowly, slightly bent. Tapping his stick on the stairs he brought his servants hastening to meet him with their torches. Then he began to descend.

In Costume

So what are you waiting for? Get dressed, you aging mountebank, you trembling old quack! Your room is full of shadows: the shadows of your youth. Youth is gone, isn't it? . . . but you can still hear its voices, like the tinkling of bells on your decrepit guest's sleigh. Off he goes, as if bowing and blowing kisses to an invisible audience, together with his servants, his magnificent horses, and his tinkling sled. He is passing under your window right now. They've swaddled him in pelts so you can't even see the tip of his nose, a gaunt and graceless figure in the depths of the carriage, wrapped in fur, protected by his rank, old and in pain, and despite what he says, however he preaches and pontificates, on the point of death. It is he who is wounded now, not as I once was, bleeding in the garden in Pistoia and at the gates of Florence: his wound is fatal. And what about you? Are you happy now, Giacomo? Are you dead? Have they already crossed your arms across your chest? If you had your way you yourself would be making bows and blowing kisses to your invisible audience, receiving their applause. Are you lost for words? Is there a sour taste in your mouth as though you had overeaten and drunk too much? Is it penance and herrings you need? It is a mad world! Now you must kill everything in you: strangle your memories, strangle every tender feeling with your bare hands as if it were an unwanted kitten, strangle everything that smacks of human contact and compassion! Is the time of your youth over? . . . No, not quite. Yes, you are missing two front teeth. You find the cold harder to bear and like to snuggle up to the fire, muttering, in fur gloves, watching what you eat and carefully rinsing your mouth before kissing anyone because neither your digestion nor your teeth are exactly perfect any more! But this does not constitute a terminal condition. Your stomach, your heart, and your kidneys are faithful servants; your hair is only just beginning to go, a little thin on your crown and your temples: you will have to be careful where your lover plants her hands when she takes hold of your hair! You are not old yet, but you have to be a little careful . . . particularly of the pox that seems to be ravaging the world, so people say. But all is not lost. That great energy, that spontaneous overflow, that all-or-nothing the old fool spoke about with such contempt, may serve you awhile yet! The virtues of caution, wisdom, forethought, and reason are nothing without the instinctive passions of youth to heat them. What kind of life is it without the desire to take everything the world has to offer and to blow all your resources at the same time, to grab and discard at once? . . . Enough of this. You are not at the carnival now. You have a different kind of appointment, a different deadline! A deadline that marks the end of youth. You are an adult now, in one of your mature moments of wisdom, the kind you get at four in the afternoon in mid-October. A fine time. Your sun is still shining. . . . Look around, take a deep sweet breath, feel the rays of the sun, slow down, pay more attention, there's nothing else you can do in any case. Your youth is leaving you . . . elsewhere people are laughing, glasses are clinking, a woman is singing, there's the scent of falling rain, you are standing in a garden, your face wet with tears and rain, the flowers are dead but your heart is wild and happy, you yearn for completeness and annihilation, all the trodden flowers lie around you . . . that's what it was like, something like that. Later perhaps, when you are an old man, you will remember it. Now get dressed, because time is passing, there are people already waiting in the ballroom and one inexpressibly tender and alert pair of eyes is looking for you because she must see you. . . . Where's the note? Yes, it's there where he left it. Let's have a look. Large writing, careful, careworn letters . . . she's not the first woman to have written to me, nor will she be the last, I suppose. And with what trembling fingers and glittering eyes that wounded old crow, her husband, explained the meaning of the letter! It really was most amusing! Sometimes it is worth being alive! I must see, yes. . . . Well, poor thing, what more could she have written when she has been literate for barely a year? He says that no one could mean more or write more beautifully, and perhaps he is right; it is an elegant note, and it might be that other women, like the marquesa, the cardinal's niece, and

M.M., who knew a great deal about both love and literature, wrote more wittily and at greater length, complete
with verses, classical references, high vulgarity, and passionate bombast, but, I must admit, they wrote nothing
more true. The jealous old fool is right to admire it. . . .
Well, my dove, you shall see me as you desire! You shall see
me, though I am not the youngest or handsomest of men,
nor, as His Excellency remarked, the greatest of villains,
either. . . . You, my dove, will see me, as you wanted and
as he, too, wanted, the ruffled old crow! What a speech he
made! What convoluted strategies he devised! All that
threatening and prodding! Could he have been the man
who betrayed me to the authorities some sixteen months
ago in Venice? . . . The council is glad to do little favors
for influential outsiders; the *messer grande* is a courteous
man and he would not deny a minor service to the cousin
of the French king. Well, my duke of Parma, you shall
have what you asked for! You made a fine job of dressing
your proposition as a gift, you spoke with feeling like a
philosopher, you wanted to be producer and patron, master and accomplice, in this curious business, and you shall
have what you want. . . . Might it have been really those
two old arthritic hands of yours that deposited me on my
straw bed in Venice? . . . he didn't say so, not in so many
words. Like a retired hangman he consulted his secret list
and simply hinted at the possibility before tucking the slip
of paper back in his waistcoat pocket and going off with it!
Chew on that! he thought. Beware, in case I do it again!
He has a point there: it was no fun in the cells. He was
right, too, in speaking of other laws and other forms of

order, though I could tell him a story or two myself, albeit brief ones, with neat punchlines. Father Bragadin is no angel, of course, when it comes to the public good or when one can gain one man's favor by selling another man's life. It is simply the way of the world. We are slow to learn its lessons but maybe it's better that way. We prepare ourselves to face the world, we find out how it works, and soon enough we discover that there is business more dirty and dangerous than a game of cards, that affairs conducted under a veil of respectability are just as dirty. Take care, Giacomo! Take care tonight! And take care tomorrow morning, too, at cockcrow, when you take your leave in the snow. This is too carefully planned to be harmless: beware the aging grandee, the ancient, august lover who prefers not to strangle his rival, but to use those hands of his rival to strangle love itself and the memory of love . . . take care! Lights are still burning in the stable, you still have a few gold coins left over from yesterday jangling in your pocket; how would it be if you quickly packed, grabbed that hot sixteen-year-old spring chicken, Teresa, whose kisses have ensured a good night's sleep these last eight days, and, true to the laws of your own being, following your impeccable logic, forgot the ball, the agreement, and the grand performance, and made off with her tonight? . . . It might be better than waiting for dawn. Perhaps you should let them get on with it, let the duke of Parma wear his ass's head and ever after fret over his precious Francesca, her memories of her literary lover, and about what he might yet get up to with her? . . . Concentrate, Giacomo, little brother! Are you in two minds? Are you thinking of staying now? Do you think your agreement obliges you to carry out your role? Can you not escape a performance that is bound to be false and sad as well as dangerous and unnatural, a performance that may end in real tears and real blood trickling across the boards of the stage, with a real corpse for the stagehands to remove? . . . But you can already feel the excitement, the involuntary shudder: everything else is beginning to lose focus, desire is stoking the fire in you. Is that desire no longer subject to reason? Do you feel you have no choice but to play the part? Could it be that the jealous old coxcomb calculated right when he appealed to the artist in you, when he drew attention to your art, so you were certain to accept even if it meant that not just the memory of the artist but the artist himself came to a sticky end, stitched up by His Excellency of Parma? But no, you must not rebel, you must not protest: accept the fact that you must stay and finish your business. You can't escape the responsibilities of your art: your entire life has been fraught with danger, so why stop now? You need the danger, you need to feel that at any moment the curtains of your bed might open and someone stick a knife between your ribs: you need to be aware of the possibility of annihilation; you need the impossible thing that the respectable citizen so desperately and helplessly craves and dreams about as he snores in his nightcap at his wife's side, while you are creeping through somebody's cellar or scrambling about on a rooftop, fighting hired assassins, living the reality that they, the virtuous, the shuffling, dare only dream about. You represent change and transformation: you are the flesh-and-blood version of what they call adventure or art. What else can you do? You will assume the part allotted to you, you will use your talent. So it is settled and you are staying! To work then! Clap three times and get them to bring water in the silver jug, let Balbi shift his horny feet and find you an appropriate outfit in town, let Giuseppe be called for to steam and pamper your face, and have a word with little Teresa, tell her to wrap her things in a bundle and to meet you at the edge of town at dawn. I will take her to Munich and sell her as wife to the elector's chief secretary. I will do things properly. Cheer up, there's nothing else you can do. The duke of Parma has thought of everything. He understands me completely and has calculated correctly; he knew I would stay and make my one-night-only guest appearance, however demanding it may be, even if it cost me my neck in the end, even if the lovely ladies of Bolzano finish up singing mournful three-part harmonies over my corpse. Yes, you greedy, clever, puzzled old man, you have calculated correctly. You firmly believe that wealth, power, cunning, and a little circumspection are enough to see the thing through. But let me send you a message, now, before I put on my costume, start painting my face, and summon every time-honored feature of my art for the performance: beware! For you, too, should take care! What do you think I am? Do you really think I am some kind of conjuror who can produce a masterpiece at a moment's notice: what an idea! You should be careful, for I am only human, and so is she. You demand, in your desperation, that we should collaborate on a single work of instantaneous genius. How could I be sure of doing that? I have never known what the morning light would bring. Not that I regret it. Half my life is over and I have never regretted anything, nor was ever bored for an instant: I have been stabbed, I have been offered drinks laced with poison, I have slept under the stars without a penny in my pocket, I have no one I could call a friend: all I have is my notoriety, but I have not regretted any of it. The best part of life is gone: I have neither house nor apartment, not a stick of furniture to my name, not a watch, not even a ring that I could truly call mine. I order new clothes in every town I visit and feel no obligation to stay in any of them, yet you, the duke of Parma, are jealous of me. You who are tied to everything and are nothing but the things you are tied to—palaces, birth, name, title, lands, possessions, sentiments, and jealousies—you, who now, when life is "almost" over, as you never tire of saying—indeed you keep repeating the word in the vain hope that by flirting with it, by saying it often enough, you might actually delay your fate and avoid your final appointment with reality—find yourself in a tangle of contradictions between what you want and what there is; are you not secretly, somewhere deep in your soul, jealous of my ability to wrap myself in clouds and travel on moonbeams, to ride the wind across borders where nobody waits or takes leave of me; of me, the man without a room, without furniture, without a single possession anywhere in the world that he can truly call his own? . . . Enough, my boy, wake up, prepare yourself. Give a nice loud whoop, the way you used to. There's an icy wind hooting and tugging at the skirts of the ladies of Bolzano:

you, too, should be like the wind, hooting with laughter! Life isn't over yet, there's no question of "almost" for you. You need not rely on conjuring tricks because you are the real thing! So beware, Duke, I am no longer afraid of the morning. Let the storm whose gusts are already blowing about my heart and through my mind carry me forward, let there be tears and vows, kisses and death, let everything be condensed or slowed down, as life will have it, let it all happen despite the morning. I shall serve you well tonight, dear Duke! You have purchased me in all my miraculous, wonder-working reality. I shall be like those ancient wrestlers who knew they would have to pay for their performance with their lives: I will not be churning out a dutifully composed text to whisper in her ear, no, I shall do better and improvise a true text! Are you not afraid, you old schemer, that the performance might turn out to be all too successful? . . . Her letter is rather imperious and the spell she casts may be more effective than the ingenious strategy you have devised for your remaining days. Do you think you will save the tenderness and affection you imagined she might offer you when you married her? Are you not afraid that human passions might not be subject to nice calculation, that the greatest of artists might make a mistake, that the game might turn into a reality, a kiss become a true bond, that a trickle of blood might spread and become a tide in which life itself ran away from you? . . . Yes, we have an agreement. So both of us should now see that it is carried out: you with your ass's head, in your palazzo, with your painstaking schemes and your squint, and I in costume, the perfect costume in which no one will recognize me except the woman for whom I wear it! Are Balbi and Teresa ready for departure? . . . Balbi! . . . Hey, Balbi! . . .

Now listen carefully! What time is it? . . . Near midnight? A good time, the time when day completes its magic round and witches reach for their broomsticks. Are you drunk? Your breath stinks of garlic, your lips are shiny with grease, you look positively cross-eyed. It must be that Verona wine. Stop staggering about for an instant and listen to me! We have a great opportunity, Balbi! There has been a wonderful turn of events! You may well rub your hands because your prayers are answered: our time in Bolzano is over and we shall set out at dawn. Tell the innkeeper to prepare the bill and hitch up some horses! You will pack and bid farewell to the kitchen maids and to all the people you gulled, you old skirt-lifter, you horse thief. . . . No, on the other hand, wait, it may be better not to say anything to them just yet. You can write your fond and amorous farewells from Munich in the morning. I want you to pack, if there is anything to pack, then to go to your room and wait for daybreak. Make sure it is the best horses they are hitching up, and have a word with the coach keeper too: it's a closed carriage I want, with fur blankets and hot water bottles! Make sure everyone is ready and everything in its place! Tell them that it's either a shower of gold or a sound beating for them in the morning, it depends on them which! No questions! Clap both hands over your mouth and listen very carefully. When I call you I want you to grab your things and to dash to the carriage. You will seat yourself next to the driver! I am not asking you to do this, Balbi, but ordering you! Take utmost care until we are beyond the reach of Venice for the palm of the *messer grande* is as itchy as your neck. I want no complaints from you! Have I had bad news? . . . You will find out about a hundred miles from here, if I judge the time to be right. Now go into town and find me a costume! What kind? One for a ball, numbskull, a marvelous, perfectly unique costume, the kind that will turn everyone's head when I step into the ballroom, but under which no one will recognize me. . . . What's that? All the costumes in Bolzano have been sold for tonight? Idiot! The kind of mask and costume I am looking for is not the traditional carnival outfit, not Pierrot or Harlequin, not Prince of Persia with Vizier, not Head Cook and Scullery Boy, not Oriental Knight, not Pasha in Turban with Scimitar, not Court Fool in pretend rags, with cap-and-bells and mock scepter. That stuff is old hat: it is boring and conventional. No, Balbi, let's find something new and original for tonight. What if I dressed simply as a knight appropriate to my name and rank, a chevalier of France fresh from the court of King Louis . . . ? No, perhaps not. Hush, don't disturb me when I'm thinking. Wait! What if I went as an author, a scholar, a philosopher, with black-rimmed pince-nez perched on my nose, a mortarboard on my head, wearing a white collar and a black cloak? Not such a bad idea, an author . . . it takes one author to know another. What do you think? Are there other writers in Bolzano? Think about it carefully, Balbi. The brotherhood of authors is a secret society, with invisible insignia: you, being uncultured, think that Monsieur Vendôme or

233

Madame Montespan might have precedence over authors in an audience with the king, but it's not like that. Messieurs La Fontaine and Corneille and even Bossuet are at the front of the line, though Corneille is a little unkempt . . . you, of course, understand nothing of this, how could you? No, the author costume is wrong. We must find something else. What if I went as a hunter, with horn, dagger and bow, Nimrod at the Chase, Nimrod and Diana in the Primeval Forest? No, the symbolism is too transparent. Have you no ideas of your own? Don't the kitchen maids like you to entertain them with your wit and garlic breath? . . . That's it, Balbi! I have it! Kitchen maids! It's perfect! Quick, call for little Teresa! And let them bring a skirt, a blouse, white stockings, a beauty spot, some Viennese cloth for a shawl, a bonnet, and a white silk mask . . . what are you staring at? . . . yes, tonight I shall dress as a woman! Take that stupid grin off your face! It's the perfect disguise. I shall want a fan and something to stuff my bodice with, Neapolitan fashion: feathers from a pillow will do. Now hurry! Wake the servants! And let's get this room tidy, open some windows, build up the fire, let's have some sweet dessert wine on the table, a little cold chicken, some dressed salad, and ham and cheese, too, with white bread, silverware, and porcelain, the best of everything. Innkeeper! . . . Where are you hiding, you old pimp, you murderer of tourists and traveling salesmen? . . . Come here and do as I say! I want that fire blazing in the grate, fresh sheets on the bed, the best and finest pillowslips, a counterpane with your best lace cover, some ambergris sprinkled on the embers, two armchairs placed by the fire, a small ebony table with flowers over there, I don't care what it costs, do you hear, red roses, yes, now, in November, in the snow! Where from? That's up to you. From the duke's greenhouse, for all I care, but now, tonight! The chicken should be accompanied by pickled eggs. I want the ham and cheese on a glass tray in one piece. . . . Wait! The bread should be toasted in thin slices, and the butter should be served on freshly fallen snow! Now let's get busy. The coachman should begin to warm the coach with hot water bottles, let the horses be given some fodder, have him polish the brasses until they glitter, and let everyone stand by at dawn, in a heated kitchen, with some hot and cold food for the journey and a cask of wine, the best of everything! During the night, though, the place should be as silent as the grave, the grave where you yourselves will be resting, I assure you, if you do not carry out my orders immediately and to the letter! No, my friend, you don't yet know me: I am terrifying when in a temper! Please be aware that my connections and influence exceed the merely mortal . . . there's no need for me to spell them out to you, since you yourself have seen the kind of people who have been waiting outside my door tonight and every night! You, you murderer of traveling salesmen, you shall have a hundred gold pieces if all is done as I demand: inform your staff that however overcast the sky of Bolzano may be at daybreak it will shower them with gold, providing everyone remains at his or her station through the night, on constant call! And let all this happen without any noise whatsoever, you understand, silently and invisibly! Are you still here? . . . Close the window now, that's enough fresh air. Sprinkle some attar of roses on the bed and draw the curtains round it. Have the flowers arrived? . . . Where did you get them? You found them in the reception room of the lady from Bergamo? . . . Tomorrow we shall send her better ones, a finer-scented selection, a whole basketful of them, a hundred, no, ninety-nine as a mark of delicacy, don't forget! Yes, you may spread the table and bring the food! The wine. . . . Show me, let's have a sniff! I am not going to taste it but you will answer with your head if I can smell the slightest trace of cask on it! I won't taste it now because I have just rinsed my mouth. . . . Giuseppe, good, I am glad you have arrived, throw the towel over my shoulders: I want some blush on my cheeks, yes, both cheeks, a little something for the lips, a beauty patch just under my right cheekbone, some rice powder on my wig, and now we shall tie it up in the little bonnet we have borrowed from Teresa. Is it past midnight? . . . Now you can go. Be off with you all. I don't want to see any of you till dawn. Not you, Teresa, my little one, you stay with me. Tie the skirt around my waist, adjust the garter on my knees, lend me the silk shawl I bought you yesterday, and arrange it across my shoulders. . . . That's right, thank you. Am I sitting properly with my legs crossed, the way a woman sits, fan in hand, when she is being attended by a gentleman? . . . I find I am not at all sure of the way women move. Is this how you hold a fan? . . . Thank you, my dear. Do you find me pretty like this? . . . My nose is too big? The mask will cover it, Teresa. Now come here, little one, sit on my knees, and don't worry if you crease the folds of your skirt.

I'll buy you a finer one in Munich, a velvet and silk outfit, as many outfits, of whatever kind you want . . . are you surprised? But that was the idea, right from the start. You don't want to fade and droop here, my little snowdrop, in the bar, in the arms of drunken travelers. Tomorrow, at dawn, I shall take you with me. We shall take Balbi, too, but we will take care to lose him on the way. It is no more than he deserves. Yes, we are going to Munich at dawn, as soon as day breaks. Why are you crying? Give me a kiss, as you have so often done before, with closed eyes, open mouth, nice and easy. Why are you trembling like that? Hush, child, prepare for the journey, for your new life which will be wonderful: there'll be gold, a fine apartment, you shall have your own pony and trap in Munich, and a servant to pull off your shoes and stockings and help you into your silk nightdress. Don't you want that? . . . Are you sure? Are you shaking your head? Have you nothing to say? You want to stay here? You want me to leave you here? . . . Still quiet? I am leaving in the morning, child. Tonight I shall celebrate, in a costume, as is right and proper, but once light breaks we will take to the road, and you will be my companion and chambermaid, but later you will be a lady, too, at least for a while. . . . Are you smiling yet? Go to your room, pray, sleep, and prepare for the journey. Wait for me at dawn at the edge of town, where the road branches north and west, by the stone cross. You can trust me . . . you know very well you can trust me. But there is something in your smile that I have seen only once before, in Verona, I think, something unself-conscious and decadent, something gentle yet dangerous at the same time. . . . I will explain that later. Scrub your hands. Wash your hair tonight, apply camomile tea to your hair and your face, then spread this cream over it . . . wait, you shall have a rose as a memento of this night. Now go and think over what I have said. . . . Go, because I myself have to go. Sweet dreams, my child. Tomorrow you will wake to a new life by the stone cross, in the carriage, in my arms, under the protection of my cloak. . . . *Addio, cara fanciulla! Addio, mia diletta! Arrivederci domani! Iniziamo una vita nuova! . . . Una vita felice! . . .* Phew! Is everyone gone? . . . Let's get going. Just the mask, quickly. It's a nice mask, familiar, Venetian style, white silk: let it cover my face as it has so often done at difficult and dangerous moments in my life. One more glance in the mirror . . . the beauty patch has slipped a little, a touch more red needed for the lips, smooth the eyebrows, and just a pinch of candle soot, the merest dab under the eyes. . . . Yes, perfect! The greatcoat will cover me as I make my way across the street. How the snow is falling! Mind your voice, Giacomo, speak with your fan and your eyes only if at all possible! Everything is in place, yes, the cold chicken, the butter on fresh snow, the wine in the engraved decanter, the roses in the marble basket, there's attar of roses on the pillow, the curtains of the bed are closed. . . . I think that should be all, yes. Perhaps one more log on the fire . . . something is missing? I can't think what it is. What was it, something important I mustn't forget . . . something more important than roses, wine, ambergris, or the roast ham. . . . Oh, I know. The dagger! Into my bosom with you, faithful companion.

Into my bosom, under the bodice, down among the feathers: an excellent costume. Only a woman could hide a dagger in such a place, and it certainly gives you confidence knowing there is a dagger just above your heart. It's much the best way of setting forth on an engagement! . . . I don't think I have forgotten anything. So get going. Wait . . . what is it now? Why aren't you on your way? You are alone. Check the mirror. The costume is excellent, everybody and everything is in place, a few more moments and the performance can begin according to the agreement, according to the rules you discussed with the duke of Parma. Why are you hanging back? Why is your heart beating so loudly? What is this feeling that has taken possession of you, grips your heart, and makes you indecisive, so you hesitate here with a dagger in your bosom, a mask on your face, and a fan in your hand. . . . What is happening to you, Giacomo? Acrobats suffer the same sense of dizziness when they look down on the crowd from the top of a human pyramid, seeking a familiar pair of eyes in the audience. . . . What unsettles you, what is it you are trying to remember? Hush, restless heart, stop this drumming. It is love you are afraid of, yes it is . . . you fear the emotion that binds, as the duke of Parma realized in his agony, in his increasing need, he who knows you all too well: it is this feeling that you fear, that casts its shadow across your path, it is the feeling you have fled ever since childhood. Don't be afraid, poor fool. You can overcome it. Don't be afraid. There is no feeling that can take complete control of you: you may suffer a few days of grief, but after a week or so of discomfort, you will find your way to the card table, or set to entertaining people the way they have always liked being entertained, playing your part in the human comedy, laughing or being laughed at, swindling or being swindled . . . and so the memory will fade. It won't kill you, no fear of that. Come the morning, you will abscond with the kitchen maid as you have done before, and will again, no doubt, in the future. There is nothing you can do about it. Let us do it without sentimentality or fear. The teardrop you are shedding will smudge the makeup on your face and your beauty patch will come unstuck . . . but I am not afraid of a teardrop or two. *I must see you.* . . . It is a beautiful letter. I don't think I have ever received lovelier. Yes, this woman and I are fated to be linked in some fashion, in a different sort of way, by a different power, a different desire. She herself cannot prevent that. So set about your task, comedian. Stand up straight, throw the cloak across your shoulder, put on your mask. . . . How silent it is. There's only the moaning of the wind. Off to the ball with you, attend to your worldly business, follow your fate, be firm, be levelheaded. Who is there? . . .

The Guest Performance

The door opened, the candles flickered in the draft. A masked young man in a party cloak stood on the threshold. He was wearing short silk pantaloons, buckled shoes, a three-cornered hat, and carrying a slender gold-handled sword at his side. He bowed and spoke in a clear, sharp, almost childlike voice as if he had brought the coolness and good temper of the snow in with him.

"It's I, Giacomo."

He closed the door carefully and stepped forward fastidiously, a little awkwardly, as if not quite accustomed to wearing boy's clothes. He bowed in masculine fashion and baldly declared, "I waited for you in vain. So I have come to you."

"Why have you come?" the man asked, a little hoarse behind the mask, taking a step and getting tangled in his skirt.

"Why? But I explained in my letter. Because I must see you."

She said this pleasantly, without any particular stress,

as if it were the only reasonable explanation, the most natural answer a woman could give a man. The man did not respond.

"Did you not get my letter?" she asked anxiously.

"I certainly did," the man answered. "Your husband, the duke of Parma, brought it to me this evening."

"Oh!" said the woman and fell silent.

The "oh" was a quiet and simple acknowledgment, like a bird call. She leaned her slender boyish figure against the mantelpiece and fiddled with her sword. The mask she was wearing stared at the floor, solemn and empty. Then, even more quietly, she continued.

"I knew it. I was waiting for the answer and knew somehow that there had been some problem with the letter. You know it is very unusual for me to write letters. To tell you the truth it was the first letter I had written in my life."

She turned her head aside gracefully, a little embarrassed, as if she had confessed her most intimate secret. Then she started laughing behind the mask, but it was a nervous laugh.

"Oh!" she said again. "I really am sorry the letter fell into his hands. I should have expected it. Do you think the groom who volunteered to bring my letter to you is still alive? . . . I should be sorry if anything happened to him, as he is still young and has a very sad and languishing way of looking at me when we are riding, and besides, he has a large family to support all by himself. Was it the duke himself delivered the letter? . . . Poor man. It can't have been easy for him. He is so proud and so lonely, I can imagine what he felt when he set out to bring you the letter in which I said I must see you. Did he threaten you? Offer you money? . . . Tell me what happened, my love."

She pronounced the last word loudly, confidently, enunciating clearly, as if she had articulated an important formal concept or subject with it. The mask was staring fixedly at the fire now, pale as death.

"He both threatened me and offered me money. Though that wasn't the main reason he came," the man replied. "He came primarily to give me the letter whose contents he analyzed in great detail. Then we came to an agreement."

"Of course," she said, with a brief sigh. "What agreement did you come to, my love?"

"He instructed me to dedicate my art to you alone, tonight. He asked me to make this night a masterpiece of seduction. He offered me money, freedom, and a letter of introduction that would protect me on the road and see me over frontiers. He told me you were ill, Francesca, diseased with love, and asked me to cure you. He told me that he was making us a present of this night, which should be as brief and as long as life, long enough for me to perform the impossible, so that we may experience in a single night all the ecstasies and disappointments of love, and that in the morning I should leave you to travel the world, go as far away as it is possible to go, wherever fate takes me, and that you should return to the palazzo with your head held high, where you may brighten and warm the remaining days of the duke of Parma. That is what he said. And he explained the meaning of your letter. I do believe he understood it, Francesca, every word of it. He did not raise his voice, but spoke calmly and quietly. And he also requested that I should be tender with you but hurt you enough to guarantee that everything should be over between us by morning, so that we could put a full stop to our sentence. . . . Those were his instructions."

"He told you to hurt me? . . ."

"Yes. But he asked me, in parting, not to hurt you too much."

"Yes," said Francesca. "He loves me."

"I think so, too," the man replied. "He loves you, but it's easy for him, Francesca. Love, as he loves, is easy, especially now that his time is running out . . . or rather, has 'almost' run out, and he kept repeating the word 'almost,' which seemed to be very important to him for some reason, if I understand him properly. It is easy to love when life is almost over."

"My dear," said the woman very gently and compassionately, like an adult addressing a child, and at the moment her unseen lips pronounced the words it was almost as if the mask itself were smiling. "It is never easy to love."

"No," the man obstinately insisted. "But it's easier for him."

"And so," the other mask inquired, "did you come to an agreement?"

"Yes."

"What were the terms of the agreement, Giacomo? . . ."

"I agreed to the terms he demanded and which you

yourself declared in your letter. That we would meet tonight. That we would embrace each other, because there is a secret bond between us, Francesca, because love has touched us both. It is a great gift and a great sadness. It is a great gift because I do in fact love you, in my fashion, and because I regard love as an art; but it is also a great sadness because my love will never be easy or happy, can never grow wings and soar like a dove . . . because ours is a different kind of love from his. So we agreed that we would 'know' each other, in the biblical sense, and that you would then finish with me, cured and disillusioned, and after the morning we would never see each other again. That I would not be the shadow across your bed and would not haunt you when the duke of Parma leaned over you as you lay on your pillows; that I would be a memory for a while, but later not even that: that for you, I would be nothing and no one. That is what I agreed. It is what I must do tonight, in words, with kisses, with tears, and with vows, using all the tricks of my trade, according to the rules of my art."

He stopped and tactfully, curiously, waited for an answer.

"Then go ahead, Giacomo," said the woman quietly and calmly. And she tipped her head on one side so the mask stared indifferently into the air. "Go ahead," she repeated. "What are you waiting for, my friend? Now is the moment. Begin. See, I have come to you, so you needn't go out into the storm, for as you may have noticed a storm sprung up at midnight, an icy northern blast screaming and sweeping towers of snow along the street.

But it is quiet here, warm, and scented. I see they have pre-pared the bed. Attar of roses and ambergris. And the table is set for two, carefully, in the best of taste, as custom dic-tates. But it is past midnight, and it is time for supper. So let us begin, Giacomo."

She sat down at the neatly spread table, pulled off her gloves, breathed on her fingertips, and rubbed her bare hands together, her posture suggesting anticipation, good manners, and propriety as she looked over the foodstuffs, very much as if she were expecting the waiter to arrive so that she might start to eat.

"How will you begin?" she asked, he having made no move, then continued, now intimate and curious. "How does one seduce and then disabuse someone who has come of her own free will because she is in love? . . . I am very curious, Giacomo! What will you do? . . . Will you use force, guile, or courtesy? It is, after all, a masterpiece you have undertaken, and that is bound to be difficult. Because, you see, we are not entirely alone, for we are here with his conscious blessing, so it is a little as if there were and will continue to be three of us in the room. Naturally, he knows that you will immediately tell me everything, or almost everything: he doesn't think you capable of crude workmanship, of lying to me, and hiding the secret of his visit, of not revealing the terms of your agreement. He couldn't have imagined, not for a moment, that events would proceed otherwise than they have already done; he knew very well that you would begin with a confession, and how we should go on from there, the two, or is it three, of us? But I myself don't yet know. After everything you have told me I am merely curious. So do begin."

Both masks remained quiet awhile. Then the male mask began talking, at first in a little boy's voice, then, slowly, as it warmed to its subject, modulating into something more feminine, as if every trace of roughness and strangeness had fallen away.

"Then perhaps I could begin . . . since I, too, am here, if not entirely according to his will nor entirely according to yours, either: I am here of my own free will, albeit masked and in male costume, in other words dressed for fun and games . . . and for all we know, the disguises help us. Do begin and perform a miracle. It should be fascinating. So this is what you said to each other, you two, the man I love and the man who loves me? . . . And by that token I must be merely obeying his instructions by being here. So, however this night turns out, it will all be according to his instructions, just as it is according to his instructions that we two, you and I, should 'know' and hurt each other? How marvelous," the voice continued indifferently. "And this is all that he could think of: this is all that you have agreed to? Could you not have devised something more ambitious, more ingenious? Two such intelligent and remarkable men as you? . . . He brought you my letter, he explained and interpreted it? But Giacomo, my love, his interpretation may not be complete. Because when I committed those words to paper, the first sensible, properly related words I have ever written in my life, and I did so all by myself, I was suddenly frightened by how much words can say when one chooses them responsibly and carefully joins the letters up. . . . Only four words, you see, and he is on his way from the palazzo, acting as postman, ascending these steep stairs, and there you stand, dressed in female costume. . . . Four words, a few drops of ink on paper, and how much has already happened as a result! All those events set in motion on account of a few words I had written! Yes I, too, wondered and shuddered. And yet I think he may not have understood the letter as completely as he thinks. He interpreted it, you say? . . . No, let me do that, Giacomo! Let me do it, even if I do it with less literary skill than you two have done. Do you think I am the kind of woman who on a whim, a desire, leaves her home at midnight to seek out a man who is only just out of jail, whose reputation is so bad that mothers and older women cross themselves at mention of his name? . . . Do you know me so little? And the duke of Parma, with whom I share a bed, is his knowledge of me so shallow? . . . Did you imagine I learned to write because I was bored and wanted to amuse myself by sending a naughty letter inviting myself to a midnight rendezvous with you? . . . Did you bind yourself to a contract that would see me come to you for a night of romance as you had planned, you two wise men, for a fling, for a single night, between two turns on the dance floor? Did you imagine that I would hurry over from my home, masked, enter a strange man's room, and then, before the dancing is quite over in the ballroom, hasten back to the palazzo to join the other couples? . . . Do you imagine that in writing to you I am seeking some childish night to remember; and that when I come to you, when I think of you, when I warm your memory with my breath, when I count the days you spend in jail, I mean to steal over to you for a night, for a secret rendezvous, just because you happen to be here, passing through the town where I live with my husband, or because once in my girlhood I knew you and there was some romantic feeling between us? . . . Is this the much-vaunted wisdom of the mighty duke of Parma and the omniscient Giacomo, who knows women's hearts? . . . Do you imagine that I am like a simple child, chasing shadows of the past, when I finally write the words that inform you, and yes, the duke and the whole world, that I must see you? It may be that I am not quite so simple and childlike, Giacomo, my love. Perhaps it was I that directed the groom's footsteps so that he should walk into the trap set for him by the duke? . . . Perhaps I, too, have struck a bargain tonight, with myself and my own fate if no one else, and this bargain may be as binding as the coffin, even if it bears no seal and contains no vows? Perhaps I know better than the duke of Parma why I should have climbed these stairs. What do you think, my love? Why did I write the letter? Why did I send the groom on a secret mission? Why did I wait for you? Why did I dress in a man's clothes? Why did I sneak from my palazzo? Why am I standing in this room? Having made the agreement, you should answer."

The other mask responded obediently, his voice flat.

"Why, Francesca?"

"Because I am not an object of seduction, my love, not material for a masterpiece, not the subject of a sage agreement. I am not the sweetheart who hastens to her lover's side at midnight. I am not some silly goose waiting vainly for a man, chasing shadows and illusions of happiness. I am not the young woman with the elderly husband, dreaming of hotter lips and more powerful arms, setting out in the snow in search of opportunity and recompense. I am not a bored lady of leisure who cannot resist your reputation and throws herself at you, nor the sentimental provincial bride who is unable to pass over the appearance of her dazzling childhood suitor. I am neither whore nor goose, Giacomo."

"What are you, Francesca?" asked the man.

The voice sounded strange through the mask, as if it were addressing the other at a great distance. The woman replied in the silence across an enormous distance.

"I am life, my love."

The man stepped toward the fire, careful that his skirts should not catch fire, and threw two fresh logs onto the flames. He turned round with the remaining logs still in his arms, as he was bending over.

"And what is life, Francesca?"

"It is certainly not running away in the snow," the woman answered without raising her voice. "Nor is it all fever and fret nor big words nor even the situation in which we find ourselves now, you dressed as a woman, I as a man, both masked, in the room of an inn, like a pair of characters in an opera. None of this is life. I will tell you what life is. I have given it a great deal of thought. Because it was not only you who was locked in a prison where powerful, jealous hands deposited you, Giacomo; I have been in prison as long as you have, even if my bed was not made of straw. Life, my dear, is a whole. Life is when a man and woman meet because they suit each other, because what they have in common is what the rain has in common with the sea, the one always rising from and falling back into the other, each creating each, one as a condition of the other. Out of this wholeness something emerges, some harmony, and that harmony is life. It is very rare among people. You flee from people because you believe you have other business in the world. I seek wholeness because I know I have no other business in the world. That's why I came. As I said, it took some time for me to be certain of that. Now I know. I also know that there is nothing perfect you can do in this world without me, that you cannot even practice your art, as you call it, for, without me, true and perfect seduction lies beyond you: the experience, the excitement, the thrill of the chase requires me; even the charm you exert over other women is imperfect without me. Why are you standing so stiffly there, Giacomo, with the poker and bellows in your hand, as if someone had hit you and you had tried to stand up too quickly? . . . Have you realized something? I am life, my love, the only woman offering you a whole life: you are incomplete without me, incomplete as a man, incomplete as an artist, as a gambler, and as a traveler, just as, without you, I am an incomplete woman, no more than a shadow among shadows. Do you understand now? . . . Because I do. If I were complete I would not have left the duke of Parma, who loves me and offers me everything the world has to offer: power, pomp, ambition, and meaning, and I am not betraying a confidence or stating something improper, believe me, when I say that it was he who introduced me to the sad, solemn faces of love and desire, because love has a thousand faces and the duke of Parma wears one of them. He is in his palazzo at this very moment, wearing an ass's head because our love has hurt him and he is mortally sick with sadness. But he knows he has no choice, which is why he tolerates me being here with you at such an hour and why he wears the ass's head so proudly. But the knowledge doesn't help him nor does the fancy dress nor the agreement: nothing helps him. He has lived by violence and he will die in vanity. There is nothing I can do for him. But for you, I would never have left him, because I, too, had an agreement with him, and I was brought up to honor my agreements. I am a Tuscan, Giacomo," said the mask, and the figure wearing it straightened a little.

"I know, my dear," said the man, the poker in his hand, and it was as if his voice were smiling. "You are the second person to say that to me in this room today."

"Really?" asked Francesca, drawing out the vowel in an almost musical manner, like an amazed, well-behaved schoolgirl. "Well yes, you have had a lot of visitors recently. But that's how it was and always will be with you, you will always be surrounded by people, both men and women. I shall get used to it, my dear. . . . It won't be easy but I shall get used to it."

"When, Francesca?" the man asked. "When do you want to get used to it? Tonight? . . . I won't be receiving any more visitors tonight."

"Tonight?" the woman asked in the same calm, child-like voice as before. "No, later, during the rest of my life."

"In the life that we shall spend together?"

"Perhaps, my love. Is that not the way you pictured it?"

"I don't know, Francesca," said the man and sat down opposite her, leaning back in the armchair, crossing his legs under his skirt, and crossing his arms under his false bosom. "That goes against the agreement."

"That agreement was verbal," the woman calmly replied, "but the other agreement, the one between us, is wordless and implicit. You will always have people around you, both men and women and that, you will not be surprised to know, will be neither particularly desirable nor pleasant from my point of view, nevertheless I shall bear it," she said a little wearily and gave a short sigh.

"And when," asked the man in a most respectful, matter-of-fact and reassuring manner, as though he were speaking to a child or some mad person it was unsafe to contradict, "when do you think, Francesca, that we will embark on this life? . . ."

"But we have already embarked on it, my love," the woman answered brightly. "We embarked on it the moment I wrote the letter and when the duke of Parma passed my message to you, at which point I put on these man's clothes. Now you are talking to me as people tend to talk to children or to lunatics. But I am neither of those, my love. I am a woman, albeit in man's clothes and in a mask, a woman who is absolutely certain she knows something and therefore acts. You are silent? . . . Your silence indicates that you wish to know what it is I know with such certainty, with such ridiculous, lunatic, deathly certainty? . . . Only that however many people surround you—men, women, probably more women—and however that is likely to hurt me, we belong to each other. My life is linked to yours, Giacomo, as yours is linked to mine. That is what I know and what the duke of Parma knows as well as I do. That is why he brought the letter, and that is why he is in his palace now with his ass's head, tolerating my presence here. That is why he hurried to make an agreement with you, and that is why you, too, Giacomo, hurried to make an agreement with him, because the agreement saves you from me, because you fear me as a man fears life, a whole life, the life that lies in wait for him . . . and everyone is a little frightened of that. I am no longer frightened," she pronounced aloud.

"And what sort of life will we have? . . ." asked the man.

"It will be neither happy nor solemn. It will not be a lucky life. There are people with perfect pitch, who can hear intervals and harmonies and recognize wholeness. You are not such a man. I know I shall be alone a good deal, and that I will seem lonely to the rest of the world, because you will often leave me. I will not be happy in the billing-and-cooing sense of the word, which is what other people mean and desire, but my life will have meaning and content, perhaps all too heavy and painful a content. I know everything, Giacomo, because I love you. I have the strength of a wrestler because I love you. I shall be as wise as the Pope because I love you. I shall be a literary scholar and an expert gambler for your sake; I am learning even now how to mark the king and the ace without others observing me. I have had packs of cards and wax brought over from Naples. We shall prepare the cards together, you and I, before you go out to take on the rabble and scum of the world, and I shall wait for you at home while you cheat them and return in the morning or maybe only on the third day. And we shall spend this money, we shall let the world take it back, because we don't need a fortune, because you never hold on to money, because that is your nature. I shall be the most beautiful woman in Paris, Giacomo, and you will see what a conquest I shall make of the chief of police when I dine alone with him: and no harm will come to you, for I shall guarantee you greater safety than the duke of Parma's commendatory letter: every glint of my eye, every breath I take will be there to protect you, to see that no harm comes to you. Should some evil woman give you the pox, I will nurse you, rubbing your limbs with lotions, making you soup out of herbs for your convalescence. I shall be as devious as the spies of the Inquisition; I shall sleep with the doge and intercede on your behalf so he allows you to return home, so that you may see Nonna and Signor Bragadin again, or, if you like, the pretty nun for whom you rented a palazzo in Murano. I will learn to cook sensibly, my love, indeed have learned that already, and I know that you should not eat spicy food because it makes your nose bleed; I can make soups that will cure your headache, and I will go to the women that wink at you and flirt with you and act as your bawd so you should enjoy a free night with the famous Julia for whom the duke of Norfolk paid one hundred thousand gold pieces, and who was so cruel to you at the last Carnival in Venice. I have learned to knit, to wash, and to iron, because there will be times in our lives when we will have no money, when moneylenders' agents will scamper after us and we will have to stay at worse inns than The Stag. But I will take care that you will always have clean, ironed shirts with decent frills to wear in public, my love, even if we haven't eaten anything but dry fish cooked in oil for four days. I shall be so beautiful, Giacomo, that sometimes, when we have money, and you shower me with velvet and silk and jewels, and you take a box at the opera in London, everyone will look at me rather than the performance, and you will sit beside me, cold and indifferent, as we gaze over the audience, because I won't have eyes for anyone but you on such occasions, and everyone will know that the most beautiful of women is yours, only yours. And this will suit you, because you are vain, inordinately vain, and everyone will know that your victory is complete, that I am the duchess of Parma who has left her husband with all his stately homes, to live with you; that I have thrown away my jewels and lands so that I may share a bed with you; that I accompany you as you flee across the highways of the world and sleep with you in damp and filthy hovels and never cast a longing look on another man, except only when you ask me to. Because you can do anything with me, Giacomo. You could sell me to our cousin Louis and his harem at Versailles, you could sell me by the pound and know that when strange men melt in my arms like lead in the fire, I remain yours alone. You could forbid me to even glance at another man, you could

disfigure me, you could cut off my hair, brand my breast
with a hot poker, infect me with the pox, and ruin my
skin, but those would be the least of my worries, for you
would soon see that I will still be beautiful for you,
because I would find medication, brew potions, grow new
skin and new hair, just in case you should sometime later
desire me and want me to be attractive for you. I want you
to know that all this is possible because I love you. I will be
the most modest of women, my love, if that is what you
want. I will live alone in our apartment: you can brick up
the windows if you like. I would even go to mass only if
you permitted it, accompanied by your servants. I would
spend the whole day indoors in the rooms you marked out
as my prison, caring for myself, getting dressed, and waiting for you. And I would be waited on only by women of
your choosing, blind and dumb women, if you want. But
if you wanted other men's desires to spice up your own I
would be flirtatious and depraved. If you wanted to
humiliate me, Giacomo, you should know that there
would be no humiliation I would not undergo for you,
because I love you. If you felt you had to torture me you
could strap me to a table and beat me with barbed whips,
and I would scream and see my blood flow, all the while
thinking of fresh means of torture to bring you greater and
truer joy. If you wanted me to rule you, I would be ruthless and unfeeling, as I read some women are, in the books
that the duke of Parma brought back from Amsterdam. I
know such extraordinary secrets, Giacomo, that there is
not a woman in the brothels of Venice who knows more
than I do about tenderness, torture, the yearnings of the

body and the spirit, love potions, small clothes, lighting, scents, caresses, and abstinence. If you wanted me to be vulgar I know such words in Italian, French, German, and English as make me blush sometimes when I am alone and think of them: I learned these words for you, and would whisper them only to you, if you wished. There is not a slave in the harems of the east, my love, who knows more about the pleasures of the flesh than I do. I have studied the body and know all its desires, even the most secret ones about which men think only on their death beds, when everything is all the same to them, and the scent of sulphur hovers about them. I have learned all this because I love you. Is that enough? . . . ."

"It's not enough," the man replied.

"Not enough," the woman repeated. "Well, naturally it's not enough. I just wanted to tell you so you knew. . . . But do not believe that I for an instant hoped that it would be enough, that this would be all. These are just means, my love, I know too well, melancholy means. I have simply catalogued and enumerated them because I want you to know that there is nothing you could want from me that I would not give or hesitate to grant. You are right: it is not enough. Because love has two arenas, two theaters of war, where the great two-hander is played out, and both are infinite: the bed and the world. And we must live in the world, too. It is not enough to accommodate myself to everything you desire, everything your whims might demand of me, no, I have to discover what makes you happy and provide it. I have to find out what it is that you desire but cannot confess, even to yourself, not even on your deathbed when everything is all the same to you: I have to find out and tell you so that you know, that you should see what the good is, so that you can be happy at last. And because you are the unhappiest of men, my love, and I can't bear your unhappiness, I have to name the thing you desire . . . though that is not enough, either, that is too little, too crude, and it would show poor skill on my part, because, should you doubt it, I, too, have my art, even if it is not quite as highly esteemed and complex as yours. What is my art? . . . Nothing more than my love of you. That is why I shall be strong and wise, modest and lewd, patient and lonely, wild and disciplined. It is because I love you. I have to find out why it is you run from deep feeling and from true happiness, and once I know why I must pass that sad knowledge on to you, but not in words, not by telling you, because such knowledge is terrifying and would not save you . . . words, however precise, can only name and catalogue the discoveries of mankind, but they solve nothing, as you, being a writer, will most certainly know. No, I must be tender, watching and waiting for ways in which to tell you the secret without words, to let you know what hurts you and what you desire, what you are not bold enough to admit: because it is cowardice and ignorance that are behind all unhappiness, as you must certainly know, being a writer. And so I must find out why you are afraid of happiness, which is not merely the touch of two hands, which is neither cradle nor coffin, but wholeness, a wholeness requiring something solemn, almost severe in our composition, the wholeness which is life and truth. I have to find out what it is you desire so badly you dare not admit it to yourself and then I have to keep that secret from you, because my words would only hurt you, and you, in your vanity, would protest and run away, cursing and denying: that is why I must stay silent, keeping the secret in my heart. And I must live so that, even without words, you should know and understand why everything is as it is, why you suffer loneliness, boredom, restlessness, yearning; why the gambling, why the orgies, why you have no home, why your art developed as it did, why all those women, why you are a seducer: and once you know all this through me, without my telling you, you will see that suddenly everything will be easier and better. You alone will be entitled to pronounce the secret. I can do nothing but wait, watch, learn, and then, silently, with my whole being, my life, my body, my silence, my kisses, and my actions pass the secret knowledge on to you. That is what I must do, because I love you. And that is why you are afraid of life and of wholeness, because there is nothing we fear so much, not the rack, not the gallows, as ourselves and the secrets we dare not face. And will all be well after that, my love? . . . I don't know. But everything will be simpler then, much simpler. We will move across our two stages, the bed and the world, as accomplices, people who know everything about each other and everything about our audience, too. There will be no more stage fright, Giacomo. Because love is togetherness and harmony, not fever and fret, nor tears and screams: it is a most solemn harmony, the firmest of unions. And I undertake that union, even unto death. What will happen? . . . I have no plans, Giacomo. I am not saying, 'Here I am, I am yours, take me with you,' because those are only meaningless words. But you should know that even if you do not take me with you, I shall wait for you forever, secretly, until you think of me one day and your heart melts and you turn to me. I don't need to make vows or promises, because I know reality, and that reality is that you are truly mine. You can leave me, as you did once before, taking to your heels like a coward, though it wasn't the duke of Parma you fled from but the terrifying power of true feeling, the recognition that I was truly yours. You did not know as much in words, nor in your thoughts, but you knew it in your heart and in your body and that is why you fled. And escape was pointless because here we are again, face-to-face with each other waiting for the moment when we can remove our masks and see each other as we really are. Because we are still only masked figures, my love, and there are many more masks between us, each of which must, one by one, be discarded, before we can finally know each other's true, naked faces. Don't hurry, there is no rush, no need to grope for the mask you are wearing or to throw it away. It is no accident that we are wearing masks, meeting, as we do, after a long time, when both of us have escaped our prisons to face each other: we needn't hurry to throw away our masks, because we will only find other masks beneath them, masks made of flesh and bone and yet as much a mask as these, made of silk. There are so many masks we have to discard before I can get to see and recognize your face. But I know that somewhere, far, far away, the other face exists and that one day I must see it, because I love you. Once, many years ago, you gave me a mirror, Giacomo, a present from Venice. A mirror was, of course, the only possible gift, a Venetian mirror, which is reputed to show people their true faces. You brought me a mirror in a silver frame, and a comb, a silver-handled comb. That is what you gave me. It was the best of presents, my dear. Years have passed, and every day I hold the mirror and comb in my hand, adjusting my hair, looking at my face as you imagined and wanted me to, when you gave me a mirror as a present. Because mirrors are enchantments—did you know that, you, a citizen of Venice, where the finest mirrors are produced? We have to look into mirrors for a long time, regularly, for a very long time, before we can see our true faces. A mirror is not just a smooth silver surface, no, a mirror is deep, too, like tarns on mountains, and if you look carefully into a Venetian mirror you will catch a glimpse of that depth, and will go on to detect ever deeper and deeper depths, the face glimmering ever farther off, and every day a mask falls away, one more of the masks that is examining itself in the mirror that was a gift your lover bought you from Venice. You should never give a woman you love a mirror as a present, because women eventually come to know themselves in mirrors, seeing ever more clearly, growing ever more melancholy. It was in a mirror, at some time, in some place, that the first act of recognition occurred, the point when man stared into the ocean, saw his face in its infinity, grew anxious, and began to ask, 'Who is that? . . .' The mirror you brought for me from Venice, a mirror no bigger than my palm, showed me my real face, and one day I saw that this face, my face, the face

I thought was familiar and was mine, was only a mask, far finer than silk, and behind it lay another face that looked like yours. I am grateful to the mirror for that. . . . And that is why I am not making promises, vowing no vows, not demanding anything, however madly my heart is beating at this very moment, because I recognized my face and I know that it resembles yours, and that you are truly mine. Is that enough? . . ."

"It's not enough," replied the man.

"Not enough?" the woman asked in the same singsong voice. "No, Giacomo, this time you have not been entirely sincere. You yourself know that this is not to be dismissed, that it adds up to something, maybe even more than something. It is not a little thing, not in the least, when two people know they are meant for each other. It took me a long time before I understood it. Because there was a time when I did not know myself, and that is the way I grew up in Pistoia, behind thick walls, a little neglected and unkept, like wild nettles—and you courted me then on a whim, with mock gallantry, but both of us knew that whatever we said, something true was passing between us! You found me various pet names adapted from plants, animals, and stars, as lovers often do when they are still playing with each other and trying out words, in the early days of love when they lack the courage to call each other by their true names, such as 'my love' or 'Giacomo' or 'Francesca.' By that time all other words are superfluous. But at that stage I was 'wild flower' and even, somewhat discourteously, 'wild nettle,' because I was wild and I stung and you said that your hands burned and came out in a rash when they touched mine. That's how you courted me. I think back to those times and feel dizzy or find myself blushing, because I am sure that I knew you the very first time I saw you, in the large hall on the ground floor of the house in Pistoia among those scrappy bits of furniture with their broken legs—I remember you were just showing the cardinal's letter to my father and exchanging a few pleasantries with him, lying about something with considerable fluency. And I knew more about you at that moment than I did later, when conversation and social games hid your real nature from me. I knew everything about you at that first instant, and if there is anything I am ashamed of, or hide from myself in embarrassment, it's the consequent period of our love, when you flirted with me using those names of animals and plants and stars, when you acted gallantly, when you were false and alien to me—it is that period that fills me with shame. You were a coward then, Giacomo, too much a coward to do as your heart commanded that first moment you saw me, before we had spoken a word to each other, before you started addressing me as 'wild nettle' or anything else. It is a great sin to be a coward. I can forgive you all those things the world will not forgive: your character, your weaknesses, your maliciousness, your boundless selfishness; I understand and wholly absolve you of all those, but I cannot forgive your cowardice. Why did you allow the duke of Parma to take possession of me, to buy me as you might a calf at the cattle market in Florence? . . . Why did you let me take up residence in strange palaces and foreign towns when you knew you were truly mine? . . . I woke at dawn on my wedding night and stretched out my hand looking for you. I was in Paris in a coach under the plane trees, on the stony road to Versailles, with the king on my right, and I didn't answer when our cousin Louis addressed a question to me, because I imagined it was you sitting beside me and I wanted to show you something. And I asked myself continually: why is he such a coward when he knows we belong to each other? He is not afraid of knives or jails or poison or humiliation, so why should he fear me, his true love, his happiness? . . . I kept asking myself that. Then I understood. And now I know what I have to do, Giacomo—it is the reason I learned to write, and to do so much else that has nothing to do with pen and ink and paper. I learned everything because I love you. And now you should truly understand, my love, that when I say the words *I love you,* I do not say them in a languishing or misty-eyed sort of way, but speak them aloud; that I shout them in your face like a command, like an accusation. Do you hear, Giacomo? I love you. I am not trifling with these words. I am addressing you like a judge, do you hear? I love you, therefore I have authority over you. I love you and therefore I demand that you take courage. I love you so I am starting again from the beginning. Even if I have to drag you from your orbit as if you were a star in the firmament I shall take you with me, I shall tear you from your natural place in the universe, remove you from the laws of your being and from the demands of your art because I love you. I am not asking you, Giacomo, I am accusing you: yes, I am accusing you of a capital crime. I am not inviting you to join a game, I am in no mood to dally or flirt with you, I am not making sheep's eyes at you or melting with tender sighs. I am staring at you with anger, with fury: I look upon you as one looks at an enemy. I shall kidnap you for love, if not now, then later, nor will I let you off the leash for a single second, whatever borders you cross, however you try to flee me with the little serving maid at your side, the one that opened the doors for me, who started back into the shadows like a fawn that scents danger, sensing that under the man's clothes I was a woman and a rival, for I sensed that she had something to do with you, too, that she was plotting with you against me, like all the other women. That is how life is and how it will continue to be. But I am stronger for my love. I tell you this directly, and I say it aloud, like a slap across your face, do you understand? . . . Do you hear? . . . I love you. I cannot help it. It is my fate to love you. I have loved you for five years, Giacomo, from the moment I saw you in the old garden in Pistoia, when you were telling that thumping lie, after which you called me 'wild nettle' and fought over me, stripped to the waist in the moonlight, at which point you fled and I despised you and loved you. I know you are afraid, are still afraid of me. Don't try shutting your eyes under the mask, because I can see through the holes: yes, now at last I can see you beneath the mask, and your eyes, which were bright before, like a wild animal's contemplating its prey, have clouded over, as if some veil or fog had descended on them. Your eyes are almost human now. Don't shut your eyes or turn away, because I want you to know that I shall not let you go, however complicated an agreement you have come to with the duke of Parma, because despite the agreement you remain the man that is meant for me, and I am the woman that is meant for you; we belong together like murderer and victim, like sinner and sin, like the artist and his art, as does everyone with the mission he would most like to escape. Don't be afraid, Giacomo! It won't hurt much! I must make you a gift of courage; I must teach you to be brave in facing yourself, facing us, the fact of us, a fact that may be sinful and scandalous, as is every true and naked fact in the world. Don't be afraid, because I love you. Is that enough? . . ."

"It's too much," said the man.

"Too much," said the woman and gave a short sigh. She fell silent, her hands against her mask, and stared into the fire.

The fire spluttered and carried on with its monotonous singing. They listened to its song, full of life, full of reason. Then the woman moved warily, as if afraid of tripping over her sword, and knelt before the man; raising her two long, slender arms and very gently and carefully laying her fingertips on the man's mask, she took his hidden face in her hands and whispered, "Forgive me if my love is too much, Giacomo, I know such love is a great sin. You must forgive me. Very few people can bear the burden of absolute love that is also an inescapable duty and responsibility. It is the only sin I have committed against you. Forgive me. I will never ask anything more of you. I will do everything to reduce the suffering it causes you. Are you afraid that boredom might one day grip you with its damp palm and strangle you as you wake beside me? . . . Don't be afraid, my love, because this boredom will be as satisfying and good humored as when you stretch and yawn, and the meaning of the boredom will be that I love you. You don't know, you cannot yet know, what it is like when someone loves you. I must explain love to you because you know nothing about it. You fear your desire and curiosity, you fear all the women who will smile at you from windows, from carriages, in every inn and in every foreign marketplace, because you fear that you will not be able to pursue them, tied as you are to me, by love. . . . It is not certain that you will want to pursue them, Giacomo, knowing I love you. But if you were to leave me one day, out of curiosity and boredom, I would carry on living and waiting for you somewhere. And one day you will grow tired of the world, having known and tasted everything, and you will wake with a sense of disgust, your limbs racked with some awful disease, your bones riddled with woodworm, and you will look around you and remember that somewhere I am waiting for you. Where should I wait, my love? . . . Wherever you wish. In the country house I may retire to after the death of the duke, in the big city where you first abandoned me, perhaps here in Bolzano, in my palazzo, to which I would have had to return and wait for you once the night was over? You must realize that I will wait for you forever. And wherever I make my bed, be certain one pillow will be reserved for you. Every dish I cook or is placed before me by a servant will be your dish too. When the sun shines and the sky is blue, you must be aware that I will be staring at the sky, thinking, 'Giacomo will be enjoying the same sky.' Should the rain come down, I will be thinking, 'Now he is standing at a window in Paris or in London, fractious and in a foul mood, and someone should really be lighting a fire in the room to keep his feet warm.' When I see a beautiful woman I will think, 'Perhaps she may afford him an hour of pleasure so he may be less unhappy.' Whenever I break a loaf, half of it will be yours. I know it is too much, this love, and I beg you to forgive me. I want to live a long time so I can wait for you to come home."

"Home? Where is that, Francesca?" asked the mask. "I have no home, not a stick of furniture, anywhere in the world."

"Home is with me, Giacomo," the woman answered. "Wherever I sleep, that is your home."

Her two palms curved very gently, as though she were holding a delicate piece of glass, and stroked the man's mask.

"You see," said the woman, her voice now faintly singing, her mask a living, smiling radiance, "I am kneeling before you, in fancy dress, like a courtly suitor attempting to charm a lady. And you are sitting before me, in a female costume, masked, because fate has playfully ordained that, for one night only, we should exchange roles. I am the gallant suitor, and you are the lady I am courting. What do you think? Is this not more than coincidence? . . . I had no idea this afternoon that I would be wearing a male costume tonight, nor did you know this afternoon that the duke of Parma would seek you out, bring you my letter, invite you to the ball, and that you would be dressing up as a woman . . . do you think this is all just coincidence? I don't understand human affairs, Giacomo, I only have my imagination, and I begin to suspect that no vital, no unique situation is coincidental, that deep down, at bottom, everybody, men and women alike, is a similar blend of feelings and desires, that our characters and roles are not wholly distinct, that there are moments when life toys with us and shifts about those elements within us that we had believed to be unique and fixed. That is why I am not astonished to be kneeling before you, rather than you before me, as the duke of Parma had ordained in his agreement, and it is I who am endeavoring to woo you. So, you see, everything is proceeding according to the agreement, even though the actors are not precisely in the parts the duke of Parma had designed for them. I am begging you, my dear, to accept my love. I want to console you because I love you and cannot bear your unhappiness. I am the suitor, the besieging force, not you. I have come to you because I must see you. And here we are now, and you are silent. It is a powerful silence, a proper, tight-lipped silence, as it has to be, considering your role, and I echo the last words of your speeches precisely as the agreement demands. But you are still restrained, Giacomo, still acting: you are too true to your part. Are you not afraid that our time will run out, that night will pass, and you will have nothing of interest or satisfaction to report to the man who commissioned you? . . . Don't you want me, my love? How terrifying you are when you keep quiet like this, so utterly in character. Not enough and too much, you said, when I offered you everything a woman could offer the man she loved. Look at the fire, Giacomo, see, it has flared up as if it, too, wanted to say something. Perhaps what it wants to say is that it is necessary to be destroyed by the fury of passion and be born anew in feeling, because that is life and wholeness. Everything that has happened might catch light and burn in our hearts if you so desired, if you took me with you or if you let me take you—it is all the same, Giacomo, who goes with whom—but we will have to start everything again, from the beginning, because that is how love works. I will have to give birth to you, to be both your mother and your daughter; my love will cleanse you and I, too, shall be clean in your arms. It will be as if no man had ever touched me. Are you still quiet? . . . Don't you want me? . . . Can I not console you? . . . How terrible, Giacomo. In vain do I offer you delight and peace, cleanliness and renewal, I cannot drag you into feeling, cannot prize you from your art, cannot change you or see your true face, the last face, without its mask, as I wanted in my letter. . . . Is it possible that you are stronger than I am, my love? Will the strength of my love break against your cold art and impregnable character? . . . I promise you peace and wholeness, and you tell me it is too much and not enough. Why don't you say just once that it is enough, perfect, just right? . . . Can't I offer you anything that will draw you out of your orbit? Can't I say anything to make you finally step out of character and cry, yes, it is enough! . . . Look, here I kneel, I am twenty years old. You know perfectly well that I am beautiful. I know it, too. I am not the most beautiful woman in the world, because the most beautiful woman does not exist anywhere, but I am still beautiful, my body is perfect, my face is alive and full of curiosity, repose, delight, understanding, cheer, and solemnity all blended together. It is the blend that gives it its beauty. Because that blended animation is what beauty is. All else is merely a malleable combination of skin and flesh and bone. You still believe in the kind of women who ostentatiously draw attention to their beauty, Giacomo, who strut about proudly, not knowing that beauty is what dissolves in the crucible of love, that a month or a year after the successful wedding, no one notices beauty any-more—face, legs, arms, a fine bosom, all melt away and disappear in the flames of love, and there remains a woman who may still be able to soothe, to hold, to help you, to offer something, even when you can no longer see the beauty of her face and figure. . . . My beauty is like that, Giacomo: I am true metal, gold through and through. Even if I were worn on someone's finger, or buried deep beneath the earth, I would be true because I am beautiful. The Creator has blessed me with beauty and he has given me the odd beating, too: I am beautiful and therefore have a purpose in life, which is to please your eyes, though it is not only your eyes I must please, Gia-como. For I cannot pass through life with such beauty without being punished for it, because wherever I go I rouse passions: I am like a water diviner who discovers underground streams, who can feel them bubbling beneath her. I have to suffer a great deal on account of my beauty. I offer you the beauty and harmony with which the Creator has blessed and cursed me and you are still uncertain, saying now too much, now not enough. Are

you not afraid, Giacomo? . . . You made my acquaintance
when I was still in bud, calling me your 'wild nettle,' but
you permitted the duke of Parma to buy me, and fled
because you feared and still do fear me, even though I represent truth and wholeness. Are you not afraid that human
ties might not be enough, that maybe I am just a woman
who may tire of waiting, of agreements, deals, and promises? Are you not afraid that I might be tired already and
that I visit you only to confirm the fact and tell you so? . . .
Because the desire and devotion that burns in my heart for
you is itself a terrifying and self-consuming passion! Are
you not afraid, Giacomo, that I have secrets of my own?
Are you not afraid that I may be able to stir feelings in you
that are not entirely tender or calm, that I might, if I very
much desired, entertain you with stories that will make
you cry out and finally demand, 'Enough!' I am truly
yours, Giacomo, nor is there anything I desire more than
to save you and to save myself, and having done that, to
live with you as people do, through whatever hells we may
have to face. But if your attachment to your art, to the
duke of Parma's contract, and to yourself demands something more, it may be time for me to weaken and to confess that, while this flame has continued to burn within
me ever since I first met you and that it is indeed
unquenchable, I was unable to resign myself to your running away, to your cowardice, but allowed other men to
kiss me before I gave myself to the duke of Parma. I could
regale you with stories about the consolations required by
a rejected fifteen-year-old girl. Shall I tell you what it was
like after your flight in Pistoia, when I threw myself at the

gardener—you know the man? Are you not afraid of hearing about that night, Giacomo? I remember it very well, in every detail, just as you, in your turn, will remember the gardener who gave me flowers on your behalf: a tall, powerful, violent man, a man of few words. Shall I tell you the story of the night after your duel and your escape? . . . Would you really like to hear it in all its detail? And what about the other things that followed as the months and years passed, when I had no news from you, and this flame, that is worse than the flames and fumes of hell, worse than the flames suffered by poor victims of the Inquisition, burned me through and through? Shall I tell you the story of the house in Florence? About the palazzo on the bank of the Arno by the Ponte San Trínita, where you will find my nightgown, my slippers, my comb, and the Venetian mirror you gave me? Should I tell you about the house I frequented that I, too, might have used as a casino, Giacomo, the secret palazzo in Murano that, like you, I once enjoyed? Should I tell you all this? Should I tell you what it is like when a woman who wants to give everything that a young body and soul has to give to the man she loves is disappointed in love and begins to burn with fury, like a torch made of flesh, hair, and blood, a torch that burns in secret, like a flame in the half-light, scorching and blackening everything she touches, so that despite all the power, strength, and wariness of the duke of Parma, he is helpless to put the fire out? Should I tell you what it is like when a woman is obliged to seek the tenderness she desires from one man alone, a man who has run away, in the embraces of ten, twenty, or a hundred men? Would you like names, Giacomo? Would you like proof? . . . Would you like to know the names of those noble lords, gardeners, courtiers, comedians, gamblers, and musicians, together with their addresses, every one of them kinder and more tender to me than you have ever been? . . . Do you want to know what it is like when a woman begins to move through the world like one possessed, touched, and branded by fate, without a scrap of peace in her heart because she loves somebody and has been rejected? Because I could tell you about that too."

"I don't believe you," the man said, his voice cracking.

"You don't believe me?" echoed the woman in her sweetest, most childlike, most astonished manner. "And if I had proof, Giacomo? . . . If you had the list of names and addresses that would act as proof, would you believe me then? Because I could give you the names and addresses. Is that enough? . . ."

"It is enough," said the man. He stood up and with a quick movement seized the dagger hidden in his breast.

The woman, however, did not move. Still kneeling, she turned the stiff gaze of the mask on the man, and spoke quietly and modestly.

"Oh, the dagger! Always the dagger, my love. It is the only answer you have for the world that inflicts itself on you! Put the dagger away, my dear; it is a one-word answer that explains nothing, it is a stupid, needless answer. And why answer me with a dagger when you are simply a coward afraid of loving me, when I can offer you neither true delight nor true pain, when all this is just a game, the pièce de résistance of a hired conjuror, a guest performance by a remarkable artist who is only passing through? The dagger is not part of the agreement, my dear. I say it again, put the dagger away, and don't bother reaching for the mask with those trembling fingers. Why should you take off the mask? What could the face beneath the mask tell me? I wrote to say that I must see you, and now I have seen you. It wasn't so much a face I wanted to see, Giacomo, but a man, the man I truly loved, who was a coward, who sold me and ran away from me. But it was all in vain. It was in vain that I knew who and what kind of man you were; in vain that, for five years, the fires of Gehenna have been blazing inside me; in vain that I made futile attempts to extinguish the glowing embers of that fire and to heal the wound with the kisses of other men while never ceasing to love you; in vain that I have carried this wound about with me like a bloody sword wherever I have gone, challenging everyone who crossed my path with it; in vain that I cursed it in secret, in the depths of my soul, a hundred times or more, for I was still hoping that one day I would have enough strength to tear the mask from your face and see you, as my note demanded, to see you and forgive you. That is why I asked the castrato to teach me writing. That is why I wrote and sent you the letter. That is why I waited for you, and that is why, when you did not come to me because, true to your art as ever, you were drawing up a contract with the duke of Parma, I came to you, in men's clothes, masked, just once more, so I could see you. I told you everything, that you are truly mine and that I am the woman to whom you are eternally bound, and you knew it was true. I offered you everything I had. And your only reply was, 'too little,' or 'too much.' But finally I have got you to say, 'enough.' That was the word I wanted to hear. Good. Now listen carefully, my love. Everything I told you is true. And now that I have seen you like this, I have no wish to see you any other way. I will go back to my house and to my guests. And you will go out into the world to live and to lie, to loot and to steal, to snatch at every skirt you come across and to roll in every bed you find. You will continue, faithful to your art. But all the while you will know, whether you are awake or asleep, even as you are kissing another woman, that I was the truth, that I meant everything in life to you, and that you hurt me and sold me. You will know that you could have had all that life has to offer but preferred slyness and cowardice: that you chose to work to a contract and that henceforth life will offer you nothing but contracts. You will know that my body, which is partly your body, will never now be yours but will belong to anybody who asks for it. You will know that I am living somewhere, in the arms of other men, but that you will never again hold me in your arms. I too am faithful in my fashion, Giacomo. I wanted to live with you like Adam and Eve in the Garden before there was sin in the world. I wanted to save you from your fate. There is no passion, no misery, no sickness, no shame that I would not have shared with you. You know what I say is true, you knew my letter was sacred. You knew but kept silent, true to your agreement with the duke of Parma. And you should know that, now that I have seen you, I have sentenced you to unhappiness, you will never again have a happy moment in your life, and whatever sweetness you taste you will think of me. You may have seen me but you do not know me in the biblical sense, and yet you do know something, if not everything, about me now. Our time is running out. Do not forget that my sex and the name I bear demand a certain modesty and tact. You know something about me and the rest I leave you to imagine at every hour of leisure between one task and another, one contract and another, one masterpiece and another. Because you will think of me, Giacomo. I am confident in the knowledge that you will think of me. That is why I came to see you, why I promised you all a woman can promise a man, and why I tell you now that there is nothing a corrupt imagination can invent that I will not turn into reality in the future, at the very moment you think of me. That is why I came to you masked, at midnight, wearing a man's clothes, with a sword at my side. And now I can go home to my palazzo and to the rest of my life, which I know for certain will be only half a life without you. Now go: live and create masterpieces, my friend. Perhaps one day your own life will become a masterpiece, a masterpiece glowing with cold, corrupt light. The laws of your being may be what most concern you: my concern, however, was for you yourself, my love, and now, this night being over, I know that your heart is condemned to eternal pain. Because it is not a matter of having seen you as I wished to: you have seen me, too, and having seen me, you will never forget my face, the face under the masks I show the world. Because revenge can console us, Giacomo. You may not understand that at this very moment, but you will as soon as I have left this room and vanished forever from your life, then you will suddenly understand and your whole life will be filled with that understanding. I am nobody in particular, Giacomo, not a great artist, not a man, just a woman, Francesca from Tuscany, unfit to occupy a leading place among your great works of art. But from now on I shall have some kind of place there, I have made sure of that. I have infused my being into yours, I have infused you with the knowledge that I was the truth you threw away, that you brought shame to someone who loved you and will always love you in whatever situation she chooses for herself in exacting the revenge she has vowed to take. I wanted to take other vows with you, Giacomo, vows for life. You rejected them. Life will go on, however, even like this. . . . But your life will not be what it was before, my love: you will be like the man who has been fed some exquisite slow-working poison and feels the pain at every moment. I have taken care of that. Because I, too, have my weapons, subtler than daggers. Put the dagger away, my love. I may not have been strong enough to overcome you through love, but I shall be stronger in revenge and your dagger will be useless. Put the dagger away. Or, if you want, you could give it to me as a memento of this night. I would look after it well, in Florence, keeping it together with your other gifts, the mirror and the comb. Would you like to exchange mementos? Look, I will draw this slender gold-handled sword that I strapped to my side this evening, and I will give it to you in exchange, the way enemies used to exchange hearts and arms when they had finished fighting each other. Give me the dagger as a memento. Thank you. . . . And receive in exchange this sharp, highly refined weapon, and take it with you wherever you go. You see, we have exchanged arms, if not hearts, Giacomo. And now we should both return to our respective places in the world and live on as we must, if only because you were too weak to step out of character and reject your art. I thank you for the dagger, my love," the woman said and stood up, "and thank you for this night. Now I, too, can live on, more settled than I have been these last five years. Shall I hear anything of you? . . . I don't know. Should I wait for you? . . . But I have already said, Giacomo, that I will wait forever. Because what we share will not pass with time. It is not only love that is eternal, Giacomo: all true feelings are, including revenge."

She drew the sword and handed it over, attaching the Venetian dagger the man had wordlessly handed over to her to a link of the golden belt she was wearing. "It's almost dawn," she said in a voice as clear as glass. "I must go. Don't see me out, Giacomo. If I could find my way here by myself I can find my way back, too, to life, to my home. How quiet it is. . . . The wind has died down. And the fire, too, has gone out, you see, as if speaking its own language, which tells us that every passion, all that passes, must eventually turn to ashes. But that is not something I want to believe. Because this night has, after all, provided us with an encounter and a chance of deepening our acquaintance, even if not quite as the duke of Parma imagined or the Bible describes. Now you have a seal on your agreement, Giacomo, that seal being your consciousness of all I have told you. It is the seal of revenge, a powerful seal, as strong as love or life or death. You can tell the duke of Parma that you were true to your agreement, that you did not cheat him, my love, nor did you fail, but have earned your fee and merit your reward. By the end of the night everything had happened as you had agreed, and now that I have got to know you I am returning to the man who loves me and is waiting for me to ease his departure from life. Travel well, Giacomo, trip through the world on light steps. Your art remains infallible and the task you took on is accomplished, not quite as you imagined, you two clever men between you, but it's the result that matters, and the result is that I know you, that I know I have no real hold on your heart, and can therefore only resign myself to my fate, the only power remaining to me being revenge. Take this confession, this promise with you as you go, for your road will be long and certain to be fascinating and full of variety. But I want something from you, too, by way of farewell. Rather unusually for me, I wrote a letter: if ever you feel that you have understood my letter and wish to answer, don't be lazy or cowardly: answer as is fit, with pen and ink, like the well-versed literary man you are. Do you promise? . . ."

And when the man did not answer, she continued, "Why will you not answer? Can the answer be so terrifying, Giacomo?"

"You know very well," the man replied, slowly and somewhat hoarsely, "that if I were ever to answer you in this life, the answer would not be given in pen and ink."

The woman shrugged and responded calmly, almost indifferently, with the trace of a smile in her voice. "Yes, I know. But what can I do? . . . I will live and wait for you to answer my letter, my love."

And she set out toward the door. But halfway there she turned to him in a gentle, friendly manner.

"The game and the performance are over, Giacomo. Let us return to our lives, taking off our masks and costumes. Everything has turned out as you wanted. I am sure that everything that has happened has happened according to some unwritten law. But you should know that it has happened as I, too, wanted it: I saw you, I was tender to you, and I hurt you."

She stood on tiptoe, looked briefly into the mirror, and with an easy movement placed the three-cornered hat over her wig. Having adjusted it, she added solicitously: "I hope I did not hurt you too much."

But she did not wait for an answer. She left the room without looking back, her feet swift and firm, and silently closed the door behind her.

The Answer

The room had chilled down and the candles had gut-
tered but were still smoking with a bitter stench. The
man stepped out of the skirt, released himself from the
bodice, tore off his mask, and threw away the wig. He
entered the bedchamber, stepped over to the washbasin,
poured icy water from the jug over his palm, and with
slow deliberate movements began to wash.

He washed the paint and rice powder off his face,
rubbed the scarlet from his lips, peeled the beauty patch
from his cheek, and wiped the soot from his eyebrows. He
splashed the water on, its icy touch burning and scratching his face: it stung him like a blow. He ran his fingers
through his hair and rubbed his face raw with the towel,
then lit fresh candles, and in the light they gave, leaned
toward the mirror to check that he had removed every
trace of paint from his face. His brow was furrowed and
pale, his chin needed a shave, and there were dark shadows
under his eyes as if he had just returned from an orgy that

had gone on all night. Then he threw away everything associated with the mask, and with quick, certain movements, began to dress.

Somewhere, bells were ringing. He put on traveling clothes, a warm shirt and stockings, and drew his cloak about his shoulders before looking around the room. The food and drink lay untouched on the damask tablecloth with its silver cutlery, only the snow in the dish had melted and futile little islands of butter were swimming about in the remaining pool like peculiarly swollen Oriental flowers on a tiny, ornamental pond. He picked up the chicken, tore it into two, and with fierce greedy movements nervously began to gnaw it. Having finished it he threw the bones into a corner, wiped his greasy fingers on the tablecloth, raised the crystal wineglass full of viscous golden fluid, and filled his mouth with it. He held his head back and watched as it went down in slow gulps, his enormous Adam's apple bobbing up and down in the mirror. He wiped his mouth with the back of his hand and threw away the glass, which struck the ground with a light chink and broke into pieces. His voice hoarse with wine, he called for Balbi.

The friar was immediately there, as if he had been ready and waiting for some time. He stood in the doorway, ready for the journey in his thick brown broadcloth coat, in his square-toed shoes, and a flask under his arm that he was nursing as tenderly and carefully as a mother might her child. Teresa followed him in and silently, without a second glance, hurried over to the shards of broken glass and assiduously gathered up the pieces in her apron.

"Is everything ready?" he asked the friar.

"They're preparing the horses," Balbi replied.

"Have you packed?" he asked the girl.

"No, sir," the girl replied, humbly and modestly. "I will not be going with you."

She stood by the fire, her head to one side, the broken glass in her apron, gazing calmly at him with wide and empty blue eyes.

"And why will you not come with me?" he asked, throwing his head back and looking down his nose. "I guarantee your future."

"Because you don't love me," the girl dreamily replied like a dutiful schoolgirl repeating a lesson.

"Do you think I love somebody else?" he asked.

"Yes."

"Whom do you think I love?" he asked curiously, as if addressing a child who was hiding a secret and was now about to reveal it.

"The woman in men's clothes, who left a little while ago," answered the girl.

"Are you sure," he asked, astonished.

"Quite sure."

"How do you know?"

"I can feel it. There is no one else. Nor will there ever be. That is why I won't go with you. Forgive me, sir."

She stood still. Balbi waited silently in the doorway, his hands folded over his stomach, and peered at him with a mildly inquisitive expression, twiddling his thumbs and blinking. Giacomo stepped over to the maid and stroked her hair and brow with great tenderness.

"Wait," he said. "Don't go yet. An angel may be speaking through you."

He opened his cloak, sat down in the armchair, drew the girl carefully to him, and sat her down on his knee, gazing deeply into those empty, watchful blue eyes.

"Sit down, Balbi," he said eventually. "There, by the table. Take pen, powder, and paper. You will write a letter for me."

The friar sat down silently, shifting and panting with his great weight. He lit a candle and examined the pen before staring up at the ceiling in anticipation.

"Address it *Your Excellency*," he said. "And watch your hand now. I want this to be beautifully written. I will speak slowly so you have time to form the letters. Are you ready? We may begin. *I am leaving town in the early hours of this morning. I am leaving without payment or reward, and all I ask is a single favor. Your Excellency has already volunteered his services as a postman once: I beg him now, by way of farewell, to undertake the task once more, and to inform the duchess of Parma that I call for help on whatever powers may be, and pray to God that He preserve us, she and I, now and in the future, from ever meeting again. I would that Your Excellency beg her, as she cares for her life and fears God, to avoid me henceforth, and to make sure that we never again look upon each other's faces, whether masked or unmasked. That is all I ask. For by most human expectations—and I say this with due courtesy, without any intent to offend—I am likely to outlive Your Excellency. I shall outlive him as nature and human destiny decree, and Your Excel-*

lency's noble corpse will soon be dust in his ancestors' tomb while Francesca and I continue to exist in the world: and, once Your Excellency is dead there will be no one to protect her, the woman we have both loved, each in his own fashion, according to our agreement and our fate. That is why I ask Your Excellency to tell the duchess, she whom I shall never again address in writing, to avoid me like the plague or the deluge; she should avoid me as she might sin and calumny; she must avoid me so that she might save that which is more important than life, meaning her soul. Only Your Excellency can tell her this. My carriage is prepared; in an hour I shall have left town and by evening I shall be beyond the frontiers of the state. The duchess of Parma will inform Your Excellency at some opportune hour, at a moment of tenderness perhaps or at some other proper confidential time, that I have carried out my obligations according to the terms of our agreement; not quite as we imagined, not quite as I usually do or imagined I would, but it is the outcome alone that matters, and the outcome is that I have kept my word and that the duchess of Parma has returned home by first light of dawn, known and cured, recovered from one who is as the plague and the yellow fever to her, and that she will henceforth dwell at the side of Your Excellency, without me, as is to be expected, with only the fading memory of my dangerous and wicked person in her heart. For that which was desire and passion between us has vanished in the performance, and now it is I who carry with me all that was feverish and resembled infection in that love, and the duchess of Parma is now free to dedicate her life to Your Excellency, gilding his declining years in

a calmer frame of mind.' Have you written it all down? . . .
Wait, perhaps we should say his declining months . . .
instead. It is more considerate in its honesty and, note
this, Balbi, and you too my child, that it is incumbent on
us to fight the great duels of life, even at moments of the
most desperate crisis, with consideration, for it is befitting
that we should be courteous while being true to the facts
and to ourselves. Now where were we? . . . *'Declining
months. For if I do not perish along the path, at the hand of
some assassin, or by way of accident—Your Excellency having
informed me that my entire life is an accident, albeit an accident that I am determined, tooth and nail, to survive—I will
live on, and every day I live will present a danger to the soul
of Francesca. That is my message to her. Everything else I
report speaks for itself. I am leaving the town, as agreed, and
the duchess of Parma is back at home after her adventure, as
pure as the driven snow or the fleecy clouds of spring. It may,
of course, be true that, according to the new knowledge, the
color white is an aggregation of all other colors, from the
crimson of blood through to the black of mourning: it is what
I read in the philosopher's book and I merely pass the knowledge on, adding only that the adventure was itself as pure as
most people imagine snow to be. Your Excellency desired peace
and recovery: he desired that the spell of love be broken and
that Francesca should live on at her husband's side without
pining, without memory. This has come to pass and I can go
my way. I do not say that I go with a light heart. Nor do I say
that I go proudly, shrugging my shoulders, rubbing my hands
with satisfaction, like an artist who has finished a commis-*

sion, stowed away his reward, and can hardly wait to cross the border and embark on new projects, with new techniques, ready to hammer out new agreements. I have looked into my heart and all I can say is that the tie we sought to sever with words and daggers is stronger now than it was the day before, or indeed ever before: the tie meaning that which binds me to the duchess of Parma. Knots tied by the gods are, it seems, not to be untied by human hands, however clever, tender, or violent. And that is why Your Excellency should look to the duchess's soul and ensure that we never meet again. Fire dies, said the duchess, and sooner or later all passion turns to ashes, but let me say, by way of farewell, that there is a kind of fire that is not lit by the spark of the moment, nor by the kindling of the senses; nor is it fanned by greed or ambition, no: there is something that continues to flicker in human life, a flame that neither custom nor boredom succeeds in putting out; nor do satisfaction or lechery succeed where they fail; it is a flame the world cannot extinguish, indeed, we ourselves cannot extinguish it. It is part of the fire that human hands once stole from heaven, and ever since then those responsible for its theft have faced the wrath of the gods. This is the flame that will continue to burn in my heart, nor do I have any wish to extinguish it: and wherever life leads me, wherever I present my character and exercise my art, I will know that the flame does not go out and that its heat and light fill my life. I could not say this to the duchess, since I did not want to break the agreement, and I will adhere to the letter of that agreement as to the rules of my art. I did not say to her, "I am yours alone, forever," as lovers generally do: I kept my word, and it is only

Your Excellency who can tell the duchess of Parma that some-
times the artist can be a hero by obeying the conventions and
obligations of performance, by not pronouncing the words
that burn in his heart and on his lips, whose meaning is in
the end, after all, "I am yours alone, forever." I did not pro-
nounce the words, and the words I did not say will now echo
forever in our two souls; that is why I report, by way of
farewell, that I have kept our agreement faithfully, to the let-
ter. The performance was a success, Your Excellency, and the
show is over. But there is something that remains and will
never be over, something upon which Your Excellency has
expended all his strength, his secret influence, his terrifying
omniscience and literary acuity, and yet is impossible to undo
or destroy, which is the knowledge that whatever flame
heaven has ignited in the human heart is not to be extin-
guished by human hands or human intelligence. And there is
something else I could not say for fear of breaking our agree-
ment: that there is a kind of sacrifice or service in love which
is more than declarations or abductions, more than "I am
yours alone, forever"'—you should write those words
within quotation marks, I think—*'There is a kind of love*
which does not wish to remove or to hurt but to protect, per-
haps even to save, and that this may in fact be the truest love
of all, and however surprised I am to feel it, it is the feeling
that the memory of the duchess of Parma prompts in me and
always will. Because there is nothing easier than to remove the
loved one from the world. There is nothing easier, for an expe-
rienced performer like me, than to produce tears and vows, to
carry out the accomplished seduction, to undertake the great
somersault, to join the circle dance of nymph and faun, com-

plete with pipes and rustic viols. I think I can say, without boasting, that I know my art, that I have performed often enough in my life, and will, no doubt, perform again should the nymphs and gods of pleasure so command. Nothing would have been easier for me—and only Your Excellency is free to repeat these words to the duchess, for I could not speak them in case the words became a reality and the reality resulted in action!—than to yield to my desires; to answer neither "too much" nor "too little" to all that a woman in love could offer me out of the depths of her pain and not to worry about her revenge, either, but to act upon desire, action, after all, having been the working principle of my life, for there has never been very much distance between my desires and my deeds, thank heaven'—I would like a semicolon there, please—'and I say this without boasting, with a clear conscience. But I knew something that the sickly child of love, the duchess of Parma, could not yet know: I knew who I was, I was aware of my earthly task, my role, and my fate, and I also knew that the flame that keeps me alive and gives me strength is death to those who carelessly touch it. There would have been nothing easier for me than to accept her gift, to exchange body for body, and soul for soul, and thereby to take possession of One'—write that with a capital O—'One who was truly mine. And there was yet something else I knew that the duchess of Parma could not yet know: that the truth can only survive as long as the hidden veils of desire and longing draw a curtain before her and cover her. That is why I did not lift the veil and bathe truth's mysterious face in the light of reality. And now I must return to my own reality, which is many-colored. I know its taste and scents so well that sometimes they seem bitter to me, and I no longer expect miracles or salvation. Let us go in peace, Your Excellency! We are mortals, and that high station imposes obligations on us: we are obliged to know our hearts and our fates. That is not an easy task. There are only two divine medicaments to help us bear the poison of reality and prevent it from killing us prematurely, and these are intelligence and indifference. We are men, the both of us: we know this secret; we have encountered reality and met our truth; we understand this. But it is not the business of a young, fiercely beating, and grievously wounded heart to understand it: that is why we must silently bear her accusations and her revenge, too, the revenge that will follow us everywhere we go. And I beg her once more, as I go, before I vanish into the mist that will now be covering the mountain paths, vanish away into cities, into time, into otherness, as my fate, which I truly regard as my fate, consumes me, to avoid me at all costs. She should avoid me if she wishes to save her soul. Because goodness, experience, skill, and compassion are only means whereby we may discipline the heart from time to time, but something underlies our intentions, directing our steps, some vast imperative whose magical power we may not transgress without being punished for it. I wish you months of happiness, Your Excellency! I hope we are not disappointed in each other. And if, a little later, when passions have died down somewhat and the miraculous balm of forgetting has eased the young heart so dear to both of us, should my name crop up in the course of some tender conversation, tell her that I have carried the rapier she exchanged for my dagger into the world, and am handling it well. That I will not bring disgrace on it. Tell her this so she may be assured. It is possible *that I might have to twist the blade she has given me in a heart or two, but tell her that she need not fear, for my hand will be cold and certain at those moments. Because this hand, that she now holds in such contempt, has trembled only once in all these years, the only time that goodness, clear sight, and compassion prevented it, and that was when I did not reach out for her, who was my truth. And when you are searching for famous last words on your death bed, Your Excellency, simply pronounce the words that mark your own farewell, the words that now remain my unspoken message: "I am yours alone, forever."'"*

He spoke the last words quietly and calmly into the girl's ear, clearly enough for Balbi to hear them, too.

Then he stood up and raised both arms high into the air before putting the girl down as indifferently as he might an inanimate object. He looked about him absentmindedly, took the rapier from the table, and stuck it in his belt.

"Now make a clean copy!" he ordered Balbi.

He went over to the window, opened the blinds, and bellowed into the faint glimmering light, his voice hard and commanding: "Bring the horses!"

He wrapped the wings of his cloak about his shoulders and strode through the door. His steps echoed in the stairwell. The yard was stirring below: horses neighed, bottles clinked, and the wheels of the coach were creaking. The girl, still carrying the shards of glass in her gathered apron, took one or two slow steps and then scuttled out of the room, down the stairs, after the departing figure, as if she had understood something, as if something had occurred to her. Now only the friar remained in the room. He wrote slowly and with great care, frowning and pursing his lips, and spelling out the end of the message letter by letter: *"I am y-o-u-r-s a-l-o-n-e, for e-v-e-r!"* . . . Then he threw the quill away, leaned back in the armchair, admired his workmanship, and, stomach shaking, fell to loud, full-bellied laughter.